Champagne & Lemon Drops

CHAMPAGNE AND LEMON DROPS

A BLUEBERRY SPRINGS SWEET ROMANCE

JEAN ORAM

Champagne and Lemon Drops
A Blueberry Springs Sweet Romance © 2013, 2018 Jean Oram
Cover design by Najla Qamber Media and Designs

Printed in the United States of America unless otherwise stated on the last page of this book. Published by Oram Productions Alberta, Canada.

LIBRARY OF CONGRESS CATALOGING-IN-PUBLICATION DATA

Oram, Jean.

Champagne and Lemon Drops: A Blueberry Springs Sweet Romance / Jean Oram.—3rd. ed.

p. cm.

ISBN 978-1-928198-77-2, 978-1-928198-08-6 (paperback)

Ebook ISBN 978-0-9918602-0-3, 978-0-9918602-1-0

1. Weddings—Fiction. 2. Marriage—Fiction. 3. Marriage Proposals—Fiction. 4. Romance fiction. 5. Romance fiction—small towns. 6. Love stories, Canadian. 7. Small towns—fiction. 8. Triangles (Interpersonal relations)—Fiction. 9. Blueberry Springs (Imaginary place)—Fiction. I. Title.

Third Oram Productions Edition: October 2018

DEDICATION

To all the wonderful writers I've met, chatted with, and worked with at the online writing community Agent Query Connect. Without your help, support, feedback, and knowledge I surely wouldn't have made it this far. And a very special thank you to my critique partners who went above and beyond and told me the things I needed to hear as a writer. Everyone needs friends who are willing to help you pursue your dream without calling you crazy—at least not to your face.

To my family who has always understood my absent distraction while writing and for allowing me the freedom and support to pursue this. You guys have never been anything less than awesome. Thank you.

I

THE NOT TOO DISTANT FUTURE

(April)

*B*eth Wilkinson worked to pull in a deep breath against her gown's sleek fit. If she could breathe properly, everything would feel exactly the way she had always dreamed it would. She would know, without a grain of a doubt, that today was more than just a reaction to the events over the past thirteen months. That *this* moment was her true destiny.

That this wasn't just a knee-jerk reaction. That she was marrying the right man. Because when life handed you an opportunity you didn't turn your back or drag your feet. You made a choice and you leapt.

Did Cinderella hesitate? Heck no. That girl took the leap with both feet.

And right now, Beth was leaping. No parachute required. Both feet in.

Well … almost.

Her sister, Cynthia, adjusted the veil around Beth's shoulders. She closed her eyes as she inhaled her sister's familiar, reassuring perfume. "Here goes nothing, right?"

Cynthia shook her head with a smile. "You know, it's funny, I thought Gran and I would be giving you away to--"

"I know." *Don't say his name.*

Cynthia added quickly, "I just didn't expect it."

"And I didn't expect Dad to be stuck overseas and unable to give me away."

"Sure you didn't." Cynthia shot her a wry look. "He couldn't make my wedding, why should he make it to yours?"

"Because he always liked me best." She stuck out her tongue, then clasped her trembling hands, trying to force all thoughts from her mind. Cynthia was stirring up unwanted thoughts and worries. Bad sister. Beth concentrated on happy images of walking down the aisle. She and her hubby-to-be would say their vows and live happily ever after in a nice home and have a family so big she'd be surrounded by people--her people--just like she'd always wanted.

Cynthia fussed with the veil and Beth batted her away. She ignored her older sister's raised eyebrow which meant she was trying to read Beth's mind--the woman always had to know everything. Beth flashed her a convincing smile and Cynthia relaxed, tossing her head in a way that tousled her wavy hair leaving it sexy and perfect and making Beth think of champagne and movie stars and an easier life. Beth patted her slick chignon and glanced in the mirror. Maybe she should have left her hair down.

"You look fine, quit worrying," Cynthia laughed.

Shouts erupted outside and Beth turned to the window, her sister leaning over her shoulder. "What's going on?"

Beth gave the foggy window a swipe with her hand. "I can't see anything." She plunked down in the church's window seat, her dress puffing up around her like a sea of whipped cream. Below, a flash of crows bobbed on the walkway. No, tuxedos. Raised voices filtered through the snow-laden trees.

Beth stood again pressing her nose against the cold glass. She gasped.

This could *not* be happening.

Stupid pigheaded, testosterone-driven men!

"What?" Her sister crowded against the glass. "What?"

Beth gathered the folds of her skirt and shouldered past her sister.

"You can't go! It's bad luck if he sees you."

"Oh, I'll show those men some bad luck," Beth muttered, wrenching open the heavy door. She took the stairs as fast as she could, restricted by her heels and fluttering tulle. She reached the front doors of the church in time to witness her fiancés--past and present--position themselves to duke it out.

One fit form ducked, dodging a punch from the other. Shoes lost traction on the icy steps and a body twisted and arched through the air. A man's mouth stretched into a perfect, comical O. In slow motion he landed head first, his body grinding into the walkway like a broken bird falling from the sky.

A scream broke the silence. Hers. She screamed, unable to stop, the terror of the scene freezing her in place before adrenalin kicked in, propelling her through the gathering crowd and toward the unconscious heap--the man she loved. Gingerly she touched the fallen man's face as the other man she loved was herded back by a dark wall of groomsmen.

She looked at her blood-covered fingers. This was going to change things. She could feel it. Her nuptial bad luck had caught up with her.

There wasn't enough oxygen. The world spun rapidly to the right and she couldn't breathe. A blurred vision of dress hems and shiny black shoes was the last thing she saw before collapsing on top of the wounded man.

II

WHERE IT ALL BEGINS

(13 Months Ago)

2

Beth dropped her purse and work ID at the door and, not smelling any hints of soup being heated in the kitchen by her fiancé Oz Reiter, entered the trailer's cozy living room. Seeing him slumped on their worn velvet couch, she plunked down beside him, her stomach grumbling for its lunch. She leaned against his arm, but instead of wrapping it around her like he usually did, his posture stiffened.

"What?" she asked. She surreptitiously sniffed her armpits. Nope. Fine.

Oz shifted from side to side, his broad shoulders leaning into her as he echoed the movements of the football player on TV. When they were teens, his size and strength intimidated her before she saw him using it to gently retrieve Mrs. Everett's kitten from the oak on Main. Watching the sixteen-year-old hand the fluffball back to its owner with a sweetness she hadn't seen in other boys, her heart had grown warm, and she'd vowed to find a way to catch his attention as something more than just his kid sister's best friend. She wanted those beefy arms wrapped tight around her. While she figured out how to go about doing that, Mandy Mattson had swooped in with her long mane of glossy blond hair, lithe body, and a knowledge of all things mechanical that Beth had absolutely no interest in matching. When Oz, smitten with Mandy and her seemingly bold sexuality as well as her divine homemade brownies, took the rival to the end of year dance Beth had bowed out gracefully--before Oz had even noticed her shy attempts. For almost eight years Beth had ignored her persistent crush and dated others, disappointed as each of them failed to compare to the man she saw in Oz.

Fresh out of college two and a half years ago, Beth returned home to take the recreational therapist position at the town's hospital which served the surrounding semi-isolated mountain and foothill areas. She'd thought she was over her childhood crush until a freshly single Oz came in to visit his elderly aunt in the continuing care wing--which was simply an old folks home tacked onto the hospital for those requiring medical monitoring and attention. When Beth began the physical therapy dance session for her patients he was still in the common room, patiently watching his aunt flip through an old photo album. Always in need of more male partners, he'd obliged her request with a broad smile and stepped in to dance with his aunt as well as a few other ladies. Watching him move smoothly around the room, smiling and laughing with her beloved patients, she'd fallen harder than a four hundred pound gorilla trying to ice skate. She invited him for coffee and pie in the cafeteria afterwards as a thank you and he'd never missed a dance session since.

Well, until two months ago when his father suffered a heart attack, forcing Oz to spend insane hours in the shared accounting business in order to keep it afloat. But beyond the busyness, something was up. She couldn't see it, smell it, or put her finger on it, but it was there like a flash in her periphery. It felt like a breakup. Which was silly. Completely silly. They were planning their upcoming wedding and even saving for a bigger home.

But she still couldn't shake the feeling.

It was as though something she couldn't see had shifted. Lately Oz had been concerned about her following her dreams even though she told him she *was* following them. Her future was mapped out. She loved her job. But Oz kept telling her there was more to her life. To their life.

She pulled her Dream Home scrapbook off the coffee table and set it on her lap as reassurance. She flipped to the photo of a wrap-around veranda with a double swing where they could sit and talk about their day. She needed a picture of a white picket fence to keep the future family dog in the yard and maybe one of a golden lab as well. Oz had sketched a floor plan that included enough bedrooms for a couple of kids as well as a guest and she studied his tight writing, smiling at the walk-in closet where she could store her wardrobe without taking over Oz's side. Two and a half months ago, Oz had given her the latest clippings that she'd added to the yard section: a hot tub and a gazebo. And that was the last time he expressed an interest.

Beth sorted through the loose clippings of 'undecided add-ons' in the back of the book. "What do you think? Oak or maple cabinets? And apple trees or lilacs in the front? Or both?"

Oz shrugged as Beth shifted to face him. There was more beyond him feeling overwhelmed with taking care of the family business. More than his father's heart attack and the fact that the air between father and son was strung so tight with live wires that she worried one of them would trip and cause an explosion.

"We lost another client yesterday," Oz said, not looking away from the TV.

Beth froze. "A big one?"

"Moved their business over to Ed's."

Beth held her breath. Lately it seemed as though the town was favoring the new accounting firm in town rather than the staid and true offices of Reiter & Son. Which was downright unneighborly of them.

"How did your dad handle it?" she asked. Despite Dr. Nesbit telling Harvey Reiter to take it easy, he wasn't the kind of man to step aside and let Oz do things his way or within his own timeframe. He was constantly telling his son how to run the place via emails, phone calls, and even going as far as sending Oz's mother, Angelica, to check up on the place and deliver instructions.

Oz fished around in the pocket of his worn dress pants and handed Beth a set of keys.

She frowned at the gift. "Aren't these your father's work keys?" She met Oz's brown eyes momentarily before he sank further into the couch, his gaze back on the screen in front of him. "Did you lock him out so you could get work done?" She smiled at the thought of Oz finally taking a stand against his father.

After a long pause, Oz replied, "He resigned."

"What? How? He owns half the business." Beth stared at the warm keys weighing heavy in her hand.

Oz shrugged, his expression darkening.

Beth leaned into the couch, watching Oz's favorite team get tackled two yards from a touchdown. Was Harvey for real, or was this one of his games to make Oz do as he wanted? And if he was actually resigning, what would cause him to leave the business he'd built up over the past twenty-five years? Surely it couldn't be the heart attack. He was supposed to be coming back to work in two weeks. He wouldn't just give it all up. There had to be something she wasn't aware of. Something big.

"Life's too short." Oz sighed heavily and wiped his face with a rough hand.

"Yeah, I know." Her thoughts immediately jumped to her late mother as they always did whenever anyone used the expression. Her mom, Wendy, used to pop a lemon drop candy in Beth's mouth, any time of day, and chirp: *Life's too short to wait for the right moment. Get it while you can.*

By the time her mother passed away, Beth's father had been long gone for eleven years and wasn't too keen to step into the unfamiliar daddy role, protesting that his work took him all around the world in a perpetual quest for new oil. Their gran had taken in the two sisters, moving them all into the big apartment over the corner store whose owner supplied the girls with free day-old donuts and Beth with an extra ten pounds she never seemed able to lose. She reached over and snagged a lemon drop out of the bowl she kept on the coffee table and waited for Oz to explain why he thought life was too short. She'd learned over the past eight weeks that if she probed him too much he'd act like a clam being chased with shuckers and a pot of boiling water.

Oz stared at the photo of the house Beth had glued to the cover of her scrapbook and sighed. "He delivered full ownership papers this morning."

Beth grinned and perched on her knees, facing him as she hugged the scrapbook. "You mean you own all of it? Oh my God, we should celebrate! Think of all the things we can do with the business as full owners. All those ideas you've had over the years. You'll make more money and we'll be able to have kids right away. This is so great! We can do it all, Oz." Her smile faded as Oz's expression remained grim. "What? What's wrong?"

His jaw clenched and he drew in a long, controlled breath, giving his head a brisk shake. "Nothing."

"Oz, what? He just gave you this amazing business that you rock at, but you look like he gave you an embalming business and told you to go at it." She softened her tone. "You finally have him out of your hair."

Oz snorted.

"We're Team Wilkineiter, remember?" She laughed, trying to lighten the mood with their bowling league nickname, which combined their last names Wilkinson and Reiter. Wilkineiter (verb): to meet and conquer. "Tell me what's going on in that handsome head of yours so we can conquer whatever it is." Oz leapt off the couch like an uncoiled spring when she touched a lock of his hair.

"You wouldn't understand. Your father doesn't expect anything of you. None of the postcards he sends come with strings attached. You still get to live your life however you want."

She squelched the sting of anger that swirled at the mention of her father and his abandonment. "So do you."

"It's hard to disappoint someone who doesn't care and is never around."

Beth sucked in a sharp breath and carefully set her scrapbook aside. She headed to the kitchen, ignoring his apology. She ate last night's leftovers straight from the container before hurrying back to the living room. Leaning over Oz, she gave him a light peck on the lips.

"Better hustle or you're going to be late for work." She wondered if that was a silly thing to say to a business owner.

His dark eyes studied her. "What would you say if I told you I wanted to trade it all in?"

She eased onto the couch beside him, knowing she'd be late for her afternoon shift. "Trade what in?"

He glanced around the trailer. "Everything. Move. Start fresh with everything. Hold off on getting married. Go explore. Find new jobs. Live off of nothing?"

Start fresh with *everything*? "Hold off getting married?" Her pulse picked up as fear surged through her.

"Yeah." He caressed her hand, a hopeful look in his eye. "There's no rush."

She pulled her hand back and lined her scrapbook with the coffee table's edge as Oz stood to pace. She swallowed a lump of dread. "Everything?"

She had a cousin who waited to have kids and now, not even thirty years old, was looking at in vitro. What if it was a genetic flaw? What if she waited and missed her chance?

Oz turned to her, taking a bold step forward, blurting, "I need to change. I need to break out. I need to ..." He pulled his shoulders up, hands bunched at his chest as if he was about to break into song, but couldn't remember the words. "I need to *move*, and I'm ... I'm trapped."

"Move away from Blueberry Springs, and trapped by what?" What the heck was he talking about? Oz loved their nosey little town, nestled in the middle of nowhere, protected by a semi-circle of mountains and rolling meadows. How could he feel trapped when this was where his family was, his new business, and where they planned to raise their kids?

Oh *no*. Her stomach lurched as the word *trapped* circled in her head. It was her. Somehow, despite their mutual talk about their future, she'd made him feel this way. Wedding plans, starting a family, building a home. She'd blindly moved ahead not realizing he wasn't in step with her. How had she missed it? It was the one thing she'd promised she would never do to a man. She'd seen the way her dad ran from their family and the way Oz ran from Mandy when she'd faked a pregnancy to keep him from leaving. And somehow Beth had gone and trapped him.

Crap, crap, crap on a stick. She was everything she'd ever dreamed of *not* becoming.

But how? He said he wanted the same future.

"Maybe not trapped," Oz said. "More like blocked. Like when you can't move where you want to in chess and you have to wait for the other player to move so you can. Except I'm tired of waiting."

"Trapped and blocked are the same thing." She closed her eyes. *Tired of waiting.* Waiting for what?

Was she blocking him?

Beth twisted her ring around her finger. Blocked or trapped-- neither were words a woman wanted to hear from her fiancé.

"What if I wanted to change my life? What if ..."

Alarm zinged through Beth like lightning. "Yes, of course." Anything to make sure he didn't feel trapped or blocked. Those words equaled losing, and she couldn't lose Oz. She just couldn't. "Let's make some changes." She stood up as though there was something she could do right now such as rearrange the living room.

Oz paced the small room, making the floor creak. "What if this isn't our life? Our true life?" He stopped and turned to face her. "What if we want different things, Beth?"

Wait a second. This wasn't a change she wanted to make. "I don't understand." Her breathing hitched up in her throat as she waited for him to reply.

"You have dreams. I have dreams ... somewhere. I don't know who I am."

"I'm following my dreams," she replied carefully. "And you're an accountant. You own a whole business now."

"A business I never wanted."

Beth's head tightened and she perched on the edge of the couch, eyes closed, trying to slow her thoughts. She needed to start at the beginning and work her way forward. "You don't like accounting?"

He gave a coarse laugh and shook his head. "I hate it. It's my dad's passion and now he's saddled me with it because he thinks I need to grow up."

Her shoulders relaxed. His dad had him feeling trapped, not her. But he hated his career? When did that happen?

Oz continued, "He's trying to trap me into a stable life--a life he thinks I should have. Not the life I want."

Beth tried to hold herself together. Stable life. Defined by career, marriage, and kids. Her stomach took a nasty swoop.

"I thought you wanted marriage and kids?" she asked, her voice unable to rise above a whisper. They'd had piles of conversations about having kids and how much he wanted a whole gaggle of them. Who was this man? And who was the idiot who conked him on the head and made him forget who he was?

Oz sat beside her and took her hand. He stared at the television, thinking for a second, before turning to her. "I don't know who I am, Beth. I can't have kids if I don't know who I am. I can't wake up ten years from now wondering if I made a wrong turn. I can't do that to you. I can't keep putting one foot in front of the other if I might be going in the wrong direction. You need to be able to marry a man who knows who he is."

"I don't understand. What do you need? What can I do?" Beth tried to block out the thought that he might not love her in the way she'd thought.

He sagged into the couch. "I don't know."

"Well, sell the business. Find something else." Her voice tightened as she said, "We can wait to have kids."

Oz pushed a hand through his hair. "I can't sell it."

"Why not?"

"If I sell in the first five years all proceeds go to my dad."

"But you own half! I mean, all of it. You guys were partners."

"I don't own my original half outright because I've only worked off about a quarter of it. So, if I sell now I get about twelve and a half percent of the business. If I wait five years, I get it all."

"Five years is a long time when you're waiting to get what you want." Boy, she knew that one. "If you don't want the business, sell it. Like you said, Oz, life is too short." Her heart stuttered at the idea of upheaval. Of Oz starting fresh in a new job with no vacation time and the possibility of them having to move if he couldn't find something suitable. Of having to make new friends and finding a new hospital to work in. It was terrifying. She finally felt as though she had the beginnings of a real home and a family here in Blueberry Springs. She didn't want to toss it all up in the air. Not for something that sounded, and felt, so uncertain.

But if she was with Oz, it would be worth it. Anything would be worth it.

Oz took her hands in his. "I love you, Beth. You know that, right?"

"Of course, I do. And I'll love you no matter what you decide to do with your life. If we have to move, then we move. I'm here with you."

"I don't know if I can do this."

"I'll be right there with you. It'll be okay."

"No." Oz's eyes grew wet and Beth's face heated from a fight or flight reaction. "I can't put you through this. I think ..." He grabbed both her hands and held them tight. "I think I need to do this alone."

Oz sat hunched on their couch, his knees jiggling up and down. He wouldn't meet her eye for longer than a split second. Beth stared at the framed photos that sat three deep on the shelf above Oz. The two of them looked so happy up there. So in love. Not like this real life Oz was slowly revealing.

"A break," she repeated, trying to make it sink in. "You want a break." She knew she'd said it a hundred times already, but her mind refused to cooperate and accept the concept. Seriously. What idiot had conked her perfectly good fiancé over the head causing this mess? And what had gone wrong with their relationship that she couldn't see?

Oz said gently, "You can't raise happy kids in a happy family if you aren't happy and don't know who you are. You can't pin your life on someone else's happiness. I've got to figure out who I am." Oz muted the commentator who was laughing uproariously at his cohost who had just predicted that the underdog team would sweep the cup out from under the favored contender. "A month. Maybe less. I don't know. I just need to figure out what I want, you know?" He arched his brows and gave her a hopeful look that made her want to give in.

Beth sat beside him, pushing her knee into the side of his leg, her hands clamped onto one of his tight quads. She squeezed her eyes shut. A month. She could give him a month to figure things out. He would do the same for her with ease and grace. This was a sacrifice she could make for the man she loved. Besides, the sex when they got back together would be utterly mind-blowing. But no quickies for a month? That was going to be hard. Harder than scaling a mountain in flip-flops.

"A break will be good for us," Oz said, tilting his head so their foreheads rested against each other. Her eyes flooded with tears and she swiveled away. She already missed him so badly her chest ached. He brought her face back to meet his, kissing her long and slow, her tears slipping between their lips. He broke off the kiss and said, "You'll have some time to follow your dreams, too."

Beth resisted the urge to push him away and snap that she didn't need time because, unlike him, she knew who she was and what she wanted with her life. Exactly. Down to the finest detail: cut and pasted in her scrapbook.

"It's been a hard couple of months. Dad ... man, his heart attack just kind of opened my eyes, you know?" Oz's voice shook. "Thank you for understanding, Beth. For not letting us turn into everyone around us."

Lungs tight, her voice barely able to strike its way out, Beth asked, "What's wrong with everyone around us?" Blueberry Springs was full of wonderful, happy people who went about their lives with an ease that came with having a contented routine that provided fulfillment. There was security and comfort in that.

Oz passed his arm through the air as though encompassing the town. "Everyone's moved forward without knowing who they really are. Like they're scared to find out. They just keep clomping one foot in front of the other, working at the same boring job all their life because it's easy and they don't know what else they would do. Everyone starts popping out kids and it's like game over. They just settle in and grow old without ever exploring their dreams and the things they could do if they had the courage. There's so much life out there."

Beth pushed away from Oz, her mind spinning.

"I mean, look at your sister. She gave up a scholarship to play volleyball for a big school. She was going to become a professional coach. She had what it took." He cupped his hand as if holding something tangible. "Both you and I know she could have competed nationally."

"But instead she raised me when Gran and my dad couldn't." Beth turned away. "Don't worry, I get it." Tears thick with guilt blocked her throat and prevented her from saying more. She knew she'd altered her sister's future. When Gran's health started failing and she had to be moved to the continuing care facility, Cynthia, who had just finished high school and was about to embark on her semi-charmed life, stepped in to support Beth through her final two years of high school instead of sending her off to be raised by their father who was working in God-knows-where.

For that reason, she had to let Oz go. She couldn't put her life before his. She began to leave the room, but Oz snagged her hand, holding her back.

"I want something more for us, Little B. I want us to enter our marriage knowing full well who we are so we don't become one of those resentful, bitter couples who always think the other one held them back somehow."

"You think I'm holding you back?"

"I think we're both capable of more." His breath was warm on her skin. She stepped back, wanting space. "What would you do if anything were possible? There's got to be a secret dream in there bursting to get out. Everyone has one."

She stalked to the room's doorway, swiping at her tears but unable to keep up with the flow. "You know what my dream is. I want a family. I want stability. To be smothered with love and a sense of belonging. I want people to lean on, and for us to be there for each other. I want to have a crowded table at Thanksgiving where everyone is laughing and shares a history. More than just Cynthia, Gran, and me reading a postcard from Dad. *That's* my dream." She flexed her hands. He didn't get what it was like not having a real family. Unlike him, she knew exactly what she wanted and had ever since she saw him rescuing Fluffy: him.

Her breathing became labored as she fought for control. *Breathe, girl, breathe.*

Oz tugged her to him and wrapped his strong arms around her, making it even harder to breathe. "I'm so sorry, baby. I'm so sorry. But we've got to. I can't see any other way. I love you."

Beth sniffed and tried not to bawl. It was only a month. She could do a month. It would be fine.

"We'll be even better than ever after."

She nodded, trusting him. She pulled in a deep breath, trying to relax and be okay with the idea. What was she going to do about the wedding? Keep planning? Or was she supposed to hold off on that, too?

Oz said quietly, "I'll move out. Just for a bit."

Beth shoved him hard, sending him scrambling to stay upright. "No. No! People don't fix themselves in *a bit*. I can't live here without you, Oz." She gestured to the shelf of photos. "This isn't a home--*my* home--without you. I can't be surrounded by happy memories knowing you weren't happy when we were together and that you felt trapped and unsatisfied. That you wanted out." It was that simple. She had to be the one who left. She couldn't be the one sitting here waiting for him to come back.

Oz reached out. "Beth, it's not like that."

"Well, that's how it feels. Call me when you want me again." She wrenched the engagement ring off her finger and set it on top of the TV, tears streaking down her cheeks. She bolted from the trailer, slamming the door behind her.

Sobs rose up in her throat as she revved her Volvo, then popped it into gear. The tires screeched as she flew away from the trailer like a tornado. She pointed the wagon toward work, wiping away her tears with the heel of her hand as she wove down the road. Son of a monkey's uncle.

How did she become *that* woman? How had she misread his cues about him wanting family and a big house? And what the heck was wrong with being like everyone else? Wasn't that the goal?

She shivered and cranked the car's heat. A whole month of being away from him and all the while living in the same small town. The rumor mill was going to lock it into overdrive and steamroll them until there was nothing left.

She flicked on the wipers, swishing the cold spring rain to the side. She slowed her thoughts to match the wiper's pacing. Her Plan A for all crises was to run to her sister. But with Oz's words still ringing in her ears, she knew she couldn't ask her sister to save her. Not this time. She had to let her sister live her life. Just like Oz needed to live his.

Plan B was always Gran. But Gran couldn't take her in. Which meant Plan C.

Unfortunately, there was no Plan C.

Plan C might be her best friend Katie Reiter who lived in a one-bedroom basement suite. But she was also Oz's kid sister meaning Beth couldn't put her in a position where it could be construed that she was choosing sides. And everyone else in town ... well, she didn't want to go there.

The problem with standing on her own two feet, which was exactly what she needed to do, was that her own two feet couldn't afford setting her up in a new place. And a new place for one month was unrealistic. She'd really screwed the pooch thanks to her stupid pride.

She hunched over her steering wheel, hurt clenching her soul as she stared at the delicate buds trying to leaf out on the trees lining the road. She stared until the world fuzzed out of focus and a car tooted cheerfully behind her. She bolted upright, forcing herself to move her car through the four-way stop and on to work. Although the wipers creaked their way across the windshield, her vision remained blurred by water. She dabbed at her eyes with the sleeve of her cardigan and wrestled with the urge to run. Run from Oz and the pain of his rejection. Run from the town and the inevitable gossip, meddling, and kind-hearted looks which would break her down piece by piece. Run from this place, so laden with memories. Run from everything.

But she couldn't leave Gran, Cynthia, and her patients just because she was experiencing a painful speed bump in her love life. It was only one month. That was all. She could do this.

A fresh bout of tears let loose as she pulled into the hospital's parking lot. She stared at the one-storey brick building. Finishing her afternoon shift while she looked and felt like a bag of run-over crap was going to suck big time. Sighing, she plopped one foot out of the car, then the other. She stomped through a cold puddle, squelching her way down the hospital's hallways seeking Katie who was on day shift. Despite knowing her friend couldn't save her, she needed some no-nonsense advice from the woman who'd been there since the day she found Beth hiding in a corner of the funeral home bawling her eyes out over her mother. Katie had rubbed her back and handed her tissue after tissue without saying a word. When Beth was finally all cried out, her new friend had pulled her down the alley behind Main Street and told her to wait outside the back door of Benny's Big Burger. With a confidence that had surprised fourteen-year-old Beth, Katie had strode into the seldom-used delivery entrance and returned a minute later with a pie plate containing half of his well-known chocolate maven pie and two forks. They'd plunked down in the alley, their backs against the rough brick wall, and dug in. When they were done with the pie, they were best friends.

Pausing in the quiet hospital hall, the smell of antiseptic clinging to her, Beth peeked around the corner, hoping to spy Katie's familiar kitten-patterned nursing scrubs. There she was at her nursing station, head bent, a slight smile tugging at her lips--without a doubt reading a romance novel. Beth checked her watch. She'd missed over an hour of her afternoon shift. Taking a deep breath, she scurried to Katie, keeping her head lowered so nobody would see her bloodshot eyes.

"Oh, hey." Katie glanced up, slipping papers into an uneven stack, hiding her novel.

"Hiding a gushy romance?" Beth asked in a gloomy voice, her attempt at humor failing. God, this was going to suck. Everyone was going to know there was trouble before the afternoon coffee break even hit.

Katie cleared her throat and cast her eyes to the side, her fingers fidgeting with the stack of papers. "Did Dr. Leham find you? He paged you, like, twenty times."

"What? Who?"

"The new guy. Dr. Leham."

"Oh, right. No."

Katie frowned at Beth. "You feeling okay? You don't look too good." She swiftly brought Beth behind the protection of the nursing station's high counter and pushed her into a chair, twisting her away from Amy, a passing nurse.

Beth rubbed her bare finger and tried to smile. "Know anyone who needs a temporary roommate?"

Katie spit out the coffee she was drinking and began coughing and sputtering. "What? Where the hell is your ring?"

Beth bit her lower lip, trying to stop from tearing up. "We're taking a break."

"Is this because of Mandy? I know she's still yearning after him, but I thought he'd learned his lesson with her ages ago."

Beth sniffed and shook her head. "It's not Mandy. It's me. He wasn't ready." She buried her head in her hands and stared at her wet sneakers.

"Men," Katie grumbled. "Such commitmentphobes. It's nothing more than cold feet." She hoisted Beth out of the chair. "You need to put on a push-up bra and stomp over there. You let him know that he's going to lose a good thing if he keeps acting this way."

Beth resisted Katie's physical directing. "I can't. If I push him on this … that'll be it. I know it. He's freaked out, Katie. Something's wrong." She met her best friend's dark gaze. "I can't lose him."

The woman studied Beth for a moment, then pulled her into a tight hug. "Well, whatever you decide, I'm with you, okay? You'll get through this. And we'll smarten him up if it's the last thing we do."

3

Beth sat at her desk, back to her office door, and stared at the small square of blank wall across from her. Sticky notes of all colors crowded the square and she jabbed a fresh magazine photo of a mountain view into the spot. She crumpled up last week's view of their proposed honeymoon destination and sighed. Propping her chin in her hands she tuned out the hospital's PA system and stared at her pretend window view until her eyes lost focus and the room swam.

Maybe it was just cold feet. Maybe Oz was freaked out by his dad giving him the business and all the responsibility that came with it. A simple case of too much, too soon. Because really, Oz had never complained about the job, only his dad riding him hard about how to do things. Once he saw that he could run the firm the way he wanted to it would all be cool again. She just had to be patient and let him see it.

But it still hurt. A lot. She slapped a nearby photo of her and Oz onto its face, spilling a container of craft supplies over her desk. She stared at the mess, flicking a few googly eyes and making them bounce back to her when they hit the wall. She kept flicking until her finger grew sore. Katie had insisted Beth crash at her place until Oz "straightened up and popped his head out of his butt." Hopefully he'd be working late so she wouldn't have to face him when she went home to pack a bag.

She needed a distraction. A good one. Or else a good strong drink. Maybe both.

Beth rested her forehead on the desk's cool surface and lolled it back and forth. She lifted her head and let it drop back onto the desk with a loud *thunk*. It was impossible to think. Impossible to imagine a day in her life without Oz. No Oz meant facing a ratty old car that depended on him to keep it running and a job where her patients were still irked with her due to Oz being too busy to come dance with them during his Friday lunch breaks.

Her weekends were going to be intolerable. Every weekend for the past two and a half years they'd done something together whether it was hiking up the local mountains, cozying up with popcorn and a movie, paddling around the local pond to see how close they could get to the ducks, or trying to outdo each other on their game system. Weekends were sacred reconnection time. Now she would see him on Sundays, for one hour, while they drank coffee at their table at Benny's Big Burger and discussed whether Oz was ready to get back together or not.

What if he was never ready? What if this break was ... No. She couldn't think about it. Positive thoughts only.

Someone rapped lightly at her office door and it creaked open, its latch failing to catch when she had banged it shut minutes ago. She snapped upright, sending papers sliding in all directions as they dropped from her clammy forehead. She attempted to pull herself together while pushing her curls off her face. She spun her chair to face the visitor. The sudden head lift combined with a spin put her off balance and she went to lean on her armrest. She missed, sending her sprawling onto the floor. She landed hard beside the occupied Italian loafers just inside her doorway.

"Whoa there." Dr. Leham placed a hand under Beth's arm and helped her stand.

"Sorry! New chair." They both glanced at her worn chair.

Obviously not new. She gave an uneasy chuckle. "Right. I meant um, I switched this one ... and ... hi."

"Are you okay if I let go?" he asked.

No. Didn't you hear? The rumor mill must be slow today, because the truth of the matter is that I will never be okay again until Oz comes running back to me.

She held her breath as the doctor's ice-blue eyes zipped over her, taking in every detail as he continued to hold her. He gave her a slight, questioning smile, and she closed her eyes against the memories floating in on a familiar scent: the same cologne Oz wore on special occasions. Reminders of him were going to be everywhere, attacking her at irregular, unexpected intervals. Like a guerilla attack to the heart over and over again. She bent over and placed her hands on her knees.

Dammit. This break better not last longer than twenty-four hours or she was going to be an extremely pathetic basket case.

Dr. Leham placed a gentle hand on her back. "Maybe you should sit down?"

Beth aimed her butt and plopped into her chair. She sucked in a deep breath only to be hit by his cologne again. "The hospital is supposed to be scent free." You big meanie.

He sat in the chair across from her. "Are you sensitive to my cologne?"

Hello, understatement.

She waved away his concerns. "I'm fine, really. Sorry." She stuck out her hand and introduced herself. "Beth Wilkinson." Why wasn't he meeting her eyes? Usually when a man had this issue his gaze was stuck about a foot lower than her forehead.

"Dr. Nash Leham." He gave her hand a brisk shake. He reached for her face with his left hand and she pulled back. Quick as lightning he pulled something off her forehead. He studied the googly eye in his palm. Still serious, he carefully handed it to her. "I've heard of a third eye, but I didn't realize it was a googly eye. I always believed it to be mythical. Your inner child was showing."

Beth burst out laughing, loving how the man took her from

bouncing on the bottom to laughter within seconds. She pushed her chair back until it hit her desk. Normally she didn't mind the smallness of her office when she was chewing the fat with Katie during breaks, but this man was seriously making it feel crowded.

She adopted a mask of professionalism and waited for him to explain why he'd come by. As the hospital's recreational therapist she was often seen as the softie with the fluff job. Some of the city doctors who came out to Blueberry Springs as part of the Rural Doctors Program actually laughed when they discovered her job wasn't a volunteer position. Which was so not funny. Her job was as important as theirs. Well, maybe not quite *exactly* as important, but you couldn't just shove the elderly and infirm into the hospital's attached nursing home and ignore them. They needed her program to help keep their minds sharp, their moods buoyant, and their health stable.

And she was that person. The diploma on her office wall proved it.

She waited for the man to speak and worked on emitting a cold, confident, business manner rather than the emotional defeat she felt. She could do this. No personal life. Just thoughts about work. This handsome doctor was a serious, top-notch go-getter who had a killer gut instinct and had been turning heads around town--for both professional and unprofessional reasons--since his arrival a few weeks ago.

City meat. That's what the nurses called him. And for the first time, meeting him up close instead of just glimpses of him hurrying off to see patients, she could see why. Hot stuff. The doctor might be the opposite of Oz, but he was still handsome with his blue eyes, slim build, and perfect hair. Whereas Oz was like a tall Hugh Jackman, Dr. Leham was more like a wiry, blond Bradley Cooper with those sharp, light-colored eyes. Both good looking, but completely different.

Beth bit her lower lip to keep it from trembling. Oz was sneaking into her thoughts again.

"Uh, is this a good time?" Dr. Leham asked, furrowing his brow.

He tucked his clipboard to his chest, one hand at the ready to push himself out of the chair.

Beth cleared her throat and smiled. She could do this and *not* cry. "It's fine." She rubbed her fingertips over the bare spot on her ring finger. The ring's absence stung like a burn.

"I see," he said, his eyes moving from her hands. "Tough day?"

She let out a brave snort, her eyes immediately filling with unshed tears. She turned away to dab at her eyes and a tissue popped up in her periphery. His gesture opened her floodgates and she rolled her eyes at herself. So much for holding it together and impressing him with her savvy business manner. Now she'd definitely be marked as the softie with the cush job. At least he was only in Blueberry Springs for a short-term contract and would be city-bound as soon as his commitment was fulfilled.

The more her tears fell, the more humiliated and embarrassed she felt which, in turn, made more tears join the chorus. She blew her nose and another tissue appeared to her left. She snatched it from the air.

"Do you want me to come back later?"

She shook her head. Doctors never came by to talk to her, so if he'd been paging her and had come all the way to the continuing care wing, it must be important. She took several long, slow breaths and thought about how strong her sister had been as a teen. If Cynthia could persevere, so could she. She would channel those sister genes and be strong. One last deep breath and she turned to see Dr. Leham watching her with so much concern that the tears almost returned full-force.

"Breakups suck," the doctor said softly.

"It's just a break," Beth replied quickly.

"Oh, well. That's not too bad then?" He quirked his brow and gave a half smile. "A reassessment of priorities."

"We were engaged." She blinked back tears. Breaks were the promise ring of breakups. An IOU that meant one day, when the timing was right and Oz had his courage shored up about him, he might just go ahead and break up with her for real. A small wail escaped and her brave front disintegrated into tears. She buried her face in her hands, cheeks burning with humiliation.

Dr. Leham patted her shoulder. She peered through the cracks between her fingers and saw another tissue being offered.

"I'm sorry," he said.

Her head popped up, tears slowing. "Why?"

He blinked, caught. "Um. Well, because it sucks."

As if he knew anything about broken hearts. She'd bet her Volvo a guy like Dr. Leham was always on the giving end. Because only crazy women would break up with a nice, handsome doctor. And there weren't that many women out there who were that kind of crazy.

"It's like your world stops," he continued. "Days don't make sense. You can't figure out what it is everyone can be so happy about when you're so miserable."

This man understood.

"You know," he said, "when my ex-wife left me, I got into exercise."

"You're divorced?" There must be more crazy women than she'd anticipated.

Nash laughed at Beth's expression. "Yeah. I know. I'm kind of young to have been through all that already, but she wasn't prepared to deal with my work dedication and I wasn't prepared to change."

"I imagine," she said slowly, "being a doctor involves a lot of long hours and last minute changes to your personal plans."

He smiled. "But it's a heart job." He tapped his chest. "It's good for the soul being able to help people."

"Yeah." She got what a heart job was. And being a recreational therapist in continuing care gave her soul hope. She was the one who brought a little sunshine and meaning to those at the end of their long lives. All it took was a bit of glue, a couple of googly eyes, and a smile. It was a fulfilling job--even though most people considered her nothing more than a glorified babysitter.

"Anyway," he began, "cardiovascular activity naturally releases endorphins and serotonin into the bloodstream which can elevate moods for prolonged periods of time. Plus," he gave her a wink, "it's a great way to get back at the ex--looking all hot."

And hot he was. His slight build had an athletic strength to it, his shoulders broad although not nearly as much as Oz's.

"So, Dr. Leham?"

"Call me Nash," he said. "Please."

"Okay, Nash." She liked the sound of that.

"Can I call you Beth?"

She gave him a look. "Of course. Everyone does." City guys were weird. She bet he asked his dates if he could kiss them goodnight instead of just going for it.

He gave her an apologetic shrug. "I'm still figuring out Blueberry Springs. People are quite casual, even in the work environment." He leaned back and crossed his arms, his clipboard balanced on his lap.

"Yeah, we're a bit more laid back than the city." Having spent two years in the nearest city, Dakota, getting her diploma, she understood how the man must feel. Those were two quirky years she never planned to repeat. If she had found it difficult moving to the impersonal city, she could only imagine how Nash must feel being thrust into a very personal and in-your-business town like Blueberry Springs. "Plus, there's no need for formalities, I'm just the rec therapist."

"Nonsense. It's a very important part of our long-term care commitment plan. I've heard good things about your program and the variety you offer. That's why I sought you out, actually." He leaned forward, full of brisk professionalism as he handed her his clipboard. "Reggie Max is a new patient of mine entering continuing care. I'd like to share my treatment plan, his health history, as well as a possible recreational therapy plan that will benefit him both psychologically and physically. I've listed a few of the activities I feel would be most beneficial."

Beth sat back, clipboard in hand. Just like that, the we're-at-work wall had come up. Not that he had been anything other than professional before, it was more that he'd returned to really, *really* professional. He was now very much Dr. Leham, not Nash.

She kind of liked Nash.

Dr. Leham continued, "He is a Type 2 diabetic and has been since he was--"

"In his forties. Yes, I know." It was only recreational therapy for crying out loud. Usually doctors let her run with it knowing their patients weren't going to get any wilder than a weekly dance session that no longer included Oz, chair yoga, tai chi, a few crafts, games, and sing-alongs. "My gran is looking forward to his arrival." Beth rubbed her eyes, suddenly feeling exhausted. "They've been dating for a few years."

"Oh. I see. Well," he began uncertainly.

"I have a bit of a rec plan laid out for him already. He's partial to card games so I'm thinking I'll reinstate bridge on Thursdays."

"Oh." He paused. "Am I out of line? In Dakota we always--"

"No, no," she said quickly, "I would love some input." She hesitated. She'd never actually worked out a plan with doctors other than during her college practicum. Out here the doctors had always been like, *Go for it, Beth. One less thing for me to worry about. It's just crafts.*

Nash leaned forward and began pointing out various aspects of his rec plans. She surreptitiously inhaled his cologne and wondered what it was that men really wanted. Was it normal for them to act as though they wanted one thing and then whip around and say they didn't? And was this pause in their relationship merely a precursor of worse things to come?

Realizing Nash was waiting for her to reply, she flushed. "Um, sorry? I missed that."

"I've noticed a genuine need for an outreach here."

Beth frowned. How much had she missed while sucking in his scent?

"I think the community and outlying areas need a recreational therapy program for outpatients. For example, people with developmental disabilities or physical issues. It could be part respite care and part therapy. I'm pretty good at finding grants for this type of thing and I could act as the attending physician for an outreach while I'm here."

Beth closed her gaping yap. He thought she should head up a new program for outpatients? She gave his shoulder a shove and laughed. "Get out of here!" He had to be kidding, right?

He looked slightly insulted as he straightened his white doctor's coat. "I've pulled the records for the patients under your care and the results speak for themselves. There is a genuine need and I think you should fill it."

Beth struggled not to look stunned. "You checked me out?"

He cleared his throat. "Of course. So? What do you say?" He pulled a folded square of paper from his breast pocket and handed it to her. "These are the details. Training this weekend in Dakota."

"Whoa. What?" She slowly unfolded the page, keeping her eyes on Nash.

"There's professional development funding that will cover your expenses. I noticed you haven't used yours this year. It's Saturday and Sunday only so you don't have to worry about missing work and finding a replacement. I know how difficult that is out here in the boonies. Go, see what outreaches are about. No harm, no foul. And if you decide to go through with it, I'll be here to help."

Beth stared blankly at the information sheet in front of her and blinked. When it came to initiating big projects such as this one she wasn't about to kid herself that her independent, big-girl pants were from anywhere other than the junior's department. Who was she to believe she could make a program go from start to finish? And even more intriguing was that Dr. Leham was acting as though this was already a done deal.

"Besides," said Nash, standing at the door, "you could probably use the distraction as well as something to dive into at the moment. Am I right?"

She hesitated and a slow smile spread across her face. This would more than fill her lonely weekends. And it would show Oz that her life didn't stop just because he wanted his to. This could be the distraction she was looking for. "I'm in. Let's check it out."

BETH PAUSED in the doorway with the last box of the things she'd need for her time away from Oz. She felt beyond exhausted--more like a deflated balloon than a human. Oz looked just as defeated. She took a step toward him, bothered that the box was keeping them from hugging. She was missing the last hug she'd get for a month.

"I wish you'd let me be the one to move out." Oz reached over and tucked a strand of her hair behind an ear. She gave him a hard look. They weren't having this conversation again.

"If you've known since forever that accounting isn't for you, why did you wait until now?" Her anger and hurt took root and words flew from her mouth like they were jet-propelled. "Why not just *dump* the business and get it over with? I thought you had respect. I thought you cared about others. I thought you were better than that. What kind of man strings along clients and then dumps them without warning after they've made a commitment?"

"I *do* have respect for people and I'm *not* dumping you." Oz grasped her shoulders and bent down so he could look her in the eye. "I'm doing this because I love and respect you. I need time to figure out how I can be the man I want to be, and the man you need me to be."

"Why can't you tell your dad you don't want the business? Why are you doing this?" She felt so weak and pathetic. She pulled her shoulders straight and put on an air of confidence she didn't feel. She had to be strong. Had to keep her pride.

"You've never had to tell your parents you hate the very thing they love after you've just spent the last few years of your life pretending it was your calling."

"Yeah, well, I wish I'd had the opportunity." Tears blurred her vision and she stepped out onto the porch.

"Beth, I didn't mean it like that."

Her nose burned with unshed tears and at the bottom of the steps she turned and said, "I won't be at our Sunday coffee, Oz. I'm going to the city." By missing Sunday, she was going to have to go a week plus a couple of days until their next agreed check in. While it hurt to be away from him for that long, she couldn't help but hope that it would be even worse for him.

She slowly made her way to the car, misery clouding her vision. The earth was greening up, preparing for spring, the mountains glowing in the evening light. With shaking arms, she lowered the box into the back of the station wagon, her alarm clock tumbling out, jangling in protest. She turned to face Oz waiting for him to ask why she wouldn't be there. He stayed frozen to the spot at the top of the porch steps. His grip was tight on the railing, and he didn't speak or blink. She thought she may have seen him sway, but she couldn't be sure.

In a low voice he asked, "Are we doing the right thing?"

"Yes," she replied firmly, surprising herself. "If you're having doubts now, what's it going to be like in six months or a year? You need to fix whatever's giving you doubts, Oz. I can't ..." She shook her head, holding back tears. "I just can't." She got in her car, her head still shaking, her breath coming out in hiccups. She had to get away before her resistance crumbled and she dove back into his arms only to find out later that he hadn't fixed whatever was bothering him. If things were going to go south between them, it had to happen now. Not later when they had kids.

4

———————

*B*eth hunched over her upturned basket of music and yawned as she matched cracked cases with their CDs. Sleeping on Katie's hide-a-bed was not a good long-term where-am-I-going-to-live solution. Especially since Katie had just switched to night shifts which meant she was traipsing through the living room--aka Beth's new bedroom--at odd hours of the day and night.

But it was only for a short time. Oz had already expressed doubts when she left him the other night. Yet, she wasn't going to allow him to end their time apart prematurely. If he needed a break, he was getting a break. That man had to get his stuffing together, because if he didn't and she let him off early, they'd surely end in divorce. She wasn't going to let him toss the turkey in the oven until she was certain he was ready.

"Beth, dear?"

Beth looked up from her CDs at the elderly woman with flyaway hair. "Yes, Lauretta?"

"You know Wolf and I used to have fights. We always found the best way to work through those rifts was to stay together under the same roof and work through it." She reached into her mouth and adjusted her dentures. "You and Ozzie love each other very much. You can't let that kind of thing go."

"I'll take that into consideration. Thanks, Lauretta," Beth said, quickly matching up CDs and cases in order to escape before others gathered around to add their sage advice.

Footfalls lacking her patient's characteristic shuffle echoed across the large room and loafers stopped at the outskirts of her scattered music pile.

"Good morning, ma'am." A deep voice addressed Lauretta.

The woman gave him a slight nod and slipped away, calling out, "Remember Beth. Same roof. Happy together forever."

"Getting love advice?" Nash asked when the woman was out of earshot.

"I didn't realize so many couples have had big fights. Blows my mind." She gave her head a slight shake, making her curls tumble over her shoulders. She flicked her hair back and accepted the cracked CD case Nash was passing her.

"Still using CDs? You could ask the acquisitions committee for an MP3 player. Convert this over to digital. Make some playlists."

Beth glanced up and was struck by the nearness of Nash's bright blue eyes. He smiled and she tried to ignore the extra heartbeat that thrummed inside her chest. Which was silly. It had only been days since Oz had asked for a break. She was in no position for heart thrills.

She obviously needed more sleep.

"I could help if you want," he offered.

"I already have an iPod. It doesn't work." Sometimes men didn't understand that old technology was easier, cheaper, and faster. And harder to lose.

"Oh. Uh, I was wondering if you were hungry." He ran a hand through his perfectly groomed hair, each strand returning to its proper place. "I was angling to grab lunch before heading back to my clinic. Would you care to join me? A side of conversation with my cafeteria gruel always makes it more palatable."

She studied him through her lashes and stuffed a few CDs in the basket. He gave her a confident, disarming grin and waited.

"My treat. Simply sustenance and company." He handed her another CD.

"When?" Beth replied reluctantly. She tipped the Ella Fitzgerald CD into the basket, wanting to snap it in half as punishment for all the dance memories it brought back. Damn that Oz. She shoved the basket onto the bottom of her cart. Her knees were aching from kneeling on the hard floor.

"Now?" His eyebrows arched hopefully.

"Yeah. Okay." Why not? She had to eat. Besides, she could use a friend who wasn't invested in her relationship like half the town seemed to be.

He laughed. "Not exactly the enthusiasm I was hoping for, but better than eating alone. And besides, we can arm wrestle over who gets to drive and claim mileage for our outing to Dakota tomorrow."

She laughed despite her mood. "I don't know, City Boy. Think you can out-wrangle a country girl? And since when did you decide to come along?"

He laughed and stood, his scrubs momentarily outlining his fit quads. God, she was such a pushover for a good pair of quads. When Oz was still playing high school football he had *amazing* quads and some nights, she used to fall asleep dreaming of where those muscles ended and what they might feel like pushed against her in moments of passion. And now she knew--and they were even better than in her fantasies.

Nash laughed and squeezed her bicep. "Hmm. I dunno if I could beat this."

She flexed her muscles and grinned. Laughing, she pushed her cart back against the wall and Nash out the door. "Come on, let's get there before they're out of the Friday special."

"So?" asked Nash sitting down across from Beth in the small, bustling cafeteria filled with staff, townsfolk and patients. "Still feeling down?"

"Sorry?" Beth glanced around the room. The clatter of dishes and hum of conversation was distracting.

"How are you and Oz doing?" He broke his tea biscuit in half and dipped it in his Irish stew.

Her shoulders sagged. "Oh, you know ..."

"I heard you moved out."

"You never struck me as a gossip follower."

"Well, I can't say I like it, but you can't get anywhere in this town without wading through it. Some of it sticks to you." He glanced at Beth, then away. "The two of you are the talk of the town, you know. Especially with you moving out."

Beth closed her eyes. Great, so much for Nash being an impartial ear who didn't know the town's gossip or everyone's history. The guy probably knew more than she did by now. She opened her eyes to find Mary Alice, the town's most active rumormonger beside their table, tray laden with desserts and coffees for a table of Beth's patients. The woman said she was volunteering, but the way she pumped those folks for gossip--knowing they spent half their days on the phone catching up with the town--she was more like a pioneer trying to fill a leaky bucket with water.

Mary Alice let out a wheezy smoker's cackle. "Ha! I heard Oz *kicked* her out, Dr. Leham." She turned a curious eye to Beth, brows raised in anticipation.

"I chose to be the one to move out. Temporarily." Beth straightened her shoulders. If there were two people in town she'd like to avoid until this business between her and Oz was over, it was Mary Alice and her older sister Liz and, in particular, their big mouths and active imaginations.

"Now why would you two break up?" Mary Alice asked, her sister sidling up beside her.

"It's just a break," Beth muttered.

Liz piped up, "Then where's your ring?"

"Oz has it."

"He asked for it back?" the sisters asked at the same time. Their eyes slid over Nash and they shared a knowing look.

Liz elbowed her sister in the ribs and whispered loud enough for Beth to hear, "Betcha Mandy moves in on Oz."

Beth shot Nash a look and avoided making eye contact with the ladies. Seriously. They were worse than a pair of soap opera writers. Beth focused on her stroganoff and entertained a brief fantasy of flying away on a private plane, away from these ladies and their gossip. She could picture a dance floor on a secluded beach with a live band playing Michael Bublé. Nash would twirl her around, her light gown flowing out around her, neither of them with a care in the world. She jabbed a noodle and shook the image from her head. She really, really needed to get more sleep. Desperately.

"I think Beth is looking to climb a new mountain." Liz waggled her eyebrows suggestively, elbowing her sister again.

Beth threw her arms in the air, trying to act cavalier when all she wanted to do was rip the heads off of everyone who had turned to eavesdrop. "You got me!" She let out a laugh. "Nash and I are bumping uglies on the side. That's why I moved out."

Eyebrows shot up around the room and whispers stirred the air like a breeze through dry grass.

"You know what?" Nash said casually, his jaw tight. "It's a beautiful spring day. Why don't we go outside to eat?" He stood and clamped a hand on Beth's arm, helping her stand. The sun shone through the floor-to-ceiling windows to her right, and small mounds of slush hid on the shaded stone benches. It was going to be chilly out there, but it would be better than staying in front of the firing squad.

"Outside would be fantastic." She hoisted her tray. "Send your husband my regards, Mary Alice. I hope his ear is feeling better soon. Lovely talking to you, ladies."

Catty cows.

Nash led her outside and past the cold tables and benches. Curious, Beth followed him to a bench resting in a patch of sun under a grove of trees. Nash worked to balance his tray on his lap, then giving up, placed it to the side and held the bowl at chest level, carefully spooning stew into his mouth.

"So," Nash asked casually, his cheeks pink. "I'm part of the rumor mill now?"

"I'm sorry." Beth placed a hand on his arm. "I was just so pissed off. But don't worry. They won't believe me." She let out a laugh. "Me with a city boy? No offense, but not on your life."

BETH SAT in Nash's shiny BMW and waited for him to finish gassing the car so they could leave town. She tried not to pet the leather seat peeking out from under her. It was so smooth. So soft and luxurious it made her feel as though she should be dressed up in a ball gown and on her way to some fancy fundraiser where people gave cheek kisses as freely as hellos. She inhaled the car's aroma, certain the new car smell enveloping her was from the interior's lack of age rather than a tree-shaped air freshener like her gran used to keep in her Plymouth. Plus, the scent of Nash's car didn't make her feel ill in the way Gran's car had on a hot summer's day.

Nash slid into the driver's seat, a gust of cool morning air following him in. "All gassed up. Sorry, I should have filled the tank before picking you up. It completely slipped my mind. I'm still not used to being so far from everything and having to worry about when and where I fill up."

"That's okay," she sipped the takeout coffee he passed her. "I'd rather wait than be stuck in the middle of nowhere."

"How is it?" he asked, waiting while she took another sip of her coffee. "I chose the freshest looking brew, but none of it looked great."

"It's fine." The coffee was a bit bitter, but it was warm and caffeinated. Perfect for an early morning drive to the city. She smiled over the rim of her cup. He seemed as nervous as she was.

He cranked the engine and an almost-silent purring filtered into the cab.

"Have you been to one of these before?" she asked. The way he had been talking about the outreach training and info sessions and had everything organized so quickly she figured he had to have been to a million of them.

"Yes. I helped get an outreach started during one of my practicums while I was in med school."

She looked out the window as they pulled out of the gas station and tried not to sink down as community members gawked at her riding alongside Nash. He nattered on about the expertise of the people running the information sessions and Beth's mind drifted. She was going to miss her first coffee date with Oz tomorrow. What if he was ready to ask her back, but she wasn't there to leap into his arms?

But he'd told her to go follow her dreams, too. And although opening an outreach for community members wasn't a dream she'd always had, the idea of doing something new with her job was exciting. Plus, maybe if she didn't show up for their coffee date Oz would realize how much he actually needed her and that when it came to the idea of marrying her, his feet were, in reality, plenty warm.

"Do you think he's going to need a long time?" Beth asked out loud.

"The speaker? They usually have three hour sessions with a break in the middle."

"I meant ... never mind."

"Oz?" he asked gently.

She nodded, watching the mountains give way to foothills and meadows as they left the steep passes behind.

"I mean, have you ever talked to anyone who had a temporary break before they got married? Did it work out?"

Nash frowned and shook his head. "I haven't. But you know, Oz has been through a lot lately. It's not uncommon for people our age to need a bit of time to figure out what they want in life. I think it's admirable that he's doing that. You wouldn't believe the people I've seen with health problems because they've swallowed the truth about their lives for so long. It's as though it festers inside." He turned to her, his blond hair glowing in the early morning light.

"He said everyone has a secret dream." She turned to him, curious. "Do you have one?"

Nash smiled, his teeth straight and narrow. "Not so secret with me. I want to move up the chain."

"Oh, right." She felt silly forgetting that maybe other people's dreams weren't so secret and under wraps--kind of like hers.

"How about you?"

"Not so secret either. I want a family."

"Kids?"

She nodded.

"What else?" he asked.

"What do you mean?" Her back muscles tightened. *Don't tell me another man is going to tell me there's more to life than a good, fulfilling job in a small town and a table crowded with people you love.*

"There's got to be something else, right?" There was a tentative uncertainty in his question. "I mean, you like to help people." She gave a noncommittal shrug, waiting to hear him out. "I can see it when you work with your patients. That's one of the reasons I know you're going to rock this outreach thing. Not only will it be fulfilling, but it'll look great on your resumé."

"And fill a community need," she reminded.

"And heck, maybe you'll discover your dream is to open a private outreach or become one of those consultants we'll see today. They've got to make some serious coin."

"I'd miss my CCPs."

"Your what?"

"Continuing care patients." How could she explain that working with the elderly settled that scared feeling she had inside? That it gave her hope seeing people live long, fulfilling lives. She'd managed to explain it to Oz once, but that's because he knew her. He knew her whole life, and could fill in the pieces that even she didn't understand. To explain everything from start to finish to an outsider felt like too much work. Besides, she liked how Nash saw her in a different light without all her history and baggage. He saw her as she stood today. Nobody else in Blueberry Springs would have suggested that she open an outreach and fulfill the area's need for outpatient recreational therapy. But he did.

And she liked that. A lot. And she didn't want to spoil it.

"But you never know," she said. "Keep throwing ideas at me. I liked the first one!" She grinned and admired the way his quads flexed under their denim covering as he shifted gears to climb the last big hill before leaving the mountains completely behind. That and the gossip and advice swirling in Blueberry Springs.

5

---

eth shifted from foot to foot while waiting outside the trailer she'd called home for almost two and a half years, waiting for her courage to catch up with her. She hesitated with her fist raised against the inner wood door. It felt odd to knock.

Tucking the dirt bike magazine under her arm she readjusted the screen door and knocked. After her fifth knock the trailer door swung inward revealing Oz, groggy and unshaven. She used to find his morning look sexy, but there was something off about his appearance that made her pause.

"Hey," she said. "I brought this for you." She handed him the magazine.

He gave her a small smile and she bounced on the balls of her feet. She couldn't wait to tell him all about the outreach program sessions. Between the speaker and Nash, they'd convinced her she should--and could--start a program. The organizer had handed her everything she needed: a program in a box. All she had to do was unpack it over the next couple of months.

"I thought we agreed we'd check in on weekends only." Oz leaned against the door, looking concerned--almost as though he was about to do something he knew he'd regret.

Beth paused, then said carefully, "I missed the weekend and wanted to talk to you about something."

He let the door swing open and moved to the kitchen just off the entry. Beth blinked as she took in the disheveled room. Beer cans and empty pizza boxes. Poker night had obviously been reinstated. She sat at the table across from Oz. He leaned back in his chair and watched her, arms crossed as though protecting himself. Feeling self-conscious in her work clothes while he was in a pair of sweats and a tee, she kept her eyes on the opened bottle of Johnny Walker. It sat next to a melted tray of ice cubes and a shot glass. Whiskey was not Oz's usual drink of choice.

"Is this a bad time?" Most mornings he was showered and finishing breakfast by now. "Maybe I should have waited until Sunday?"

"It's fine." He continued to stare at her.

"Aren't you going to work?"

He shook his head. He seemed sad.

She opened her mouth to tell him he had to work, but quickly switched to something less likely to cause a fight. "How was your weekend?"

"Fine." His arms tightened across his chest. "Yours?" His jaw flexed and Beth drew in a long, slow breath, feeling as though she had parachuted into a minefield.

"I wanted to tell you about that," she began. All weekend she'd wanted to text him about her plans and ideas, but had held off as part of their agreement. This morning, while getting ready for work, she'd just about bubbled over from excitement thinking of how she was heading over to share her news with her best friend. But now she wasn't sure how to dive in when he seemed inexplicably peeved.

"I've already heard all about your weekend," he said, his voice hard. His eyes shut as though he was dealing with a sharp pain.

"Are you okay?"

"Fine."

"Are you sure? You don't look too good."

"I'm fine."

She really wanted his advice and approval about the outreach--especially since it would affect his weekends once they were back together, too. "Do you think it's a good idea?"

Oz gave her a hard look that was difficult to decipher. The vibe coming off him told her something was terribly off as well as really, really wrong.

"What?" Unease settled over her like an itchy wool sweater.

"Giving your ring back, moving out, then telling the town you're doing it with the new doctor followed by taking off to the city to spend all weekend with him? Don't you think that might be what's wrong?"

Beth's skin grew cold. "I was joking."

"Nobody's laughing."

Her face heated with guilt. She never would have guessed that he would assume the worst from any rumors. He was usually so good about saying there had to be another side to the story.

"It was a training session. I'm starting an outreach program." She tried to meet his eyes, begging him to believe her. To trust her. To know her heart was still his.

"It's only a break, Beth. We're still exclusive. We're still engaged."

"I know that! Could you trust me a little?"

"I'm finding it a little difficult right now."

"Oz. I was joking! Mary Alice and Liz were hounding me." Beth slammed her hands on the table and stood.

"You're not the kind of girl who jokes about that kind of thing." Oz stood, face red. He grabbed the bottle of whiskey and took a swig, his face contorting as he swallowed.

Beth planted her hands on the tabletop and leaned forward. "Do you know how hard the rumor mill is working me over right now? Do you have any idea how much their probing and speculation hurts?"

He pointed a finger at her. "You're the one who chose to leave your ring here. You're the one who chose to move out. You're the one who chose the doctor."

"I didn't choose him. Do you really think I could have stayed here without you and that I'd choose some city man? I moved out because you wanted me out of your life!"

He stood, echoing her posture, bringing them almost nose-to-nose over the table. "I don't want you out of my life, dammit!"

"You broke up with me. You didn't tell me until it was too late that you wanted to change your life. You didn't give me a chance."

"It's a goddamned break so I can get my shit together!" His breath pushed against her face.

"You don't even love me--"

Oz grabbed her face in his large hands and shoved his lips against hers, silencing her. He kissed her slow and with meaning. Legs trembling from the effort of leaning over the table, she collapsed against the tabletop when he released her.

"What was that?" she whispered.

"The truth."

She looked up at his soft brown eyes, the burn of Johnny Walker still on her tongue. She slid into her chair, trying to make sense of him, his thoughts, his actions. Why was he kissing her with his 'I want to take you to bed' kiss when he'd been so blatantly clear about them being chaste? About her not tempting him because he needed space to think. Maybe she should have asked the same of him.

Still leaning over the table Oz said, "You can't move on, Beth. Give me a chance."

"I'm not moving on." She kept her head down. She knew if she looked up into those warm brown eyes that she'd beg him to take her back. More than ever she realized how much he needed space to figure out what he wanted. The old Oz would have laughed at rumors about her being with Nash. He would have been overjoyed with her outreach plan. This was not her Oz. Her Oz was MIA.

It was like the family Christmas photos her mom used to send out as their Christmas card. Every year, wearing a new festive sweater, she'd hand Cynthia and Beth their own kid-sized versions and instruct them to try them on without removing the tags. They'd try them on in the living room and her mother would be so pleased with how they looked, she'd pull out her camera and pose the girls in front of the decorated tree. Every year. And every year when Beth went looking for the sweater to wear on Christmas Eve she could never find a trace of it. The garments disappeared just as they had appeared--hers to wear briefly, to revel in the joy of having one just like everyone else, but then it would slip away when she wasn't paying attention.

And right now, that's how their relationship felt. The snapshots and memories were proof of its existence, but she couldn't hold it in her hands or ever truly own it. She feared that, somehow, she had looked away for too long and it had disappeared.

"You need longer than a month, don't you?" she asked quietly.

Her fiancé withdrew to the chair across from her, shoulders rounded with defeat.

Silence pleated the air between them and Oz's legs began jiggling. He stood and moved to the patio door, bracing his arms against its frame. He hung his head so his forehead rested against the glass.

"You can't rush this." His voice was barely audible.

"You can't kiss me like that and then push me away." Emotion cloaked her voice and she stood. "I'll wait for you, but don't toy with me."

———

BETH BURST into Katie's basement suite, her body aching as though she'd run a marathon. "He kissed me," she announced before realizing her friend was watching a chick flick. The kind of movies Katie mocked at great length. She froze in the doorway and her roomie flicked off the TV, turning to her with a massive smile.

"He did?"

Beth fell onto the couch beside Katie. "I don't know what it means."

Even though she'd had all day to settle her feelings, she still felt as though her world was resting on a bed of loose marbles. Somehow their relationship's short-term break had turned into an open-ended disaster.

49

"He still looooves you," Katie said in a sticky sweet voice.

Beth touched her lips. The pressure of his mouth was still hot and furious against hers despite the hours that had lapsed since the kiss. "I can't shake the feeling that there's something wrong. Really wrong." She turned to face her friend. "He drank Johnny Walker right from the bottle and the place is a mess. He isn't going in to work."

Katie frowned.

Beth wove the hem of her sweater between her fingers. "I think he actually believed the rumors about me."

"Maybe that's a good thing." She nudged Beth and smiled.

Beth shoved her back, unimpressed. "How is that a good thing?"

"If you're out flirting with other men, he'll get over his cold feet and come marching back. There's nothing like knowing another man is after your cherry pie to make you hustle."

"Katie," Beth sighed. "He totally misinterpreted me attending the training session with Nash. We're moving away instead of closer." Panic swelled inside her and she jumped up to pace across the small living space, making the floor-length curtains flutter.

"I hate to say it, but if your relationship is as great as you think ..."

Beth felt Katie watching her and she bristled, dreading what her friend's next words might be and if they might be those same dark worries she'd been persistently shaking off at every turn for the past week. Katie continued, picking her words carefully. "Wouldn't he want you by his side if he's going through a premature midlife crisis or whatever it is?"

Beth blinked back tears. "I thought so, but Nash said--"

"Nash?"

"Dr. Leham."

"I know who he is, but you were talking to *him* about your Oz problems?"

"What?" Beth asked defensively. "He's a good listener. And he believes Oz is trying to protect me. That Oz needs time to sort things out alone. I mean, it's pretty noble of Oz to stand up and say he needs time and not just bury it all."

Katie squinted at Beth. "He's protecting you by making you homeless?"

"I could have stayed." Beth worked to fight the coming tears and wandered over to Katie's shelf of snow globes. One by one, she picked them up and gave them a shake, making snow fall down on tropical scenes, snowmen, cityscapes, and fairytale settings. "What if everything changes? What if after he finds himself we aren't compatible any longer?"

She watched the snow drift and swirl down, and how within seconds the snow globe world was back to normal. Envious. She was envious of a snow globe's world. She sighed and turned to Katie. "He already seems like a different person." She slumped back into place alongside her friend.

Katie scratched her cheek, her eyes showing her worry. "Well ... don't you think it's worth waiting to find out?"

Beth thought of her lonely nights on the hide-a-bed and how much she missed hearing Oz tell her about his day while wrapped in his arms. How during the day she'd start to text him about something he'd find funny and have to stop, or how she'd pick up something in the store, thinking of him, and have to put it back again. How empty and sad she felt. It was like mourning him except he was still alive. Living a life without her.

"Of course it's worth it." She sighed. "I just need to find a way to help him while still giving him space. He's struggling and I want to show him that I'm still here if he needs me. He doesn't have to push me away. I can handle whatever he's going through."

***

BETH CRADLED the career and self-help books in her arms and bumped her office door open with her butt. She dropped the books on top of her filing cabinet and grinned. Her lunch break was over, but the inspiration and hope she'd felt in the fresh April air hadn't ended. Something flowery had been blooming near the library, tinting the breeze with a gentle sweetness that had made her never want to stop inhaling. The scent had made the world feel new and as though anything was possible. Even getting back together with Oz. She slipped her cardigan off her shoulders and hung it on the hanger by the door. All she had to do was take the books to Oz during their coffee on Sunday and that fresh spring air would do the rest. He'd be convinced that it was time to figure out what his dream was--really and truly--and he'd etch out a plan and follow it. His world would be lit on fire and he'd yank her back into his arms where he'd never, ever let her go.

And unlike Katie who thought she should flirt with other guys to motivate Oz, she knew she had time. She was young and free and the desperation she felt a week ago had ebbed away. There was no rush, especially now that she was crazy-busy organizing her new outreach program. Only two measly months until it would open. She grabbed an overstuffed file folder off her desk and flipped through the top couple of papers, looking for the permit form she needed to complete and drop off at town hall after work.

She scooted to the door, pushing it closed. The latch failed and it drifted open a few inches. She nudged it again and within seconds it creaked open again. Sighing she put down her papers and logged into her computer. She fired off a quick work order to maintenance to fix her door and finished filling out her outreach permit.

Rubbing her eyes, she placed the completed form in her purse. Wasn't she the gal getting stuff taken care of today? Two things off her plate and she'd only been back in her office for ten minutes. And yesterday she'd done pretty well, too. She'd used half her paycheck to replace the alternator and repair a few things on her car she'd been waiting for Oz to take care of. When word got back to him that she'd gone to the shop instead of him he'd see that she was giving him the space to try being someone else. They could both change and still love each other. Her grin grew even further. He was going to be stinkin' proud of her. Maybe this week would even be the one where he ended the break.

Voices drifted down the hall and Beth rolled herself over to shut the door. As she reached out to give it a tap, she caught a glimpse of blond hair swaying like a satin cape and she quickly scooted behind the door, her heart hammering. That hair could only belong to one person: Mandy.

"Why don't you date him?" a voice asked Mandy. Beth held in a gasp, clenching her chair's armrests to keep herself from sprinting into the hall and saying something she'd be sure to regret. The latest monsoon of rumors said Mandy was Oz's new confidant and that they were hanging out around town together. Everyone was waiting for Beth to go screaming into the streets to yell at her rival. She could feel it like Gran could feel rain coming in her joints.

Mandy laughed. "What men want and what they need are two totally different things. Sometimes it's up to us women to do what's right for a man."

"Are you talking about Frankie or Oz?" asked the voice as they drifted down the hall.

Beth stood and put her ear to the hinge side of the door, but could only make out laughter and murmurs as the two women continued on their way.

Beth rubbed her temples, a massive headache closing in. *What did that mean?*

She glanced at the career and self-help books and put her head in her hands. Did Oz want or need space? Were the books what he needed? If Oz was hanging around Mandy, was she a want or a need? Beth needed to figure out what to do. Both for Oz as well as herself.

6

The ring shimmered in the June sunlight. Beth gazed at it, emotions churning. A happily ever after. A perfect proposal and dedication of love for the whole town to see in the square on Main Street during the annual Sports Day carnival. Bells jangled as a teen won an oversized teddy bear for his girlfriend. Envy rose up, rubbing a raw spot in Beth's chest.

"Isn't it amazing?" her sister asked.

The constant crush of people swilling around them combined with the stench of overheated frying oil became too much. Beth choked back her envy and pulled her sister into a fierce hug. "I'm so happy for you." This was what Cynthia needed: a reward at the end of a long stint of taking care of everyone and growing up too soon.

Beth swiped at her eyes as she released her sister.

It wasn't fair. Her sister was naturally strong and independent. She didn't have to work at it. Both Cynthia and Katie were happy, free, and independent without men. But Beth was in an unhappy limbo without her man. It had been almost three months since Oz asked for his break and nothing had changed. Nothing. Oz hadn't read the library books. He still didn't know what he wanted to do with his life and it looked as though everything was falling to pieces around him. And yet he still pushed her back, not allowing her to stand beside him or help clear a path.

She was frustrated with herself because, terrified of rocking their sinking boat, she kept giving him one more week before she pressed him into taking some sort of action--any action--and kept hoping that this would be the week where he figured everything out. Meanwhile, everywhere she looked people were hooking up, getting engaged, and falling in love.

Oz needed to make an effort she could see. Straightening her back Beth decided today was the day when she would take definitive action and push Oz out of his rut and into real life again.

Somehow.

Her sister, beaming like crazy, waved to her new fiancé, Dan, who was leaning against the oak, grinning like the dog that had finally caught the mailman. Cynthia hugged Beth's arm. "He convinced me that you'll be okay. That I can let go and live my life." Her sister rested a cool hand against Beth's cheek. "You will be okay, won't you?"

"Yeah, of course." Beth tried to shrug off her sister.

"It'll all work out for you, Beth."

"Go give your man a kiss, Cynthia." If they kept talking Beth would end up bawling in the center of town--just when the rumors were finally beginning to die down around her and Oz.

She watched her sister jog over to Dan and flop herself into his arms. Beth wandered off to watch the baseball games, settling herself in the shade of a large tree. She waved to Katie who was on the other side of the diamond chatting with her father. Her friend had spent the past two months nudging her into other men in the movie theater's lineups and trying to set Beth up with blind dates, double dates, and plain old dates in an effort to make Beth look like a hot commodity her brother was about to lose if he didn't spring into action. But each time Beth would blush and step away, refusing the hook up.

Beth turned to take in the craziness of the carnival behind her. She needed to do something that would spin Oz around. Fast and hard but in a way that wouldn't cause him to freak out. Through a break in the crowd she caught a glimpse of her sister and Dan making out and the band of muscles across her chest tightened as though they had become part boa constrictor. She caught herself scanning the crowd of familiar faces in an effort to spot Oz.

And there he was. Tall, handsome, ambling along, shrugging off congratulations with a smile as he cruised through the crowds, a massive teddy bear tucked under his arm. Spotting her, he drifted toward her side.

"Hey." Oz stood above her, his free hand tucked in the pocket of his jeans.

Beth gave him a nod of acknowledgement, squinting against the splashes of sunshine poking through holes in the branches above him. What would he do if she stood up, grabbed his face and gave him a long, passionate kiss? Would he reciprocate? She hated to admit it, but the comment she overheard Mandy tell her friend about what men wanted and what they needed being two different things was still circling around in her head. Did Oz need space, or did he just *think* he needed it? How could she help? How could she take action to change their lives? She pondered that every day but was still stumped.

"I heard the news." He tipped his head toward the carnival. "Your sister and Dan, huh?"

"Yep."

"Was it cheesy?" He sat beside her on the grass, propping up his new stuffed friend. She resisted the urge to reach out and wrap her hand in his. Everything about him right now was familiar and comforting. Like it always had been. Except … it wasn't.

She shook her head. "She said it was romantic and personal and just the way I always said it should be." She looked away from Oz, remembering their own engagement and how they'd made an ordinary day special. Made it theirs. No tacking onto holidays. That day was all theirs.

"Good," Oz said.

"But they picked Valentine's Day for their wedding." Beth raised an eyebrow and Oz burst out laughing, leaning back to prop himself on an elbow.

"For real?"

"I know. Cheese alert, right? I tried to convince her to move it to the seventeenth." Beth batted her eyelashes and twisted a bare shoulder his way. "I will be a lovely bridesmaid, of course." She tried to smile, despite the pain of talking about someone else's wedding.

"Of course," he said quietly, his eyes focused on the baseball diamond in front of them.

The sat in silence, watching the two baseball teams rearrange players in order to even things out again. Most years Oz was traded back and forth to even out the teams.

"You're not playing?" Oz shook his head. "Why not?" He shrugged. "What's up with the teddy bear?"

Oz rubbed its blue ear. "Habit."

He hadn't given it to her yet. Apparently that was no longer a habit.

"What are you going to do with it?"

"Charity, I guess." Beth reminded herself that she didn't need another teddy bear. A token of Oz's affection, yes. But another bear, no. "What's that one you always give to?" he asked.

"I give them to whichever kid has been in the hospital overnight. If there isn't anyone, I give them to Katie and she passes it on."

They sat in silence for a moment. "I heard you got your car fixed at the shop?"

"Yeah, a few months ago." She turned to him, hoping to see a look of pleased relief on his face. Instead she saw pain. "What?"

"Why didn't you come see me?"

"Because you're ... busy. And I can get things done on my own." Plus, she didn't want to spend their precious weekly check-in talking to whatever part of his body was sticking out from under her car. Not being able to see his face made it difficult to gauge how he was feeling about his life and their relationship.

He tilted his head. "You don't want me to work on your car?"

"Oz, we only see each other for an hour a week. Paying someone else to fix my car is a small price to pay."

Oz leaned back on his elbows and studied her for a moment. "You're different."

She shook her head, her ponytail tickling the back of her neck. "No, I'm not."

"You are. I think you needed a break, too."

"I most certainly did not!" Beth stood up, dusting off her bottom. "Just because I'm not sitting around with my finger over my life's pause button doesn't mean this is a good thing." Oz popped up from his spot on the ground as she raised her wobbling voice. "And like you're one to talk. What have you done over the past three months other than drink more beer than usual? This was supposed to be time apart so you could find yourself. You're wasting my life. You aren't even working."

"Ed is taking care of my clients so I can think."

Beth tried to hold her ground when Oz stepped closer, his nostrils flaring slightly. She couldn't help but wish he'd kiss her even though they were starting what was sure to be a good fight that would blow out all the frustration she was feeling. "Of course he is! He's your direct competition. He's going to take your clients. It's irresponsible and--"

Chest to chest, Oz's warm breath blew over her. "You know what's irresponsible? Going to the office and not taking care of myself. My needs."

"And what exactly are your *needs*, Oz?" She leaned back and poked him in the chest. "You think you're important enough you can screw over everyone who depends on you? Why don't you just waltz around town saying, 'Sorry, this is *me time*, folks' then sit at home and do *nothing*? How many people do you have waiting in limbo because you're a big chicken shit who can't dump what he doesn't want any longer and move on?"

Oz grabbed her wrist and held her body tight to his. "Don't push me Beth. Don't make us say things we'll both regret. I'm trying. You have to trust me." He held her chin in his hand, his gaze softening. "Do you trust me?" he whispered.

She sniffed back tears and nodded, even though she didn't want to. She just wanted him to release her and stop feeling like everything was whirling through her life like her body was on spin cycle.

"Then you have to believe that I'm working as hard as I can. And right now I have to figure out if some of the things I took for granted are missable."

"Am I missable?" Oz sighed and gave her a tired half-smile. "Am I?"

He gave her a light kiss on the forehead and released her from his grip. She held her anger in check, waiting for him to tell her he loved her and missed her desperately, as desperately as his eyes sometimes showed. But he remained quiet.

Oz scooped his hands through his hair and turned away. "I need to go. I can't talk about things right now. Maybe in a couple of weeks."

She watched him stride across the grass, his head lowered. She sat against the tree and hugged her knees, burying her face so nobody would see her wet eyes. Slowly regaining control, she leaned back against the tree and ground her teeth. Without seeing, she watched the baseball game until a shadow moved across her legs.

She looked up to see a decent distraction. Her friend looking as handsome in his around-town garb as he did in his scrubs. "Oh my God! Who's manning the hospital?" she half joked, trying to smile.

Nash laughed. "Everyone seems to be here. Besides," he tapped the phone hanging from his belt, "I have this."

Beth pointed to a fair-haired lady playing shortstop. "Well, you'll be treating her in a few hours." She smoothed her hands over her bare knees, trying to dissipate the residual hurt from her conversation with Oz. "If you see her heading for the parking lot, consider yourself paged."

"What? Why?" He studied the woman in alarm.

"She gets heatstroke every year." She bit down a smile as his gorgeous eyes flicked around the park before sneaking a peek at his phone, his shoulders stiff.

Once certain he hadn't missed a message, he asked, "Can I get you an ice cream?" He gestured to the ice cream truck parked on a sunny patch of grass. "I was going to get myself something."

"An ice cream would be great." She reached into her pocket, pulling out a crumpled five.

"My treat. What would you like?"

A way to motivate Oz into fixing whatever the heck was wrong with him. Someone to take her to lunch and make her forget her problems. Maybe show her the world. A little wining and dining. Someone kind, generous, and caring. Someone to snuggle. Someone to take the edge off of being heartbreakingly almost-single. Unfortunately, she was pretty sure Mandy wasn't serving that up in her cousin's ice-cream truck and it was all a bit much to ask of Nash.

"A Creamsicle would be fabulous," she replied, finally. "Why aren't you playing?" She tilted her head toward the ball diamond.

"I don't play."

"It's just for fun. Non-competitive."

He shook his head. "Nope. Not for me."

She frowned. Two outfielders were piggybacking, yelling for the batter to hit the ball to them. Not exactly competitive. "You have to compete or you won't play?"

"I meant baseball isn't the sport for me." He held up his baby-soft hands. "These are my instruments. I can't afford to injure them."

"Well, you get a mitt. I'm sure you'd be okay."

"There are no guarantees. Better safe than out of work for six weeks."

"Right." Beth nodded. "So, uh, a Creamsicle?"

"Orange?"

"Is there any other?" Beth asked playfully, slipping out of her funk.

"There is also pink and blue."

She lowered her gaze to her tank top's spaghetti strap and slipped it off her shoulder, pretending to check for signs of sunburn. She snuck a peek at Nash through her mascaraed lashes. His face turned a lovely rouge, and his eyes appeared stuck gazing at her bare shoulder. "Orange is fine, thanks."

"Me too. I like orange. Orange Creamsicles." He smoothed the front of his shirt and ran a hand through his hair. "Well, uh, I'll ..." He cleared his throat and tore his eyes away from her tanned shoulder with apparent effort. "Just go over and ..." His voice trailed off and he pointed to the ice-cream truck.

"Thanks." She gave him a shy smile, feeling guilty for flirting as a way out of her funk, but relieved that at least someone still found her appealing. Oz was seriously not good for the self-esteem these days. She glanced over her shoulder, worried that maybe Oz had been coming back to spill his thoughts and had seen her flirting.

There was nobody paying attention to them other than Mary Alice who was stuffing blue cotton candy in her yap. Great. That woman could spread gossip faster than the flu in a whorehouse. She closed her eyes hoping if word got back to Oz he'd know Beth was just being a goof and not seriously after Nash. He was a city boy, after all, with plans to return there. It was pretty obvious she was just playing around.

Her gaze wandered over Nash who had joined the ice-cream lineup in his crisp chino shorts, his athletic legs bearing just the right amount of hair. Despite herself, she had to agree with Gran: the man had a nice tush. And when was the last time he had a girlfriend? Judging from the way he threw himself into his work, it had probably been a long, long time which made flirting with him all that much more fun.

And dangerous.

"Were you just *flirting* with *Nash*?" Katie whispered as she joined Beth in the grass.

"What? No." She gave a little start and a laugh. "I work with Nash. Like I would flirt." She made a disgruntled sound.

But oh, yeah. She would flirt. She would flirt his shirt off and keep on going if she were carefree and single. She scanned the crowds again, hoping to spot Oz's broad shoulders heading back to her.

"I happen to work with him, too, but I don't expose flesh for him."

"I was checking for sunburn. The UV index is very high today."

"Right, Roomie." She flipped Beth's strap back onto her shoulder.

"I heard the place above the laundromat is available next month. I'll take it and let you have your space back finally."

"Just keep staying with me--that place is already taken. I don't mind the company."

Beth struggled against a storm of frustration. Every time she found a place, it was already gone no matter how fast she moved.

"Anyway, the guy has to come around eventually, right?"

Beth squeezed her eyes shut. As much as she wanted to believe her friend, she was fairly certain her man was shoring up his courage before cutting the last cord between them. But to be sure she had to push him one last time.

***

"So, nobody got sunstroke? That must be a first," Beth said, as she sauntered down Main Street with Nash. While she knew she shouldn't be hanging out with him because of the rumors they would start, a part of her wanted to prove to the town, as well as Oz, that she could be friends with a man and not have anything untoward happen. Besides, Oz was either going to see them together and decide he really did miss her, or he was going to see them together and decide he didn't. Either way something would happen.

The streets were still busy at four in the afternoon and every so often they had to dodge clumps of pedestrians, but it wasn't nearly as bad as in the square where the band had started up, the baseball games were still going, and the mini carnival was making such a racket it was almost impossible to speak without shouting--even while tucked under a tree watching Katie play ball.

"Nope." Nash tapped his phone. "And I'm off call now."

"You're almost like a true member of Blueberry Springs. Going to a town event. Careful or our warm country ways will get to you. You'll wake up and find yourself happily married to a country bumpkin and driving a beat up old truck." She gave him a teasing shove.

Nash laughed and slung an arm around Beth's shoulders, steering her into the ice-cream shop. Beth blushed as a few people she knew looked the two of them over, their gaze lingering on Nash's arm.

"I'm not the country bumpkin lovin' type. And besides, I'm not going to start anything serious until I'm back in Dakota." He opened the fridge near the door and waved a Coke in her direction. "Drink?"

She nodded. If she didn't want a city man and Nash didn't want a country bumpkin they could remain perfect, platonic friends. Which was great because she'd come to rely on his shoulder to cry and laugh on when she had a tough day or simply wanted someone to sit with in the cafeteria.

"So, you're going to put your whole life on hold?" she asked Nash, lightly touching his forearm. "Because having your life on hold sucks the big one."

"Well," he paused, considering her comment, "nothing in life is guaranteed. I've seen how fast things can change in a person's life. My life's not on hold, but my focus is on my career. Right now I need to gain as much experience as I can so I can leverage it when I return to Dakota. I'm planning to move into administration."

"Why?" She frowned. "You'll never get to work with patients." From what she'd seen and heard, Nash had talent combined with great instincts. Plus, patients generally trusted him--even though he was an outsider.

"It's the next step up the ladder. You should really consider finding more ways to move up with your own career. You don't want to stagnate."

Moving up the ladder was exhausting. Despite the thrill of organizing her own outreach program, she couldn't imagine doing this extra work *all* the time. She missed having her whole weekend to chill out and relax like she used to do with Oz. Today was the first full day off she'd taken since the info session and next week she opened the outreach, meaning her life was suddenly going to kick into high gear.

"The experience I'm getting here is great. There aren't any specialists so I get to dabble in a lot of areas before sending patients to Dakota."

"But wouldn't you miss working with patients? I can't see admin being a heart job."

Nash shrugged.

"But what about all those years of med school? You've got talent you wouldn't get to use in an office."

"Wouldn't be wasted. Good doctors make good administrators. Usually." He smiled down at her. "But not always. It is important to have someone in the position who understands what it's like on the floor." He placed a hand lightly on her lower back and directed them to the cash register where a few people were lined up buying cones.

Nash tilted his head toward the row of farmers and town folk drinking coffee out of plain white cups at the beverage bar at the back of the shop. "Think I should get some local head gear?"

Beth glanced at Nash's perfect hair, barely mussed by the sunglasses perched on top of his head. All the men at the bar wore caps, even though they were indoors. "Where are your manners?" she called out to them.

Hats popped off in unison as the men realized she was speaking to them.

Grinning, she shook her head and waggled her finger at the men. A few smiled sheepishly while Nash stared at her with a mix of mock fear and true awe. Laughing, she reached over to the nearby hat rack and dusted off a cap that had been there for ages. "How about this?" She turned it to face him.

"Chevy?" he asked with distain. He spun the wobbly rack. "Is there one that says BMW?"

"Careful now." She glanced around the busy shop as though he'd said something offensive. The man seriously needed to learn what was cool and what wasn't in a small town. "If you want to fit in, it's either this one, or this one, or this one." She added a green John Deere cap and a blue Ford hat to her collection.

Nash grimaced. "Maybe I can be an uprooted city boy a while longer?"

"Well, then how about this?" She held up a hat advertising fertilizer, and snatching Nash's sunglasses, popped it on his head.

"Don't you let him go paying good money for that hat, Beth," said a man joining the line behind them. "I can get you one for free at the elevator. Got a whole box of 'em behind my desk. Ranchers don't want 'em. They just want their feed."

"Thanks, Alvin." Beth set the hats back in the rack. "Sounds like you're set, City Boy."

Nash tried to smile and moved up to the counter to make their purchases. "The elevator?" he asked in an undertone.

"Grain elevator."

"You're kidding. There's farming out here?"

"Not much. More ranching. The elevator is actually a feed mill."

"So ... this is your new man. I've been hearing about him all over town." Alvin eyed up Nash.

"Nash and I *work* together, Alvin." She turned to introduce them. "This is Dr. Leham."

Alvin leaned back, sizing up Nash who was paying for their drinks. "Thought you and Oz were getting married." His eyes lingered on her bare finger. "That's what my old lady was telling me when you were running that playground bake sale all those months ago."

"Oz is taking some time, that's all." She turned her shoulder, trying to politely end the conversation.

"I s'pose he's got some business to attend to with his old man leaving him the business." He shook his head to and fro. "Sad to see Harvey retire so young, but heart attacks can be real life changers." He waited until Beth met his eye. "Oz needs a good woman by his side while he works on filling some mighty big shoes."

"I know." Beth bit the insides of her cheeks and calmed her

breathing, hoping to quell the humiliation and rage brewing within her, ready to spew forth like lava.

"I heard he's been losing clients."

"He's contracted some to Ed," she managed in a tight voice. "He has a big workload."

Nash gently took Beth's elbow. "Shall we?"

Beth nodded and Alvin stepped up to the counter, his gaze still on Beth and Nash. "Send Oz my regards," he called as they made their way to the door. Beth stiffened but kept walking.

On the street Nash let out a breath. "Wow. That was hardcore." He dropped her elbow and turned to face her. "You okay?"

Beth pushed past him, her thoughts streaming through her head like an old VCR stuck on fast forward. How could Oz put her in this humiliating position? Why couldn't he either get back together or dump her outright? Limbo was like Hell and all its subsidiaries rolled into one.

Nash snatched her elbow when he caught up. "Whoa. Slow down."

Beth stopped on the street corner and forced herself to take a chill pill. "Why can't he just figure out what he wants and either marry me or dump me?" Her eyes filled with tears and she sagged against Nash when he put an arm around her for support. He brought her close against his chest in a one-armed hug.

"Sorry." He released her. "I hope hanging out with me isn't making things tougher." He gave her a sympathetic look. "Do you want me to head out?"

"No." She swiped at her tears and straightened her spine. "Screw them and the horse they rode in on."

Nash let out a laugh. "Whoa! What do you have against horses?"

She laughed and tried to shake off her mood.

He opened a bottle of Coke and handed it to her before opening the second bottle. They took a swig and watched each other. Feeling self-conscious, Beth began walking allowing Nash to fall into step beside her. His shoulder bumped against hers as they walked and before long she found herself nudged up against the buildings to her left. He was a nice guy, but city folks must be used to having less personal space. Every time she looked over at him he was right up against her like he was trying to avoid being separated from her in the nonexistent crowds.

Nash rested a hand on her lower back as they stepped off the curb to cross the street. Beth forced herself to relax and enjoy having a man looking out for her. Holding doors. Buying her a drink. Standing close.

In the next block, he stopped to point out a fancy coffee maker in the hardware store's window. "That's nice."

Beth dropped her empty bottle in a recycle bin. "Looks a bit over the top. Seriously. That thing could send monkeys to the moon."

Nash let out a bark of laughter and slung an easy arm over her shoulder. "I've been looking for an espresso maker like this. It makes everything you could ever want."

"Does it make black coffee?"

Nash chuckled. "You'll never want black coffee again."

Beth shot him a skeptical frown and slipped out of his embrace as she continued walking. "Want to check out the museum?" she asked, walking backward as he caught up. "It has some interesting old farming and ranching stuff. Some of the meadows used to be farmland. There's also some old expedition equipment and mining stuff. This mountain town has been a bit of everything."

Nash's eyebrows perked in interest. "I like museums." He guided her through a line of people piling into a hay wagon to take them to the exhibition grounds for the tractor pull.

"Or we could go to the tractor pull," Beth said as they passed the wagon. Tucking a tendril behind her ear, she tightened her ponytail. She hooked her arm through his and pulled him through the crowd, trying not to care who saw them and what they thought. "There's also going to be a logging competition."

"Actually," Nash said when they reached the other side of the crowd, "how about we grab a bite to eat?"

"Okay."

"Shall we clean up and meet somewhere for dinner?"

Beth glanced at her outfit, then at Nash's. "What's wrong with what we're wearing?"

Nash gave her a blank stare before blinking a few times. "I was thinking it might be nice to go out for a real dinner."

Beth stopped short, panic racing through her. "Like a date?" A formal date was not safe. It was not innocent. It was not above board. She had been certain he knew they were only friends and that was all they would ever be.

Nash met her eyes with his calm, blue seas. "Sure. If you'd like."

She looked down the street.

"Nothing official," he said. "I know you and Oz are on a break and you're not single. I'm thinking, sort of like friends on a dinner date. I don't want to get involved with anyone. And you're waiting for Oz. We're both lonely and bored. We could use a treat, and it sucks treating yourself alone. What do you say?"

"Yes," she blurted. She grew dizzy with visions of Oz morphing into a primal alpha male who would charge in and carry her off to his den when he saw the competition closing in. The thing to spur change. To push him into action at long last.

Happily ever after, here we come.

BETH ENTERED THE RESTAURANT, still dressed as she was for Sports Day. Glancing around the bustling place she said to Nash, "It's a good thing we came early. It's going to be packed by six."

Nash nodded, his face lighting up in recognition and delight. "Mandy! You work *here*, as well?" He gave a laugh. "I never pegged you as a workaholic."

He gave her the kind of smile that made Beth want to blurt out that she took work home, too. Even though she never had until she began working on the outreach program. In fact, it had never even occurred to her before then.

Mandy grinned at Nash, her Lusciously Pink lipstick making her already full lips tantalizingly kissable. She clutched the plastic menus to her chest in a way that made her breasts lift higher, exposing more cleavage. Beth had to admit, if she was a guy looking for a hot number, Mandy would be the first girl she'd hit upon. But she wasn't and the urge to slap Mandy was so unreal her palm tingled.

"Just started my shift," Mandy said as she waggled closer to Nash, eyes never leaving him. "Can't miss the busiest night of the year." She let her shoulder bump into his. "I like to satiate men whether it's with ice cream or something else."

Nash smiled back. "Table for two, please."

"You two are together?" Mandy raised an eyebrow at Beth as though she couldn't possibly imagine someone like Nash with someone like Beth.

Beth smiled and linked an arm through Nash's. "Yep. We're moving up from cafeteria food. We intend to write a book on the best and worst dining establishments in the area."

Nash let out a chuckle and patted Beth's hand. "Will you rate the restrooms? I hear that's often missing from eating guides."

Mandy's mouth tightened. She gave a crisp, "Follow me," and strode away.

Nash ushered Beth with a hand resting lightly on her back. "Next time we'll have to go to Dakota. McKenzie's has amazing crème brûlée. Although, that might be out of our book's range. Maybe we'll have to go for fun."

Beth laughed, wondering why she felt so jittery and nervous. It was as though this was a real date and impressions were being made as to whether they'd be suitable mates. A blush seeped over her cheeks at the thought of Nash as more than a friend and wearing less than his shorts and shirt.

"What do you think?" He leaned in to speak in her ear.

She gave herself a shake, removing the thoughts from her mind. They were strictly friends dining together with a possible added benefit of showing her fiancé that she was something missable. "I've heard good things about the place."

Nash's warm hand lingered on her waist and she struggled to ignore the looks being shot at him by other diners.

Mandy stopped them at the window table with a smug smile. "Here you go." She slapped down the menus.

Beth froze and Nash stumbled into her from behind. "Mandy, this table? Could we--"

"Best table in the place, Beth," she chirped and spun on her heel, leaving them to seat themselves.

Yeah, best table in the place for starting rumors. She and Oz used to sit at this exact table every Wednesday night and watch the town mosey by. And every Sunday for the past three months they'd met at this table to check in on how life was going. To sit here with someone else felt wrong, wrong, wrong. It was one thing to hang out with another man, but this was making a statement about territory and intentions.

Nash pulled out her chair, the familiar wood armrests and the worn padded seat waiting for her. How many times had she sat in that chair and laughed and dined with Oz, not a care in the world?

"Maybe we should go somewhere else?" she said quietly.

"What's wrong?"

She glanced at the pre-dinner crowd. As she met eyes, they quickly looked away. Anger burned inside her. She straightened her back and raised her chin. She was not going to run away or act guilty. She wasn't going to let the town run them off. She was going to sit down, with her friend, and eat dinner. She plunked herself in the offered chair and opened her menu, giving the nearest gawking table a little wave. Their heads bent down immediately, attention absorbed in their meals.

"So?" Beth asked Nash. "What shall we have? The pizza is good, but Benny is known for his burgers. And his chocolate maven pie."

Nash sat across from her, his eyes wary as he glanced around the room. He opened his menu. "Burgers you say?"

"It's called Benny's Big Burger for a reason. But they branched out a few years ago when the so-called date restaurant closed down."

Nash raised his eyebrows in question.

"Fire. Benny seized the moment and expanded." She pointed to the spot where the carpet changed from mauve to beige a few tables past Nash. "You can see the new addition." She laughed at his unimpressed expression. "I've had everything on the menu, so if you have questions, I'm your gal."

Nash raised an eyebrow. "Everything?"

Beth scanned the menu to double check. "Yep."

"Really?" Nash leaned forward, elbows on the table. "Intriguing."

Beth let out a snort, back at ease with their companionship. "Not really. The town has two real restaurants and two fast food joints. This place is the best."

Mandy sidled up to the table. "Can I get you something to drink?" She kept her expertly made-up eyes on Nash, her shoulders doing the weird flirty thing that she usually reserved for Oz.

Oh, game on, Mandy, game on. It was country bumpkin vs. country bumpkin. There was no way Mandy was getting the man first this time. Even if it was just as friends.

Beth carefully tucked a tendril behind an ear and pasted her most relaxed smile on her face. Game. On.

"I'll have a glass of your house wine," Nash said, flipping his menu to the back page.

Mandy looked temporarily confused.

"They don't serve wine," Beth said.

"Nobody orders it so Benny nixed it. We have beer on tap."

"Their cocktails are generally good, too," Beth added.

"I'll have a gin and tonic, then," Nash said.

"Right-o," Mandy said, turning to leave.

Nash rested a hand on Mandy's arm to stop her. She leaned over, her cleavage at eye level. "Yes, *doctor?*" Nash blinked rapidly and quickly looked away, appearing startled that boobs had been thrust in his line of vision.

Nash asked Beth, "What would you like to drink?"

"I'll have the same, thanks."

Mandy glanced at Beth. "Since when?"

"What?" Beth asked, daring her.

"You usually have a beer or a Coke," Mandy said, a challenging saunter entering her voice.

Beth smiled and ran a hand down Nash's arm, her eyes resting on his. "I feel like doing something ... *different.*"

Mandy blinked, battling something inside. Beth ignored her as the waitress spun on her heel and marched off. Nash leaned back in his chair and sized up Beth. "A G&T makes you different, huh?"

"Around here it does." She toyed with the salt shaker.

Mandy returned, slamming the drinks on the table without a word, Beth's drink sloshing over the rim. Beth raised her eyebrows at Nash and gave a light cough of amusement.

"Wow. History and subtext," he said when she'd left.

"I'm sure she's a nice enough gal, but we've been ... never mind." Beth adjusted her ponytail and mulled over the wisdom of messing with Mandy. If she wasn't careful she'd challenge the woman right into Oz's arms.

Beth took a sip of her drink. Not bad.

"Did you enjoy getting to know Blueberry Springs a bit better?" she asked. The number of people walking outside on the street had slowed as most of the day's events came to an end. Only about eighty percent of them paused for a double take when they realized Nash wasn't Oz.

"Yeah. And thanks to you, I'm lined up for a free hat." He patted her hand and gave her a grin. "I had some fun getting to know this beautiful bumpkin as well."

His hand lingered on hers and she resisted the urge to snatch it away. People who were just friends weren't physically affectionate like this.

"You flatter me," she said, embarrassed that she was blushing. "Tell me something interesting."

Nash gripped her hand and flipping it over, lightly traced her palm's lines sending tingles racing through her like NASCAR contenders. "Did you know that you can't tan your palms?" He continued to stroke her palm, his fingers running down from palm to fingertips. "As well, there are no muscles in the fingers. The muscles that move your fingers are located in your palm."

She tried to tug her hand back, his insistent strokes teasing her.

He gave her a wicked grin and kept a strong grip. He slowly traced her palm's lifeline. "There are tendons--"

A deafening bang shook the window beside her. Beth jumped back, the feet of her chair jamming in the carpet. She stumbled as she tried to stand, Nash lunging to steady her. Outside, Oz reeled backward, his head shaking back and forth, his face wrinkled in pain.

Beth froze, staring at him.

She shook off Nash, her eyes locked on Oz's. There was no possessiveness. No alpha male ready to stride inside and carry her away like she'd dreamed. Just pain and disbelief.

Guilt crept upon Beth, weighting her as she struggled to get free of the table. She broke eye contact with Oz in order to toss her chair to the side. When she looked back he was gone. She turned to the doors, ready for him to carry her away. The restaurant's doors remained closed.

She'd blown it. Big time.

"Do you want to go after him?" Nash asked quietly.

Beth kept staring out the window. Waiting to see Oz. Waiting to know what to do. She crashed down into her seat. He wasn't following his dreams. He wasn't taking her back. It was as though he wanted her out of his life but didn't have the courage to let her go, to let her out of his heart. But why the jealousy if he wouldn't ask her back? If she was the right woman for him, why wouldn't he allow her by his side?

She looked up and heads quickly turned back to their meals, the restaurant's sounds slowly resuming. "There's nothing I can do, Nash. Nothing but move on and see what happens."

7

"I don't care." Beth turned away from Cynthia and snatched a bag of Doritos off the corner store's shelf. She strode to the cooler and grabbed a bottle of Pepsi. She would wash away her woes in a river of sugar and altered cheese.

"How can you not care what everyone is saying?" Cynthia asked, grabbing a bottle of raspberry flavored sparkling water. "You care about *every*thing."

"Do not."

"Do too."

Beth turned to face her sister, her free hand on her hip. How could she explain that she *couldn't* care what the town was saying about her and Nash's so-called hand-holding incident because she was completely freaked out by the look on Oz's face when he'd fled? She'd heard he wasn't doing well and she couldn't get him to answer the door when she stopped by. He hadn't shown up for their Sunday coffee or replied to her messages. How could she express to her sister that a mixed bag of emotions was still haunting her two days after the event?

She'd destroyed her one chance at getting back together with Oz by being impatient and insensitive. And the only person she felt she could turn to over the past two emotionally grueling days was Nash, the one person she should be avoiding.

She grabbed a bottle of Gaviscon off a nearby shelf, hoping it could relieve the pressure she had in her chest, the burning in her stomach, and the raw, gnawing feeling that was working its way through her system.

Cynthia blocked Beth's path and lowered her voice. "Dan wants to ask Oz if he'll be his best man."

Beth's ears rang and her heart did a gross feeling swoop.

"I wanted to ask you first. Since ... you know."

"It's fine," Beth said quickly. There was no way she could rain on Cynthia's wedding parade with her problems. "Of course it's fine."

"You would have duties together. Like dancing."

"I said it's fine." Beth pushed past her sister.

"It's still over six months out ..." Cynthia said, uncertainty lacing her words.

"I can handle it, okay?" Maybe they'd even be back together by then. Maybe instead of irreversibly breaking Oz, she'd motivated him in some slow, undercurrent kind of way and he'd be asking her back within a week.

Not likely, but a girl could hope.

Mary Alice waited for Beth at the cash register with a grin. "Ready to check out, dear?"

Beth piled her items on the counter and nodded.

"Heard Oz hit the bottle," Mary Alice said, giving Beth a raised eyebrow. Her heart sank. "What's up with the two of you, anyway? Everyone thought you'd be back together by now. Is that city doc elbowing his way in where he doesn't belong?"

Beth slapped her money down on the counter. "He's a friend."

"I didn't realize you two were seeing other people." Mary Alice raised her brow again.

Beth let out a frustrated grumble and bolted her lips shut. Nothing she'd say to Mary Alice right now would make things any better.

"That boy's been on a two-day bender from what I heard. Coincidental?"

Beth turned on her heel and slammed her way out of the store, the door's bells jingling merrily. Tears pricked at her eyes. She would *not* let the town get the best of her. She would hold her head high. She would not let the guilt slowly kill her.

Probably.

Katie walked by and paused with her hand on the door to the store. "What's wrong?"

Beth forced her voice to come out in an even tone. "You told me hanging out with other men would work."

"Whoa!" Katie stepped back from the door, eyes wide. "I didn't say hold hands with the town's most sought-after bachelor in the busiest place you could find."

"I'm ruining him." She glanced toward the store.

"Oh, for heaven's sake, Beth. You can't trust what that woman says."

Beth turned from Katie's flashing eyes, reminded of how Oz's eyes had been filled with so much pain two nights ago. How she was the one to blame.

Her friend stepped closer. "What's up between you and Nash anyway?"

"Nothing. We're friends."

Katie let out an unconvinced harrumph.

Beth fought the urge to downplay their friendship, but the truth was now, more than ever, she needed his friendship and the confidence he held in her. She enjoyed the time she spent with Nash as well as his doting attention. He made her feel special and alive again. Plus, he dared her to step out of her small town roots and try something new--even if it was only a drink or starting an outreach program. There was something exhilarating in being daring for a moment in time.

This morning he'd shown up in her office with a fancy coffee concoction--super delicious--made with his new coffee machine. It even had whipped cream and chocolate shavings on top. Well, the whipped cream was nothing more than a melted puddle skimming the top of her mocha by the time she'd received it. She'd tried to turn it away, to distance herself from him, but she couldn't. Partly because sometimes, it felt as though he was the only one on her side. The only one who would support whatever decisions she made and act as the voice of reason when things got too crazy in her head.

Beth focused on Katie. "Look. I didn't mean to hurt Oz. Or intend for him to misinterpret things."

Cynthia slowly exited the store, her eyes flitting between them.

"Why didn't hanging out with Nash motivate Oz?" Beth asked them. "Why didn't he sling me over his shoulder and take me home?"

"He needs time? He's confused?" Her sister pulled her in for a half hug. "It'll all work out."

She really wished her sister would stop saying that. She was happily planning a wedding and knew nothing of the dark side of romance.

"Where do I go from here?" Beth asked.

"You wait," Katie said firmly.

"For how long?" Beth said, annoyed that a whine tinged her voice. She'd felt rejected when Oz asked for a break, and now she could add unwanted seeing as she seemed to be someone he didn't miss. Add that to another half-dozen, self-pity-inducing adjectives that tormented her late at night and she had a self-esteem that had taken up bungee-jumping.

The air sucked out of Beth's lungs as a familiar-looking blue bicycle wobbled by on the opposite side of the street. Her old bike. With what looked like a half-consumed bottle of rum in the flowery basket.

She watched silently as Oz wove his way down the street. The three of them turned to follow his progress. As Oz parked the bike at the end of the block, Katie asked quietly, "What is he doing?"

Oz lumbered up the steps to town hall--all two of them--and spread his arms out at his sides. His chest expanded as he took in a deep breath. Then he bellowed for all the Monday evening foot traffic to hear, "Bethany Wilkinson is a good person."

"What the ...?" stuttered Katie.

Beth turned and bolted up the street, humiliation dogging her steps. Oz continued his speech and Beth clasped her hands over her ears. The odd face she passed turned to her in pity and curiosity before turning back to Oz and his public proclamation.

Cynthia caught up with Beth and wrenched a hand off Beth's ear. "Listen."

Beth paused. The streets were quiet, other than a lone bird singing in the square half a block away. A diesel muttered its way toward them, oblivious to what precious words it might be drowning out.

Benny came out of his restaurant and smiled at Beth, nodding toward Oz. "He's been doing it all afternoon, on the hour. First here, then over at the church, the library, and finally at the corner in front of the diner." He gazed thoughtfully in Oz's direction. "He spends the remaining forty-five minutes at home cradling that bottle. Wanda went over at four and watered it down some. Might be too late to make a difference though." He addressed the women. "If you're driving, keep an eye out. He's a tad bit unsteady." Benny, hands clasped behind his back, returned to his restaurant. The stale, greasy smell of burgers and fries with a hint of bacon wafted into the street before the door closed behind him.

Beth watched the closed door, wondering what she could do to fix Oz and stop him from humiliating them both. She needed to find the stop cord to cease this emotional merry-go-round before one of them fell off and got hurt.

"Oz still loves you," Cynthia said, a slight smile tweaking her lips as she gave Beth's arm a hug. "He's defending you."

Oz climbed back on her bike, the frame dipping toward the pavement before he managed to pull it upright at the last second, zigzagging raggedly until he built enough momentum to straighten out. She watched him until he was out of sight, then said softly, "If he cares enough to defend me, why can't he care enough to ask me back?"

"BETH, HONEY?" Angelica peered through Beth's open office door. "Do you have a moment?"

"Sure." Beth hesitated. Oz's mother had never, in all of Beth's years working here, stopped by. Not even a quick hello while dropping off baking to help speed a neighbor's recovery. But there she was in the doorway, her long skirt's sequins sparkling under the fluorescent lights. Beth started to stand, but stopped. She gestured to the chair by the door. "Come in."

Angelica stepped in and cast a slow glance around the office. Her eyes lingered on a photo of Beth and Oz which was still staring out from its spot on top of her bookshelf.

"Are these for me?" Beth asked, indicating the plate of brownies Angelica was holding. "Do you want coffee? I can grab some from the common room."

"I'm fine. Thank you." Angelica eased into the hard guest chair, looking uncomfortable in Beth's cramped space. She passed the plate to Beth.

"Still no recipe taped to the bottom?" Beth asked, peeking at the plate's underside. "What's a girl gotta do?"

Angelica clutched the straps of her purse, her face lined and tense.

Beth slowly peeled back the plastic wrap, offering Angelica one-- who declined--before sinking her teeth into a gooey chocolate heaven. "Oh my god, these are even better than usual!" Her eyes rolled back as she savored the richness before bolting upright, her eyes opening wide. "This is Mandy's recipe!"

Angelica perched on the edge of her chair. "Just trying something new. You really think they taste like Mandy's?" Her eyebrows arched hopefully.

"Are you going to try and dethrone her at the fall bake off?"

Angelica, seemingly pleased with herself, ignored the question. "You're looking well. Are you sleeping better?"

"Dr. Leham prescribed sleeping pills."

A line appeared between her brows. "You be careful with those things."

"I only take them when I can't fall asleep." Which was fairly regularly. It was now the end of June and her one attempt at getting Oz to react and take her back had backfired spectacularly. She was at a loss on what to do next.

"Dr. Leham seems like a nice fellow." Pause. "Katie says he's very efficient. A real go-getter."

Beth wiped brownie crumbs from her lips. She wasn't even going to entertain what this conversation might be code for. A week later, she was still hearing rumblings from Oz's bike and bottle adventure.

"Nash is very caring," Beth said. "A good *friend*." Angelica frowned at her hands. Beth blurted, "We're not dating."

Angelica looked up slowly and Beth felt her face heat. Mentally, she slapped herself. Could she act guiltier? Now Oz's mom was going to think the rumors were true.

"Could I ask a favor?" Angelica asked quietly.

"Of course." Beth tried to relax. Angelica was the first to give, the last to take--making the idea of her actually asking for something a bit of a nerve-wracking experience.

"I'm not sure ..." Angelica's grip tightened on her handbag.

Oh, no. It was about Oz. There was no way she'd be able to help Angelica if it had to do with him. Things still felt precarious and if she did anything more than leave him messages, which he resolutely refused to acknowledge, things could get worse. Much, much worse. Assuming that was still possible.

"Oz won't talk to me anymore." Angelica wrung her handbag's plastic straps. "If it was only for a day or two I could understand, but it's been too long. I'm afraid I'm not going to get him back. It's not how it used to be between us."

They could start a club.

"He's letting the business go and to see him let it slip through his fingers ..." She paused to sniff. "Harvey is so upset I'm afraid he's going to have another episode. He so desperately wants Oz to settle down and succeed with the business. Why Oz would do this I just don't understand."

They could start a club for that, too.

"I know you two are having a rough patch," she continued, "but he seems so unhappy. So lost. Maybe you don't see it because you're so busy with your new job, but it's there."

Beth held back a snort. Busy was almost funny. After three insane months of getting things in place for her drop-in outreach one person had shown up, Gran. She said Reggie would have come too, but his daughter had stopped by at the last minute. Nash told her that this sort of thing always happened and building an effective outreach took time. He was full of ideas on how to recover from the humiliation; from not making it a drop-in so people would value it, to doing more advertising. As if nobody had a clue what she'd been up to for the past several months. But, he told her it provided an air of legitimacy.

"The light in his eyes is gone, and that worries me," Angelica said. "A mother can't sit by and watch that happen. Oz needs you."

Beth blinked back tears. "I need him too."

"Maybe you could talk some sense into him. He's always listened to you."

Beth bit back a bitter laugh. "He won't return my calls or answer the door. I don't think there's much hope, Angelica."

Angelica leaned forward. "He still loves you."

Beth flicked a crumb off her chair's armrest. Everyone kept saying that and it was starting to tick her off. The Oz who loved her had changed. Her hopes of him taking her back were waning to the point where she was left with a mere shred of a flickering hope. One puff and it was gone. She should move on, but her soul was resolutely clinging to one last hope. All she needed was a sign that there was still a chance that he might come back to her.

"I've been researching a really nice rehabilitation center on Google. Maybe if you and I talked to him, he would go?"

Beth almost stopped breathing. "*Rehab?*"

Angelica smiled. "Yes! Exactly."

"Uh?" Rehab was for druggies, alcoholics, and starlets who needed a break from their crazy realities. Not Oz, who was feeling lost and angry. Having his mother pull a stunt such as sending him to rehab would not help--unless, of course, Beth was missing something and he actually needed that kind of help.

Angelica sat primly, her face bright. "I think we need to get together and talk to him. It's what's best."

"Wait, like ... an *intervention?*" That was difficult to wrap one's mind around. "Have you been watching Oprah reruns, Angelica?" She tried to say it kindly, but she knew how some shows could influence Angelica and make her see her own world in a way that simply wasn't accurate.

"Exactly! An intervention." Angelica grinned at Beth. She pulled a folded sheet of paper from her purse. "Here are some tips I found online."

Beth cautiously accepted the paper. How could she explain that an intervention could cause Oz to clam up like he'd chugged Crazy Glue? An intervention spelled trouble with a capital T. Beth slid the plate of Bribe Beth Brownies and info sheet onto the filing cabinet beside her desk and stated matter-of-factly, "I can't do this."

"It will be a surprise."

"This seems a tad premature." Misguided. Ill-informed. Wrong. Whatever she needed to get him to come back to her, this wasn't it. "I don't think this is a good idea. We need to give him time to get over last week."

"It will be a calm conversation about his reckless behavior and how he's damaging his relationships," she paused to let that point hit home, "and that we know he is hurting and that there is help. He's starting to hurt himself."

Beth's pulse sped up. "What do you mean hurting himself?"

"He's in a self-destructive cycle. He believes he's protecting you, but his all-about-town rant and boozing isn't good for him, and it isn't cute or harmless." She gave Beth a hard look that made her want to crawl under her desk for protection.

"Action needs to be taken *now.*" Angelica stood waving her fist in the air as though shaking a maraca. "An intervention is the answer. It will open him up. Start the conversation. Ease his troubles."

"He needs to do this on his own." Beth studied her hands. "As difficult as it is for the rest of us."

"We have to help."

"I can't," Beth said in a quiet voice. "I can't do this to him." Beth shook her head, pushing back in her chair as though Angelica was going to forcibly make her confront Oz.

"How would it look if you weren't there?" Angelica asked softly. "It would look as though you don't care." In a low, even voice she added, "After *that* weekend, I think it is especially important that his fiancée be present."

Beth gazed at Angelica--a small, quiet, but very determined mother bear. She thought of Oz and all the hurt piling up between them. Her voice shook as she said, "I don't think this is a good idea."

"I'll arrange everything for tonight. All you have to do is show up and be present." Angelica placed a warm hand firmly over Beth's and gave her a long look that made Beth lower her eyes in shame. If that was what it was like to have a mother pissed off and disappointed in you, then it was a good thing she'd been raised by her gran and sister for most of her teenage years.

Angelica gave Beth one last look before opening the door. "Timing is everything, Beth."

"But what about Katie and Will? They're out of town for Will's conference. They won't be home until tomorrow and they should be there." Plus, Katie would totally talk sense into her mother. She'd tell her exactly how this was a bad idea and that Oz would take it the wrong way. And even if Katie did agree to go along with it, she would make sure things went right because nobody messed with Katie. Not even a big brother and his boatload of problems.

Angelica shook her head. "Timing is everything." She stepped through the doorway and turned. "I'll pick you up at seven. By eight we'll have you back in Oz's arms like nothing ever happened."

She closed the door behind her and Beth sat in the silence of her office, afraid to move, afraid to think what the consequences might be if she showed up on her old step tonight.

THAT EVENING, instead of relaxing in the theater's air conditioning watching a romantic comedy like she'd planned, Beth found herself standing in the day's lingering heat, banging on Oz's door. Something felt off and it was more than the group shifting nervously behind her and the small pack of onlookers tittering on the sidewalk. Something in the heavy summer air was warning her like a bird's screeching call of danger.

Basically, she wanted to pee her pants. But being the one thrust to the front of the intervention's gang of eight--even though Angelica had promised her a nonspeaking role--she had to stand tall even though she knew her night was not going to end in Oz's arms like his mother had promised.

She squared her shoulders and turned to the group. "He's not home. Let's go."

"His truck is in the driveway," Oz's father pointed out.

"Maybe he's taken your bike," Cynthia offered with a smirk.

"Try again, Beth," Angelica told Beth.

She turned to the scarred wood door and thumped on it, waiting for it to swing open. She traced her finger over the small 'B' Oz had carved into the door the night they'd signed the mortgage papers. He was going to carve their initials, but she'd stopped him, feeling self-conscious. It was a door, not a tree.

She pulled in a long, calming breath. Maybe if she was the one he saw first when he opened the door she could make sure it turned out all right. She could act as though this was a social call to see how he was doing and she could somehow shield him while redirecting everyone away. Away. Away. Away. Yes, she could do it.

She could feel it.

Okay, she couldn't quite feel it, but she was hoping a lack of good feelings wasn't a bad omen. She bit her lower lip. Maybe he was trying a new career or hobby right now. What if they were interrupting some sort of 'find yourself' epiphany?

She turned to the group. "Hey, has anyone heard of Oz trying any new hobbies lately?"

The group looked at each other in question, everyone shaking their heads. "Nope. Why?" asked Cynthia.

"Just asking," she said with a sigh. She rubbed her throbbing hand, wishing they'd installed a doorbell like Katie had frequently suggested. She'd give anything to have Oz's strong, warm arms pull her in right now. To have him kiss her deep--in that way that made her feel like she'd finally come home. Like she belonged somewhere special. How he'd look her deep in the eyes, his face's lines relaxing as he told her he loved her.

She tried the doorknob. Locked.

It figured. He thought to lock it now that he lived alone and not back when they were getting friendly all over the living room and risked people popping in at inopportune moments. She selected the correct key on her keychain, slightly bothered that she still had it even though it signified the hope she kept secreted away. She released the lock and let out a breath.

He hadn't changed the locks.

Hope swelled along with relief and she swung the door open.

She could do this.

She stepped over the threshold and just about melted as the trailer's heat pummeled her. She faced the group and tried to ignore the way everyone stared at her with raised eyebrows, acting as though she had the right to play welcoming hostess rather than unwelcome intruder.

Harvey gave her a nudge. "Lead the way."

Peeved, she stepped inside the small entry and cast a cautious look around. The place was a disaster. Apparently Oz was also discovering whether he missed living in a clean place.

"That boy needs to grow up and clean up or else hire a housekeeper," Harvey grumbled from behind her.

Beth cleared her throat and called, "Oz? Are you home?" Her voice caught on the word *home*.

The blinds were drawn in the living room to her right and the room's heat created a suffocating sensation. She pushed her way between the couch and coffee table which was littered with take-out bags. She opened the blinds and cranked a few windows, letting a cool evening breeze enter the room. She turned to the group who was crowded in the entry acting similar to a herd of deer caught in a big rig's headlights. "For crying out loud you guys, come in," she chirped.

People trickled in, quietly seating themselves on her favorite velvet couch and standing at the edges of the room. Framed photos of her and Oz that had once lined the shelves were either missing or face down. But the bowl of lemon drops on the coffee table was as full as ever.

"This place heats up so fast," she said to nobody in particular, ignoring the candy. "I swear you take a nap and wake up in a sauna a half hour later. It cools off quickly though. We should be fine in a minute."

Angelica shooed Beth out of the room as though she would ruin a surprise party if she didn't go grab Oz. Footfalls landed on the porch steps and Beth paused as Scott, the town's police officer, took up post just inside Oz's front door, taking up much of the entry.

"What are you doing?" she asked.

"Serve and protect," Scott said. "That's my job."

"Who are you going to protect? And from what?" She shook her head. This was getting ridiculous. Why not just invite Mary Alice and get the humiliation over with? Everyone could have a grand old time at her relationship's expense.

"Um," he replied uncertainly.

"I think you should go," Beth said gently.

Scott frowned in Angelica's direction. "I think maybe I should stay?" He met Beth's eye, his expression serious. "In case."

"In case of what?" She narrowed her eyes, hands on hips. "Someone breaks the law?"

Scott gave a few rapid blinks and straightened his back. "I'm staying."

"Fine. Whatever." Beth's flip-flops stuck to the kitchen's linoleum as she went to find Oz. The muffled sound of a toilet flushing drifted from the opposite end of the trailer. Seconds later Oz staggered into the kitchen, ruffling his messy hair. He yawned and grabbed a carton of milk from the fridge and in one fluid movement, cracked it open, guzzled it, and tossed the empty in the sink. He grabbed a fresh carton before noticing Beth standing at the far side of the room.

He froze as if trying to determine whether she was an apparition.

Several months ago she would have believed a week's worth of stubble would be a sexy look on Oz, but right now he merely looked broken. She resisted the temptation to walk across the room and pull him into her arms.

Oz pulled his T-shirt over his gut and stepped toward Beth. "What are you doing here?"

"There are people here to see you."

Oz cocked his head and slowly made his way to the living room, his bare feet making small shucking noises as he crossed the room. Beth let go of the chair she'd been using for support, flexing her hands so the blood would return. She crept to the living room doorway to listen. She remained a few feet behind Oz with Scott, a solid wall, to her right.

His parents spoke in quiet, careful tones, a light breeze drifting through the room. Beth stared at the floor, deaf to their words. Angelica and Harvey went silent. Oz slowly turned on his heel, shoving an accusing finger at Beth.

"An *intervention?* Why can't you let me have the time and space I asked for?" He turned back to the group. "You've all watched way too much TV if a man can't go on a weekend bender without this bullshit."

Scott made shushing noises from the doorway.

"Oh, Scott. Buzz off already," Oz said, tilting his chin up in challenge. "This is my house. You should all be tossed out for breaking and entering and ganging up on a guy who's trying to enjoy his evening." He looked Beth straight in the eye. "Alone."

"Oz." Beth struggled to find her courage, the word *alone* hitting her hard. "We're here because--"

"Give me the key." He held out his hand and Beth heard the whispers begin. She slowly fumbled his key off her chain and handed it to him, ignoring the pain. He fished through the pocket of his track pants and held out his fist, palm down. Hesitantly, she held out her hand and he opened his fingers, dropping her engagement ring. Her eyes flicked up to meet his, hope bubbling up.

"Keep it or not. Whatever you want--"

"Oz!" snapped his father as gasps and indignant murmurs spread around the room.

Beth wobbled on weak legs as she stared at the ring resting on her palm. She placed her other hand on the wall for support.

"I thought you were on my side," Oz said quietly. "I thought you understood."

Her head snapped up and she searched his tired, haggard face, seeking a connection. "I *am* on your side." She took a step closer and Oz shook his head, stepping away. His jaw was so tight, the muscles in his cheeks were bunched liked marbles. "I'm always on your side." Her voice broke and tears streaked down her cheeks.

"I need more time, and you need someone. I can see that I can't be who you need right now. I can't bear to hold you back from your dreams, Beth. I'm setting you free, because I love you."

"I don't want to be free," she blurted. She ignored the gathered group and through her tears said, "Neither of us is worth anything without the other. We're our best when we're together."

Angelica joined them in the doorway, her face pinched with worry. "Don't do anything you're going to regret."

"Mom, butt out," Oz said evenly, his eyes never leaving Beth.

"Oz!" barked Harvey. "Show some respect."

"I want to be there for you." Beth touched Oz's arm. "To help you."

"And you need help, young man," added his father. "What you're doing to our business--"

"It's not *ours* any more, Dad." Oz whirled on his father, his eyes flashing like a caged animal seeking an exit. "Let me live my goddamn life!"

Beth gently laid a hand on Oz's arm. "It's okay to need someone."

"She's right," said Angelica.

Scott nodded and a chorus of um-hmms came from the living room.

Oz dragged his hands down his face. "You guys are never going to get it. I need to do this alone." He let out a shaky breath.

"But you're not doing anything," Beth replied.

"Just because I'm not telling everyone every little thought and detail in my life it doesn't mean I'm not doing anything. Some people prefer privacy so everyone will stop their fucking interference and won't offer opinions or advice every damn second."

"Language," warned Oz's father.

His mom piped up, "We're just--"

"Completely nuts! All of you. You're going to drive me around the bend." Oz's voice rattled like a loose muffler as emotion coated it. "All I ever hear from everyone is when am I going back to the business? That I can't give it up. That I'm wasting--that I'm making a mistake-- that I can't let Beth ..." He caught Beth's eye and slowly seemed to shrink half a size as he let out a shaky breath. He leaned past Scott to push the door open. "Just go. Everyone just go."

Beth crossed her arms over her chest. "I'm not leaving."

Oz opened his mouth, stopped, closed his eyes, then gripped Beth's hands in his and said carefully, "You need to move on. I can't give you what you need right now."

"Yes, you can," she said in a sure voice, stepping closer. She gave his hands a squeeze, hope surging through her. "I don't need anything. I can wait. This isn't about *me*, it's about *you*."

Amber sparks lit up in Oz's brown eyes and he snatched his hands from hers. He took a step back, his linebacker build shaking with pent up emotion. "If you can wait, then why are you with *him*? You don't even realize what you need."

Beth felt as though he'd spit in her face. This was where he was supposed to sweep her up into his arms and carry her into the back bedroom and pour his soul into hers. Not this. "I love you, Oz." Her voice trembled. "I love *you*. And I have for years. That's not going to change."

"We need more space." He took another step back.

Someone said, "How can she give him more space? They're already on break and he just gave her ring back!"

"There is something wrong with that man," someone else whispered.

Cynthia piped up, "Oz, you treat her right!" She shouldered her way through the clustered group, but Angelica held her back.

Oz focused his fiery eyes on Beth. She tried to speak but all that came out were confused sounds. Her legs shook as though she was standing on a shifting fault line. Oz looked her straight in the eye. He shoved his big hands through his brown locks. "Staying together isn't fair to either of us. I know us, Beth, and we're not working. This isn't who we are. I might be what you want, but I can't be who you need."

Mandy. He'd been talking to Mandy.

Tears clogged Beth's throat. "But ..." He was drowning on his own. He needed someone to stand beside him, hold his hand, and let him know it was all going to be okay in the end. He needed her. He needed *family*.

"What if this is the *real* Oz now?" He pointed to his chest, then looked to the group. "Have any of you thought of that? That this might be the *real* me?"

"No," she whispered. She shook her head and leaned away. This wasn't the real Oz. Not even close. Unable to stop shaking her head, she barely felt the next emotional blow.

"I can't give you what you need, Beth." Oz's voice grew weak and he swayed, eyes closed. "You need to move on. We're over."

The room spun, the light fading in and out as she turned and fled, her heart on fire.

TEN MINUTES LATER, Beth was sobbing into Nash's crisp Polo shirt. She'd fled on foot, his place only a couple of blocks away. He had greeted her at the door and wordlessly drawn her into the safety of his condo as well as his arms. He asked nothing as he let her cry until she could speak.

"He doesn't want me. He's turned into a-a-a ..." She hiccupped, her chest aching as if something inside had torn free. "He told me to move on. It-it's over!"

"Shh, shh." Nash rocked her gently, his cotton shirt fresh against her skin.

When her crying subsided, he gently pulled her off his leather couch. "Come." He led her past the kitchen island that separated the living room from his immaculate kitchen. Despite being friends, it was the first time she'd been in his condo. She knew where it was, of course. Everyone knew where everyone was in a small town such as Blueberry Springs. And while she'd expected his place to be lovely and neat, she hadn't been prepared for how modern and put together it truly was. He'd obviously done more than hang a few pictures when he moved in. The kitchen looked like he'd gutted it and replaced it with something from one of Katie's design magazines.

"I take it you don't remodel locally," she joked, trying to crack a smile as she wiped her nose on a tissue. She gestured to the marble counter tops, and the track lights aimed at sculptures and smooth pieces of pottery. She'd never met anyone with art in their kitchen that couldn't be held in place with a magnet.

Nash smiled. "I have specific tastes. Do you like it?"

"It's very sleek."

"Modern."

"Katie would go ga-ga for this place." She ran her fingers lightly over the solid wood cupboard doors, testing a small glass knob. "Why would you spend money redoing a condo you plan on leaving in a few years?" Nash didn't seem like the type to waste tens of thousands of dollars redoing a kitchen when he'd only get a partial return from the condo's increased resale value.

"Why live somewhere that isn't your own personal haven?" He

opened a cupboard and, to Beth's surprise, fog billowed out as he pulled out a small tub of ice cream. "Why not surround yourself with things that make you content? After all, there's no place like home."

Beth rubbed her eyelids which felt as though they had swollen to four times their normal size. He had a point. There was nothing like having a cozy, comforting cave to curl up in. Something she was missing more and more with each night she spent in the open living room at Katie's. She needed a home. And now it seemed as though there was no reasonable way to delude herself into waiting any longer.

They were officially broken up. As official as the ring burning a hole in her pocket.

She blinked back tears as Nash held up the small container. "Nothing but the best. It's organic, old-fashioned, homemade ice cream from this great little place in Dakota. Very expensive."

"Obviously doctors earn way too much. Ice cream is ice cream." In the mood she was in, she could sit down and eat the whole thing. Three times over.

"It's very rich. You couldn't handle eating more than a few spoonfuls. I have them double the flavoring and it's pure cream, straight from the cow. Well, a little pasteurization first. There are no guarantees in life, but we can always improve our odds a little."

He peeled off the lid, pulled out a spoon that looked like it was made of blue glass, and fed Beth a nibble.

"Oh. My. God." She closed her eyes, letting the rich chocolate delight all ten-thousand of her taste buds. "I think my taste buds are having an orgy!"

Nash laughed and pulled out a second spoon and two tiny bowls. She sat attentively at the island, waiting for more. She would seriously follow Nash to the ends of the earth for more of this stuff. There was a month's worth of healing in each spoonful. She needed more. A lot more. And she needed it now.

"Come. Let's feed your soul." He led her back to the living room, tucked them shoulder-to-shoulder under a cashmere throw, and flipped to a cheesy comedy on his large TV. She never wanted to leave the sanctuary of his condo. Everything matched. Everything was deliberately chosen. It was like a show home, only absent of salesmen, and she could put her feet up on the couch. And yet, it all somehow still felt like a home. Nash's home. His little haven where he was sheltering her from the storm.

A few hours later, and feeling a bit better about life, Beth slipped into her sandals, knowing it was time to go, but for some reason wanting to stay.

Nash ran a hand through his hair and asked, "So, are you, uh, seeing other men?"

Beth shrugged and heaved a huge sigh. "I guess. Eventually."

Her chest ached at the thought of kissing someone who wasn't Oz. Letting someone else into her heart. Into her bed. The very idea felt as wrong as Cheez Whiz and peanut butter smeared together on a piece of celery.

She gave Nash a big hug. "Thanks for putting me back together."

He held her close. "Is it okay?" He tilted her head back with a gentle finger placed under her chin. "If I do this?" He softly kissed her lips. "If it's too soon," he said, watching her with calm blue eyes, "I can wait."

She didn't know what it was. All she knew was her head was screaming *run* while her legs were calmly replying *leave a message.*

8

*B*eth turned from her patients, put a mixed CD in the hospital stereo, and hit shuffle. "Okay everyone, partner up! Let's get this dance show on the road!"

She glanced at the doorway to the common room as she often found herself doing since Nash's kiss last week. For whatever reason, she kept expecting him to appear in the doorway even though they hadn't spoken since. She'd spent the week curled up with her wounded heart on Katie's stupid pullout bed and hauling herself out only for work. Which meant she had to get out of bed a lot more often than she wanted to.

Her breath wedged somewhere deep in her chest as the first notes of "A Kiss to Build a Dream On" floated from the speakers. Oz used to put their song on repeat and they would dance around and around the living room until their feet grew tired. Happy and blissful. Before he felt lost. Before he told her to move on. Before. Before. Before.

Despite the bravado, men were actually scared little boys inside.

She ignored the stabbing in her heart and turned to face the group. A few residents had begun shuffling around in their slippered feet, their geriatric version of dancing. The outnumbered men were already being coaxed from their chairs, creaking, moaning, and groaning. To Gran's disapproval, a pleased looking Reggie was already swaying to the rhythm with Lauretta.

Beth turned to the closest woman. "Mable, would you care to da--" Her jaw dropped, her words forgotten as a familiar form filled the common room's doorway.

It worked. He was here. He wanted more than he'd admitted at the intervention. He wanted her back in his life. And she didn't care that her ring was buried in a pile of crumpled tissues beside the pullout bed, her answer was *yes*!

Oz stood clutching a rose. His scruffy hair had been washed and cut by someone who obviously didn't know what they were doing and an endearing amount of razor burn speckled his neck. His mom knew him better than Beth had realized. Thank Goodness.

She smiled, her shoulders relaxing. Happily ever after.

She was barely able to resist the urge to tear across the room and launch herself into his strong arms and never, ever let go.

The rectangular doorway swayed. Beth blinked and looked again.

Disappointment and anger fell across her and she stomped across the room. "Oz," she hissed, "are you *drunk*?" What was he thinking? She would get put on probation if she allowed him to interact with her patients while intoxicated. She had to get him out of here.

His smile faltered and he looked momentarily lost before stating, "Nope. I ..." He lowered his voice to a whisper when it became obvious that everyone had stopped dancing, other than Elsie--but she never stopped--and was listening eagerly. "I know what I want."

He proudly held his arms out at his sides, a confident grin gracing his face.

"What's that?" she asked. She braced herself in case he stabbed another needle in his Beth voodoo doll and his next sentence didn't include her.

"Dancing. Katie told me I needed exercise."

"What?" She placed her hands on her hips and tried not to cry. "This isn't the gym, Oz. I can't let you dance. You're drunk."

"What? No, here." He briefly grasped her upper arms and leveled his best, honest look. "You're getting it wrong. I can save you."

Her voice thickened. "I don't need saving." Other than from a broken heart, of course, because she was fairly certain this wasn't going to end well for her heart. Again. Although, come to think of it, she wasn't sure how much more of it there was for him to smash. "I need a sober you, Oz. You have to stop destroying yourself. You're a good man. People will still love you if you sell the business."

His tired eyes roamed her face. Slowly he said, "This is my first step."

"Your first step to what, Oz?" Hope lifted the pain in her chest and she tried not to act too eager in case she scared him away. She had to play it cool.

He spread his arms out wide and his brow furrowed. "I'm not sure. But you were right. I wasn't doing anything. Nothing real or meaningful. I was wallowing because it's hard. I need to explore more. I need to dance and see where my feet take me."

She wanted to pummel his chest and scream at him for the injustice of his timing, but instead she quietly said, "You can't dance today. Maybe next week."

"My father told me to smarten up and that I was losing out. I am here. To dance."

"We can't get back together unless it is *your* idea, Oz. If that's what you're saying." She met his eyes which were filled with panic. Her voice grew thick. "You have to make the decision from your heart. It has to be for the right reasons. It has to be what you want." She blinked back tears, knowing if she played her cards right she could go home with him tonight. *Home.* But she also knew she had to let him do it on his terms if they ever wanted to truly make it.

He clipped the rose between his teeth and whirled around, storming across the room. Beth stepped after him. Oh, God. What if he left? What if she just blew off her only chance?

Oz whisked Gran out of her chair before Beth could raise a protest and her grandmother let out a delighted, "Oooo!" She beamed at Oz and patted his shoulder affectionately as he began to dance her around the room.

"What makes me the lucky gal?" she asked.

Beth hurried after the fast dancing couple. "Oz! Stop. You can't. Not today."

"We're fine," he snapped over his shoulder as he swiftly dipped Gran.

"Oh, would you look at that move!" Elsie exclaimed, clapping her hands.

Beth squealed and covered her eyes as Oz snatched his dance partner back upright. "She's elderly! You can't do that! She'll break something."

"Who are you calling elderly?" Gran waved her off, laughing. "Quit your fussing. We're fine. Nobody's danced me around like this in quite some time! And I must say I *like* it."

Beth paused. She was raised to listen and respect her gran and she trusted her, but this kind of spirited activity was most definitely not in any recreation plan her grandmother's doctor would sign off on. Something bad was going to happen. And it would be her fault. She'd lose her job and her outreach. She'd have nothing. She grabbed Oz's shoulder. "Oz, really. Not today."

"Listen to your beautiful grandmother and quit fussing." He beamed at Gran and picked up the pace to dance them across the room, leaving Beth behind.

"Gran? You have to stop. He's *drunk*." Beth ran her hands through her hair and visually checked up on her other patients. Everyone was smiling, watching Oz spin his partner around with confidence and grace.

"It's lovely watching him move," Lauretta said, her hands clasped over her chest. Beth remembered when her patients watched her and Oz dance like that, and how lucky she'd felt to be his chosen one. "Such ability."

Oz mumbled "Shit!" and a crack ruptured through K.D. Lang's deep crooning.

Beth whirled to check on the couple. Gran lay awkwardly on her back: evidence of a deep dip gone terribly wrong.

Beth rushed to her side. "Gran! Oh my God, Gran! Are you okay?"

She snapped her head up to look at Oz. "Get out of here you ... you ... *get out!*" She blinked back tears and took Gran's hand.

Oz backed up a step, his eyes glued to Beth's grandmother. Face pale, he turned and fled.

"Gran, can you move? Oh, God. Call a doctor. Someone, call a doctor."

Please, don't let it be Nash on shift. Please, please, anyone but Nash.

***

BETH SWORE GOD HATED HER.

Why else would Nash be the doctor on shift? Why else would he be there to witness another of her horrible moments with Oz and to watch her career dissolve? God hated her. It was the only viable answer.

Yeah, yeah, people said life wouldn't throw more at you than you could handle, but she knew that was a great big, massive load of smelly crap.

Minutes after the accident Nash had rushed into the room looking as crisp and proficient as ever. With athletic ease he'd dropped to his knees beside Gran and grasped her hand.

"Ozzie dropped her," Elsie sang as she pirouetted by.

"Dammit, Reggie," Gran griped from her position on the floor. "If you hadn't been dancing with Lauretta, this wouldn't have happened."

"If you chose to spend a little more time with me, maybe I would have reserved the first dance for you," he snapped back. "I'm a hot commodity, you know."

"It's not my fault!" Lauretta's voice rose above their squabbling. "It was Oz! Beth shouldn't have let him dance. He's *drunk!*"

Beth felt Nash's eyes on her as she hovered over Gran, praying her tears wouldn't become large enough to fall. And most of all, praying that Nash wouldn't judge her for what had happened on her watch.

"Leave Oz out of this!" Gran said.

"He's a troubled lad," added Reggie.

Finishing his gentle probing, Nash said, "I think your hip could be broken Mrs. Wilkinson. We're going to gently move you onto a stretcher, then a gurney, and take you over to x-ray."

"Great Scott! A broken hip!" bellowed Gran's boyfriend. "Now look what you've done. Who's going to give me snuggles if you're off in a sling?"

"You did fine without me while I was stuck in here and you were still on the outside, you big baby!"

"Enough!" snapped Beth. "Everyone just shush for once."

Silence enveloped the group clustered around Gran. "Do you want to go with her?" Beth asked Reggie as Nash and a few nurses wheeled Gran out of the room.

He shrugged and shuffled after them muttering, "May as well. Life's too short for the doghouse."

"Can we talk now?" Lauretta asked as soon as they left. "Because I don't think I should take the fall for Oz. No pun intended. It's not my fault there aren't enough available men. Blame biology. I didn't do a thing wrong. It's still perfectly legal to dance with a taken man." She tugged her dress into place and lifted her chin. "Last I checked."

"Lauretta, nobody is blaming you," Beth said wearily. "Everyone, back to your rooms. The dance is over."

"Oh, but Louie is singing my song," Elsie complained.

"Let him dance you to your room. I promise I won't turn him off until you shut your door."

Beth slowly rounded everyone into their rooms off the common room, although many vanished eagerly, no doubt to get on the horn to spread the latest gossip about Beth and how her life was a pile of steaming doggie doo. She gave the stereo cord a good yank, abruptly cutting off Louie Armstrong in mid-croon. The room filled with silence and she dropped into a nearby chair. Sighing, she rubbed her eyes.

What next?

A noise caused her to look to the doorway and a chill raced through her. Nash was watching her with a grim expression.

"What? What's wrong?"

He shook his head. "She'll be fine. It's a fracture, like I thought." He walked slowly into the room. "I'll see that she gets a room close to continuing care so her boyfriend can still get his snuggles. Although with her hip, he'd better not hope for much." He rested a hand on her shoulder. "You okay?"

Beth studied the floor. "Not really. But I will be. Eventually." Maybe.

"If you need someone to talk to, I'm here."

"Yeah." She looked up at him, his blue eyes sympathetic. "Thanks." The problem was, whenever she spent time with Nash, Oz went wild and something bad happened. Which then caused her to need Nash's support even more. It was a cycle she wasn't sure she was strong enough to break.

"Here." He handed her a clipboard holding an incident report, his voice taking on a crisp, professional tone. "You're going to need this. I have to get back to your grandmother to tell her the news, but I can sign off on this for you."

"Thanks."

She clutched the clipboard, her knuckles white. An incident report. She was so screwed.

A second after Nash left, hospital security entered, his eyes scanning the room. "I haven't located Oz. Has he come back?"

"No, why?"

"Dr. Leham requested Oz be removed from the site. Forcibly if need be. He is officially banned unless seeking emergency care. Persona non grata."

"He's not here," Beth stated darkly and turned to her clipboard.

By the time Nash returned Beth's hands had ceased shaking, but her mood had yet to lift. She understood there were protocols to follow, but she still felt as though Nash had pulled away his friendship and smacked her hard across the face with her own professional incompetency. It was as though he didn't believe she was capable of preventing another situation like this from happening and, therefore, banned Oz as a preemptive measure.

And Oz? She didn't even want to consider how she might be feeling about him right now.

She handed Nash the report, not meeting his eye. She ignored the few patients trying to sneak their way back into the common room. It wasn't as if she could keep the little gossipers locked in their rooms forever.

Nash signed the form with a flourish and gave her a smile. "Lucky thing it was your grandmother."

Her hands clenched. "Pardon me?"

"Allowing an unauthorized person--"

"I was trying to stop him, Nash," Beth said in a hard voice.

Nash's cheeks flushed slightly, and he continued, "--take part in an activity in the continuing care area could land you in serious trouble. At least it was your relative, meaning the family isn't likely to sue you or the hospital. With any kind of luck there'll be nothing more than a few hard feelings and temporary probation."

Beth swallowed hard. "With any kind of luck."

* * *

BETH GLANCED up from rearranging the common room's tables and chairs back into their normal rows. Her quick meeting with the hospital's bigwigs had left her on probation due to "patient endangerment and allowing a non-authorized person to partake in continuing care activities." Yeah, a great way to finish off her afternoon. All she wanted to do was go home and cry into her pillow until she fell into an exhausted sleep, putting space between her and this day. Instead she had two more hours of work and a steamed sister striding across the room. She instinctively backed up, placing a chair between her and her advancing sibling.

"What were you thinking letting Oz in here?" Cynthia said.

Beth cast a quick look around the room. Onlookers perking up at the hint of possible gossip? Check. Hearing aids being cranked? Check. Biggest gossipers shushing others? Also check.

"Let's go into my office." Beth sidestepped toward the door.

Cynthia remained in place, hands on hips. "I can't believe you let him hurt Gran. What is happening? You need to distance yourself from that man. He is not the Oz you fell in love with."

Beth avoided the curious stares from her patients, wishing her sister's aversion to hospitals was strong enough to prevent her from ever coming in. "Maybe we should go see Gran."

She ducked into the hall and moved slowly toward Gran's new room, waiting for Cynthia to follow.

"I can't believe you didn't stop him," Cynthia said when she caught up. "Being on probation goes on your file along with a copy of the incident report. Incompetence as well as--"

"I tried! Okay?" Tears filmed her eyes. "I tried. But he wouldn't stop, Cynthia. You don't know how horrible it was to see him like that. To think he was coming back for you, but he was only trying to get his parents off his back! To watch him *hurt* Gran and to be powerless to stop it."

Cynthia chewed on her lip, then reached out to give her a hug. "It's just really freaky." She squeezed Beth tight. "Broken hips can lead to some pretty serious complications at Gran's age."

"She'll be okay. Nash is taking care of her and he's--"

"Thorough."

"I was going to say diligent and kind and one of the best doctors in Blueberry Springs."

Cynthia faced her sister with crossed arms. "Do you have a crush on him?"

"No." Her cheeks heated. "And I wish everyone would stop assuming we're a couple just because of last month."

Cynthia rolled her eyes, the movement of her head making her curls sway. "Well, you guys *were* holding hands."

"We weren't holding hands!" Beth shouted. She glared at her laughing sister.

"She doth protest too much," she sung. She waggled a finger at Beth. "You crafty girl."

"Shut up." Beth shoved off the wall and paced a few steps closer to Gran's room.

"Oz isn't your one anymore," Cynthia called after her. "He's changed, and he gave back your ring. He's admitted he can't give you what you need." Beth's throat constricted from emotion. "Meanwhile, you've got this total hottie following you around, playing rescue hero. Maybe he's your new one. Have you considered that?"

"Cynthia I've only been single for a week." Wow, it still hurt to say that.

"I've seen the way you look at each other. I think he's a real contender if you open your eyes and give him a chance."

"We're not like that." Beth's cheeks heated. She knew she shouldn't feel proud or pleased for snagging the attention of a man like Nash. But it felt strangely validating and empowering to know someone like him thought she was worth attention. Plus, he was a good man. But a good man who wasn't looking for the same things she was. It seemed as though none of them were. She heaved a sigh and slid to the floor, her head propped in her hands.

Her sister joined her. "You're so absorbed in Oz and his problems you can't see it, but Nash is totally crushing on you. You have a chance with him, you know."

Beth rolled her eyes and tried to shrug it off. "Nash doesn't like country girls and isn't looking for a relationship." She lightly touched her lips. But there was that kiss. That unexplainable and unrepeated kiss. What did that mean? Beth added quickly, "Besides, Oz doesn't really want us to be broken up. He still loves me, he's just not ready for what I want. He thinks he's being a good guy by setting me free. If I love him, which I do, I should wait."

"He broke Gran's hip, Beth." Her sister gave her a look that implied stupidity on Beth's part.

"By accident!" Couldn't her sister see that? Today's actions said he still loved her and that there was still hope. Maybe buried under an avalanche, but it was there. He wouldn't have made the effort otherwise.

Cynthia stared at the framed print on the opposite wall, her brow furrowed in thought. "Did he say anything?" Cynthia asked, still focused on the print.

Beth studied her fingers.

"Well?" her sister prompted.

"Yeah. Sort of."

"What did he say?"

"It's not important."

"Did he ask you back?" Cynthia gave her a hard look. The kind their mother used to give her when she was lying by omission. "Did he give you *any* indication that he was there other than to get out of the house and do the things he used to do in order to get his parents off his back?"

Her mind leapt to his comment about his dad saying he needed to smarten up. Another snow boulder in the avalanche. "He brought a rose."

Beth caught her sister flashing a raised eyebrow as if to say, *That's all? You're going to hang your hopes on a flower?* and the fight boiled up within her. "He's a *guy*. He can't just blurt out his feelings. He came to dance and to do something we both used to enjoy. He was telling me to wait." She was sure of it.

"Oz used to write you poems, Beth. I think he could muster up a few words to ask you back if that's what was on his mind." Cynthia turned to face her, her expression kind. "He doesn't want his mom sending him to rehab. You're failing to see the whole picture. You can't wait forever and he's not changing. Despite him saying he loved you at the intervention."

Beth sunk her head into her hands. Her sister's argument felt a lot more solid than the one her heart was whispering in her ear. His words and actions failed to add up to happily back together again.

"I'm sorry, Beth. And the fact that he was drunk ..." Her sister gently took her hand. "It doesn't say good things about his intentions." Cynthia's voice was low and convincing. "I say screw it all and make your move. Nash is hot shit and someone will grab him if you don't." Cynthia let out a low chuckle and said somewhat wistfully, "A doctor who knows how to dress *and* how to listen? If you want to have that family you've been dreaming about, you need to seize the moment." She patted Beth's knee and stood up. "You don't need Oz for that dream. You need a man. A good man like Dr. Love Buns who can make those dreams come true." She snapped her fingers. "Easy-peasy like he's buying a new Beemer."

Beth massaged her bare ring finger and tried not to imagine having a family with someone other than Oz. Thoughts like that felt out of place. Greedy, even. Especially since Nash was the kind of man she could fall for. He was patient, kind, and stable. He'd make a good husband and a good father. And he believed in her in a way nobody else seemed to. And the way he saw her through a fresh point of view gave her confidence. Add in the way his blue eyes danced when she tickled his funny bone and she was almost smitten.

But they were just friends and that's all she'd ever allow it to be.

"I'm right about Oz, aren't I? Just like I was with you going off to college."

Beth gritted her teeth, she didn't want Cynthia to be right about Oz this time. Going to college to get away from Oz and Mandy had been one thing, this was entirely different. She stood and dusted off her pants. She'd think about it later over a thick slice of chocolate maven pie. "Shall we check on Gran?"

Cynthia gave Beth a look she couldn't decipher, then entered Gran's room first, her legs moving stiffly. "Hey Gran!" Cynthia turned all smiles, her voice strained and overly perky. "How are you feeling? Can I get you anything?"

"I'd like a cup of tea," Gran said. She was flat on her back, eyes cast to the ceiling, tubes running into the back of her hand. "Make sure it's cool enough I can slurp it through a straw."

"I'll get it," Beth said, turning to go. She'd already checked in on Gran twice, and figured Cynthia might want a chance to visit Gran alone.

"No," said Cynthia shoving past her, face pale. "I've got it."

Gran shook her head sadly. "That Cynthia. I can't believe she's still so bothered by hospitals."

"She loves you, Gran. That's all." She took the chair beside Gran. "She can't see that some people leave happier and healthier. She can't see the hope that resides here."

"Well, quite frankly, neither can I. I hate the smell. I hate the industrial bedsheets, and most of all," she said, her voice rising, "I hate the fact that everything is so bloody controlled and mandated that I can't get a decent sip of sherry!" She smacked the bed beside her with her free hand. "I need a goddamned bootlegger!"

Beth bit her lips, trying not to smile. "Maybe there's something I can do?"

Gran gave Beth a slight smile, her fight gone. "I'm okay. That city doc will look after me just fine. Even said he'd see what he could do about getting me some sherry." She raised an eyebrow at Beth and waited half a beat. "However, I don't think you need to go chasing after his love buns just yet."

"What?" Beth jolted as if she'd touched an electric fence with a wet hand.

"I heard the two of you girls out in the hall. I'm not deaf, you know." She gave Beth a stern look.

"I know," Beth said quickly. She scanned their recent conversation in her head trying to think what all Gran may have overheard.

"It was my decision."

"What was?" Beth asked.

Gran winced as she shifted her position. Beth stood to help fluff a pillow, guilt clinging to her like a thick fog. Her issues with Oz were affecting others, endangering her gran, and the town was going to rightly blame her for it. Gran was one of their own and she'd allowed her come to harm.

She had to make it stop. She had to cut the cord even if it meant starting over.

"I *said*, it was my decision. My decision to dance with Oz."

"Gran. I should have--"

"Oh, enough already. We're all adults." Gran gave her a disgruntled frown. "I know you got in some serious trouble from Justin--he's a rule follower you know--but don't you go thinking for one second that it changes anything between us. You are *not* my babysitter no matter what those numbskulls in their fancy offices think."

Beth gave Gran's hand a light squeeze. "I love you, Gran."

Gran waved her off with a frown. "Enough. You're going to make me vomit. Now ..." Gran had her business face on. "Damn, I wish I could sit up." She wiggled her shoulders, snuggling into her bed.

"Can I help?" Beth reached over to help fluff or adjust.

"Sit! Quit fussing over me." Gran pointed a long finger at Beth. "And don't you let me die of boredom in here. You wheel this goddamned bed into the common room every morning, you hear me? I can still chat, play cards, and do crafts while lying on my back. Plus, I'm going to need to keep an eye on Reggie. He's got a wandering eye, that one."

Beth lowered herself into the chair and nodded, unsure how she'd get past the protesting nurses and their rules.

"If I stay in here my brain will rot and then what good will I be?"

"I'll bring guests by, Gran."

"I want to be where the action is, you hear? There's a good reason they pay you to provide recreational therapy. Now. About these men of yours. I asked Dr. Leham--my heavens, that man has a nice tush--I asked him to check under that chair for my slippers more than once, I tell you." Gran made a satisfied sound. "Mmm-hmm."

"Gran!"

Gran gave her a silencing look and continued, "I asked him not to ban Oz. But that was all for naught. Rules this. Regulations that. Add in Oz's cousin Justin in his big office and--" She made a whooshing sound. She raised her voice like she did when making a point. "However. I do *not* agree with Cynthia. As smart as that girl is, I disagree. Dr. Leham is a fine specimen of Y chromosome and fun to spend time with while Oz gets his life sorted, but it should end there. For now." Another stern look. "Oz is not the type to take kindly to you spending time with another man."

"He told me to move on. He's not--we're not ... anymore, Gran."

"Sure you are. And if you think spending time with the lovely doctor is going to swing that man of yours around, you've got another think coming."

"But Gran--"

"Shit storms are no fun to walk in with your mouth open. And don't you *but* me, young lady. You listen to what I have to say."

"Yes, Gran." This felt like the time Gran found out she'd gone to the doctor for birth control while in high school. She'd been so sure she was going to hook up with Ricky Fallows and she wanted to be prepared. Gran, on the other hand, had laid into her for settling for less, and so early in life. How Ricky was less she never found out because once word had gotten out that Gran didn't approve, that was it. Ricky had avoided her as if she'd been sprayed by a skunk. It had taken her a long time to forgive Gran for that. Well, at least until she'd spotted Oz.

"I know Oz suggested you move on while he works through his issues. He's doing the honorable thing because he's realizing he has more issues to work through before he is ready to start a life with you. You can't figure out what your dreams are in a half a second. You kids think everything should happen on your own terms like it's one of those grand TV recording thingies and you can fast forward to the parts you want right now. Give him *time*. You're young and have time. You don't need to rush and have regrets later. Anyone else you may be thinking of, if they're worth it, will wait."

Beth clenched her hands into fists as her throat closed.

Gran's smile softened like it did when she saw Reggie. Beth looked over her shoulder, thinking he'd entered the room, but nobody was there. "Actions speak louder than words and sometimes that's all a man has. Listen carefully to his actions, not his words. The two of you were good together."

"Like what kind of actions?" Beth prodded.

"He tried to dance with your patients and especially with me. And the rose? Actions. Signs."

"But he was drunk. I asked him what he wanted and …" Beth tried to bite back the bitterness seeping into her voice. "He said he wanted exercise. He didn't come because he wanted to. He's still trying to please his father. Not himself."

Her grandmother laughed. "Oh, Beth, dear. He's a big ship. You can't turn one of those on a dime."

Beth shot Gran a look.

"Men are much more complicated than we give them credit for. You and I both know he didn't show up for exercise. He's reaching out in the only way he can without wounding his pride. Men can't always say the words we need to hear."

Beth paused. That would mean her gut was right and Cynthia was wrong.

Except the real Oz wouldn't have let his pride stop him from saying that he'd come for her.

"I'm right, aren't I?" gloated Gran.

Beth brought her attention back to her grandmother. "I don't think so," she said slowly.

Gran's expression grew grim. "Don't rush one of the most important things in your life. Trust yourself, Beth. Trust your instincts. Trust your heart."

9

<hr>

Beth sat in her car with the window rolled down. Being July, her car's air-conditioning had decided it was truly an option. An option her car no longer had. Parked in the shade of an old elm, with the steering wheel clammy in her grip, Beth thought of the overnight bag waiting experimentally in her trunk. All she had to do was start the engine and head down the road, take a left onto Second Street, another left onto the highway and straight out of town and into a new life. A life where she wouldn't burden her sister. A life where she wouldn't put Gran at risk. A life where Oz could do whatever he needed to do without feeling an obligation to her.

A clipping for a new apartment building in Derbyshire lay beside her and she glanced at the address once again. A nice part of town on a quiet street, not far from where Katie's boyfriend, Will, grew up. She'd be far enough away from the gossip and guilt, but she'd be close enough to visit Gran, Cynthia, and Katie whenever she wanted. And Nash.

She would miss their long chats on the phone, his awesome ice cream, and the way he made her feel relaxed, special, mysterious, and elegant. When she was with him it felt as though there was more to her life than just Blueberry Springs and her past. It felt as though

110

there was a completely unwritten future just waiting for her to walk into it.

It was silly. Dreaming about Nash was similar to a girl dreaming about being adopted by movie stars.

She sucked in a deep breath. It was time to make a choice. She could either keep deluding herself that there was hope in Oz's actions--just like everyone in town seemed to believe there was--or she could move on such as Cynthia had suggested.

Beth gripped her steering wheel and sweat trickled down her back. Oz was right. There was a new Oz in town and he wasn't at all like the old one. She should start her engine and go. New life. She reached to start the car.

"Nice wheels."

Beth jumped. "Oh jeez, Nash! You scared me."

"Sorry." Nash propped his arms on her open window. "Where are you off to?"

Beth casually flipped over the apartment ad.

Nash gave her a grin. "When the going gets tough, the tough gets going, huh?"

She shot him a sheepish smile.

He slid over her hood as if he was one of the brothers in *The Dukes of Hazard*. A thrill raced up her spine. She had no idea he could do that. He had athletic, nimble, agile, and sexy hiding behind his professional doctoral visage. Slipping off the edge of the hood, he landed hard on the ground and she laughed. He popped into the passenger's seat, looking embarrassed.

He snagged the ad he'd almost sat on, giving it a quick once over. "Nothing for rent in town, I take it?"

"Everything seems to be taken by the time I get to it." She focused her attention out the windshield at the leaves wiggling and dancing in a light puff of air. The leaves showed their pale underbellies, then hid them again.

"So? You're heading out?" He checked the backseat. "Reconnaissance mission?"

She nodded and they sat in silence.

Nash, hands clasped between his knees, shot her an apologetic look. "Sorry about your job."

"I didn't lose it." Although being on probation was almost the same thing when you were searching for a new job. Being on probation wasn't considered a positive strike during the inevitable reference call. It was one of the several small things keeping her from turning the key and driving off into a completely new life. That, and the fact that the nearest hospital, other than theirs, was well over an hour away and wasn't in need of a recreational therapist. Plus, she couldn't leave her outreach now that people were actually coming besides Gran. Nash had been right about holding a grand opening and advertising in the paper. She now had about sixty percent of her spots filled, making it worth getting up early every Saturday.

"I feel partially responsible for you being placed on probation, and I'm sorry."

Why was he apologizing when Oz hadn't?

It was another sign. And another reason why she needed to distance herself from Oz, despite what Gran had said, and what her heart wanted.

Nash continued, "If there had been a way for me to avoid reporting it, I would have." He rubbed the back of his neck. "But I can't admit a patient, especially one from continuing care, without writing up a report." He gave her an uncertain look. "You know?"

Some of the tension riding in her shoulders eased away. "Yeah, I know." Her mind shot down a new avenue. What if she followed her sister's advice? What if she leaned over and kissed Nash? Placed her warm lips against his soft, pouty lower lip ... closed her eyes and dreamed of the future? A whole new her. A future where Nash made her feel smarter and elegant just by being him. She'd no longer feel as though she was yanking both ends of her life together in furious hopes that one day they might connect.

"What?" Nash asked, a bemused smile lighting his face, a twinkle in his eyes.

She held her breath and leaned forward. His eyes changed and

Beth couldn't tell if it was longing or uncertainty. She lowered her gaze and reached across to open the glove box.

Big chicken.

She bit her lower lip. She deserved to be stuck in romance limbo. She didn't have the guts to pull up her pants and make a real decision about Oz other than to perpetually give him more time in hopes that he would change and ask her back. And she didn't have the courage to kiss Nash.

"What are you looking for?" Nash asked as she rummaged around.

A real life.

She straightened suddenly, bumping Nash's nose on her way up. He made a pained sound and Beth reached for him. "Oh, my God. I'm so sorry."

Nash clutched his nose.

"You're bleeding!" She scrambled in her glove box for a mini pack of tissues.

He took the tissues, jamming them against his nose. "Don't worry about it," he said in a plugged-up voice.

She sat helplessly. "I'm such a moron."

"Relax. It's just a nosebleed. Why don't you drive me around town--in your non-domestic car--and give me the full local's tour with history and insider jokes included."

A warm smile grew, its heat working through her in a way that told her that maybe, just maybe, things could be different in her life. Should she choose it.

"Volvo is owned by Ford, you know." She grinned and cranked her engine. "Hold on to your hat, Farmer Nash." She frowned and looked him over. "Wait, where's that freebie hat I worked so hard to get for you? Not just anyone can get one of those out of Alvin's box, you know."

He ran a hand through his hair. "I, uh."

Beth laughed. "I'm kidding." If she'd been walking she would have grabbed his hand and skipped down the street, her heart felt so light. "Let me show you the town."

And then you can show me the world.

BETH SLIPPED into the cool air conditioning of Benny's Big Burger just before the lunch crowd. She paused at the counter near the door, scanning the large room to see if she could spot Benny talking to customers.

Driving Nash around town yesterday had given her an idea of how she could take control of her life right here in Blueberry Springs. While running away to Derbyshire was still as tempting as all get out, she didn't want to have to deal with Bear's Pass during winter storms nor rely on her old car for a twenty-minute, mountainous commute. What she needed was a roof over her head-- which made Benny, who owned several rental properties, the man to see.

Mandy came out of the kitchen to Beth's right, carrying a tray of pizza that smelled divine.

"I'll be with you in a minute," the waitress said. She barely looked at Beth as she slipped pizza slices into the counter's revolving glass case. She adjusted the Pizza-by-the-Slice sign and turned to Beth, eyebrow arched. "Party of one?"

Some party that would be. A lovely pity party.

"Actually, I was hoping to talk to Benny."

"Need a job?"

"Have one thanks," Beth retorted.

"Barely."

"Just get me Benny." Beth turned her back to avoid the look she knew she'd receive from Mandy.

"You know Oz is seeing other people."

Despite herself, Beth found herself turning around.

"That's right," Mandy said with an evil glint in her eye, which was echoed in her grin. "He's back with me."

"Yeah, right." The liar. There was no way Oz was seeing her again. No. Way.

She tucked her trembling hands in her armpits. Mandy had to be lying.

"He said you were bad for him," Mandy whispered. The hair on Beth's neck moved as though Mandy was leaning over the counter for the full torture effect. Beth whirled, but Mandy had already backed off.

Beth glared at Mandy. "When?" she asked, despite herself.

"Oh. I'm sorry. He asked me not to tell anyone that he felt pressured by his father to get back together with you." She put a manicured hand against her lips and gave a cutesy look. "Oops."

"Liar," Beth whispered. She shut her eyes against the hurt and listened to the swish of Mandy's polyester pants as she went off to find Benny. She felt like a broken water balloon with all the water gushing out of it. Her sister was right. Oz was being pushed by his parents, not by a genuine need to be with her again. That's why he'd been drunk. That's why he didn't say the words she needed to hear.

"Beth? What can I do for you?" called a soft male voice.

She slowly uncurled her fists, rubbing the indents her nails had left in her palms. "Benny! Hey, I noticed Anna moving out of the apartment above the mechanic's shop. I was wondering what you're charging for rent?" She waited for his reply, her breath held. *Please, please, please quote me a low number so I can afford it and a bed. And maybe a few air fresheners so the place doesn't end up smelling like oil and gasoline from the shop.*

"Well ..." Benny rocked back on his heels and avoided looking at her. Beth bit her lower lip and waited for him to turn her down. "I was planning on renovating the space."

"That's okay," she said quickly. "I don't need it renovated."

Benny gave her a long look. "How many months do you plan on living there? My leases are for six months. You lose a month's rent if you move out before then."

"That's okay."

Benny frowned. "Aren't you planning on moving back with Oz?"

Beth perked up. "What?"

"I thought you two were just taking a timeout before your I Dos."

She swallowed hard, then pulled out her checkbook, pen poised. "What's first month's rent?"

Benny gave out a short laugh. "You've never seen the place, Beth."

"I don't need to."

"Not to be nosey, but I haven't seen you out with that doctor fellow as much since--"

"Oh, for Christ's sake!" Beth slammed down her fist, wincing as the impact stung her hand. "Are you going to rent me a place or not? Katie's tired of me sleeping in her living room and I really don't want to move into Mary Alice's spare room nor Angelica and Harvey's." She gave Benny a sad look. "I need a room of my own, Benny. Now."

Benny hesitated. "I can't," he said at last.

She blinked back tears of disappointment. "Why not?"

He leaned back on his heels, arms crossed. "I have to renovate it."

"Benny, I don't care what it looks like. I need a roof over my head. Help out a desperate girl."

He avoided her eye.

"What?" she asked in a low voice. Something was happening. She could smell it. And it wasn't just his pizza-by-the-slice deal rotating in the case beside her. It was something else. Something not so yummy.

Benny placed his beefy hands on the counter and leaned forward. He looked her in the eye and said quietly, "I promised someone I wouldn't." He reached out and patted her hand and turned away with a sad smile.

"Who?" she demanded. "I'm a good tenant. Who blacklisted me?"

He turned back, his eyes sorrowful. "I'm sorry, Beth. I never thought I'd have to come through on such a promise."

"Who did you promise?"

He cut his eyes to the side as if looking for people listening in. "Angelica."

She felt a sharp pain in her chest. "But she offered me Katie's old room. This makes no sense."

"Just keep on with Katie, Beth. It's for the best."

"But--" Beth stood at the counter, sputtering words that made no sense as he returned to the kitchen.

Mandy strode up to the counter, her expression surprisingly sympathetic. "Want a slice or something?"

Beth blinked. "What?"

Mandy pointed to the revolving pizza. "On the house."

Beth shook her head and slid out the door. Why would Oz's mother ask Benny not to rent to her? Why did Benny think it was best for her to stay at Katie's? And for how long had Angelica been whispering for favors?

BETH STORMED DOWN MAIN STREET, aiming for Cherry Road in order to take a shortcut to Oz's childhood home. She blasted past the ice-cream shop and clothing boutique which carried crap clothes that she hated only slightly more than driving into the city to buy something half decent and stylish. Rounding the corner to take Cherry, she paused. She backed up a step and stared through the boutique's large corner window.

It looked like she wouldn't risk cooling down during the long walk to Angelica's after all. She could get it all off her chest ASAP. She shoved the boutique's door open, the stupid frog ornament set by the door croaking as she tripped its motion sensor.

She strode up to Angelica, a cool wave of air conditioning fluttering over her bare arms. She tapped the woman sharply on the shoulder. Angelica turned, smiling until she saw Beth's expression. She dropped the chunky suede skirt she'd been petting and stepped back.

Beth, fists clenched, faltered, not knowing where to begin. Women milled about the shop, their attention piqued by Beth's stormy entrance. They circled like hungry sharks sensing blood in the water.

"What's wrong?" Angelica asked weakly.

"What's wrong?" Beth's voice scratched through the air. "What's *wrong*?" Angelica grew pale under her tan. "How about *you* tell *me*?"

Beth stepped forward and the older woman shrunk but held her ground. "How could you interfere like that? You've trapped me at Katie's."

Angelica smoothed her hair and looked away, her lips a thin, bleached line. Women whispered, trying to decipher Beth's words.

Fran, the shop owner, stepped between the two women. "Now Beth let's go have a cup of coffee over by the register. You look thirsty."

"Do you know what she's done?" Beth shouted, turning on Fran. "Do you?"

Fran gave Angelica an uncertain glance.

Beth pointed at Oz's mother and raised her voice. "She had me blacklisted."

"Blacklisted?" the shop owner asked. "Surely not."

Beth turned to Angelica and demanded, "Where else am I blacklisted other than with Benny? Who else have you been talking to?"

Angelica pulled herself up to her full height. "I am looking out for you, Beth."

"How on earth is blacklisting me and keeping me trapped in Katie's crappy basement suite looking out for me? I can't even sleep through the night there without sleeping pills because of the stupid pullout bed's bar digging into my back."

"I'm looking out for you and Oz."

"Last time you did that he gave me my ring back and told me we were through." Women whispered in agreement, their heads bobbing up and down. "You have no idea what our best interests are. Blacklisting me is not looking out for me." She turned to address the shoppers who hurriedly tried to act as though they hadn't been eavesdropping. "You *all* need to quit interfering and let me live my life. And let Oz live his."

"You are making a mistake, Beth," Angelica said quietly.

"With what?" she spat.

"Moving on without Oz."

"You think I'm moving on?" She let out a harsh laugh. "God, I wish it was that easy." She stared at the ceiling, trying to draw patience. She didn't even know where to start turning this woman's head around. "Why does everyone think I have a choice? That I have the power to influence Oz? You all act like I can snap my fingers and everything will be hunky-dory again. Don't you think I would have done that already if it were possible?"

"Setting up your own place means you're moving on, Beth," Angelica explained calmly. "You and Oz are only on a break."

"He *broke up* with me, Angelica. He's seeing *Mandy*." Around her, shoppers gasped. "He told me ..." Beth's voice wavered as she pulled in a deep breath to finish her sentence, "to move on. That we were over."

Angelica's eyes flashed. "He is *not* seeing Mandy."

A woman across the store hesitantly offered, "I, um, saw them kiss yesterday."

Beth's knees lost strength. She closed her eyes, willing herself not to cry. Damn that Mandy. Damn the ugly truth.

A small hand gripped her arm. It was Angelica giving her a pitiful look. "I'm sorry. I--"

"For what?" Beth pulled her arm free. "For Oz getting screwed up and dumping me? For him leaving me homeless? Or for the way Harvey is interfering and acting like Oz is his personal marionette and a way for him to make his own life worth living? Doesn't he see he's destroying his son?" The more she talked the more rage surged through her, fueling her muscles with adrenalin. "Or are you sorry for trying to force him into getting back together with me before he was ready? For him getting drunk and hurting Gran and putting my job in jeopardy? For him breaking my heart?"

The room blurred as the blows she'd received over the past four months broadsided her again. How could the man she had loved so dearly be so devastatingly destructive? She swiped at the tears streaking down her cheeks and women gathered around with *there, there's*. Angelica stared at Beth with a strange look.

"What?" Beth sniffed, the vacating adrenaline leaving her weak and trembling.

"I'm sorry Beth. I thought …" Angelica paused. "I thought he still loved you." She met Beth's eye. "I thought everything he was doing and saying meant he still cared. I thought he simply had to get things sorted out so you could get back together. I didn't want you running away and starting a new life." She pointed to the ground, her voice strong. "I wanted you to be there, ready and waiting for him when he got it together." She gripped Beth's hand. "I want what's best for Oz and I've always thought that was you."

Beth released a hard sob and wiped her nose with an offered tissue. She turned from Angelica so she wouldn't get hugged and fought against the compelling need to continue sobbing.

"I'm sorry, Beth. I'll talk to Benny and the others."

Beth nodded. She looked up as the frog croaked at the front door, and quickly turned away, wiping her wet face with her hands.

"Hey, Mom," the man called, "your chariot awaits."

Beth heard him move across the store, his steps faltering as he reached the spot where she was cowering, attempting to hide behind a rack, his mother floundering beside her.

"Right!" Angelica said brightly. "I'm glad you got my text, Oz. I ended up buying more than I can comfortably carry and I knew you were out and about. Did you see last year's winter wear is still on clearance?"

"Beth?" Oz asked gently, ignoring his mom's attempt to move him along. "You all right?"

Beth heard whispers to her right as women gathered closer so as not to miss a thing and a warm hand landed lightly between her shoulder blades. Knowing her face would be horribly blotchy and red, she ducked her head as she turned to push past Oz.

Oz lightly grabbed Beth's bare arm as she moved past. "Beth? Are you okay?"

"No, I'm not okay." She wrenched her arm from his grasp. "And what do you care, anyway?"

"Because we're still friends."

Beth's heart took the express elevator to the basement. *Friends.* She could never be friends with the man who held her dreams within reach only to snatch them away so he could return to his ex, not caring if rumors splattered into her like buckshot.

Friends was right next door to impossible. Friends was a lovely corner office in Hell's deepest pit.

10

*B*eth placed bags of Chinese takeout on Nash's kitchen island, tired of moaning and groaning to him all week about Angelica's blacklisting stunt as well as the difficulty of finding a place to live, even after the rent-to-Beth ban had been lifted. By the time she'd circled back to Benny to snag his vacant apartment he'd convinced himself that a bit of renovation work was truly a good idea. He had already ripped up most of the water-stained parquet flooring, and as Beth stared at the upheaved space, trying to find a way to expedite the renovation process, Katie had excitedly started suggesting a few more things to update such as replacing light fixtures and repainting the kitchen cabinets and walls. By the time Benny and Katie had sketched out all the changes, Benny figured he'd have the place out of commission for at least two to three months and would have to increase the rent significantly in order to cover the updating.

She'd come to Nash after seeing Benny's disaster zone, her head a whirlwind of confusing thoughts. He'd sat her down, with ice cream of course, and had her write out everything she was thinking and feeling about Oz and moving on with her life. Looking at it written in front of her she knew what she'd felt earlier was correct, it was over and it was time to move on. There were too many little things to ignore.

Beth perched on a tall stool and watched Nash dish himself a plate of lukewarm Chinese food. He handed her a set of bamboo chopsticks from his cutlery drawer. "I can't believe nobody in town works on a BMW," he said. "You would think *someone* would work on foreign cars."

"Well, how many foreign luxury cars have you seen around town?" she asked, spearing a piece of lemon chicken with a chopstick. She was getting tired of him complaining about how Blueberry Springs wasn't the city. She wished he'd see the bright side of small town living instead of all the bad things like rumors and interference. For example, if someone's house burned down, less than twenty-four hours later they'd find themselves set up in a new, temporary place with everything they needed. But he always seemed to focus on little things like how Cody just about ran him off the road. Which totally wasn't Cody's fault. Everyone knew he always swung left to turn right because he was used to hauling his long cattle trailer behind his truck and needed the extra room in order to make the corner. But Nash had chosen that moment to blast past the truck and almost got sideswiped. It had taken him weeks to get over the incident.

"They aren't exactly up there with Chevys and Fords for popularity, you know." She stabbed the chicken again, trying to keep it on the chopstick like Nash did with ease. "You know, I didn't pick up the disposable chopsticks at the restaurant for a reason." Her food was going to be mutilated and cold by the time she managed to get any of it in her mouth.

Nash finished chewing and balanced the chopsticks on his extended pointer finger. "Eating with chopsticks makes it an experience." He winked and went back to his meal, delicately scooping rice to his mouth like the stuff was glued to his sticks.

"How do you do that?" she asked, feeling amused that he had such quirky hidden talents. She'd never met anyone who could wrangle a set of chopsticks like City Boy.

He held out his hand, demonstrating his grip. "It's all in how you hold them."

Beth tried to imitate the hold, but her chopsticks tumbled from her fingers. Nash reached over and wrapped his hand around hers and she was surprised at how big they seemed when enveloping hers. She watched his eyes as he plucked her fingers into place. Concentration. Ease. Confidence.

She liked it.

And she also liked how Nash would make a most excellent rebound man. While he was a bit like the old Oz, he was different enough that he left her in a state of anticipation. Plus, the fact that he wasn't constantly in contact, despite how close they were becoming as friends, made his attention feel all the more special. The problem was how to leap from friends to rebound man without damaging what they had.

"There. Try that." He maneuvered her fingers as if she were a puppet, the chopsticks picking up the mangled chicken. "Now ... just lift to your mouth." He released his grip, mouth opened slightly as he tipped his head back, watching her move the chicken to her mouth.

It landed in her plate's puddle of cherry sauce with a dull splat.

She stared at her meal and contemplated asking for more lessons so he could wrap his hands around hers again. However, by the time she got any food in her mouth the sauces would be all cold and gelled and completely gross. "I cry uncle. Gimme a fork."

Nash laughed and handed her a fork from the drawer. "You know, I met a girl named Chevy the other day. *That* was a small town moment." He raised his hands as if to ward off an argument. "I'm not wholly against vehicle names as I've always thought the name Mercedes had a certain ring to it. It's just ... *Chevy?*"

Beth let out a short laugh. "Mercedes? That's better?"

Nash cut short his sip of wine in order to protest, "It's a lovely name!"

She grinned and took a bite of her lemon chicken, courtesy of her fork. "I prefer traditional names like Jennifer--Jenny, and Benjamin--Ben."

Nash nodded in approval. "Those are nice names. I could see a couple of cute kids with your curls named that." He tugged lightly on one of her curls and she tried to hide her blushing. "You want kids right away?" he asked, head tilted and chopsticks momentarily silent.

Beth's stomach did a couple of jumping jacks as she tried to act casual. "I do." She did some mental math and sighed. A year to find a man and for them to get to know each other. If he was the right guy, then at least another year for engagement and marriage. Then another year before kids. She was at least three years out from having her first child if she found herself the right man today. The grand age of thirty would be staring her in the face by the time she got to baby number two. What if she had troubles conceiving like her cousin had? What if it took years to conceive? She'd be screwed. And not in the mutually satisfying sense of the word. "I'm not getting any younger."

Nash tipped his head back and laughed. "And how old are you, exactly?" He refilled her wine glass from the bottle of sweet white wine he'd picked up especially for her.

Beth batted her lashes. "Shouldn't you know better than to ask a lady her age?"

Nash laughed again and threw up his hands. "Got me. I'll have to sneak a look at your driver's license after I get you drunk."

She took a sip of her wine, rolled her eyes, and laughed. "Seriously though, I have a cousin who is only a couple of years older than I am and she's having troubles conceiving. It makes me nervous. What if I can't have kids? What if I don't find the right man until I'm thirty?" She took a calming breath. The life she wanted felt so out of reach.

"Of course you'll have kids. Medicine has astounding capabilities these days." He pushed a container of food toward Beth. "Annual exams and ensure your husband wears boxers, like I do, and I'm sure you'll be just fine. And, really, most women don't have to worry at all until they're well into their thirties."

Beth's fork halted halfway to her mouth. She really *was* running out of time. Especially since she wanted at least two kids, maybe more.

"You see ..." Nash said, acting doctorly, "you've got to keep the testicles away from the body's heat for optimal sperm count." He snatched two chicken balls from the container in front of him and cupped them in his hand. He laid a spring roll between them. "That's the biggest source of the sperm count issue for many men, their choice of underwear keeps their testicles snug up against the body. The testes become overheated." He tossed the chicken balls back in their container and took a bite out of the spring roll.

Blushing, Beth focused on her plate. Great. Now all she could think about was what she'd find in Nash's boxers, white picket fences, a precious baby girl sporting Nash's bright blue eyes, and a rough and tumble tyke running around the yard trying to place a stethoscope over the family dog's heart. It didn't help that Cynthia kept teasing her about Nash. Or that Gran had pretty much given up on Oz already. Beth blinked, realizing she'd broken out in a sweat of longing.

Why did she always seem to grow a crush on guys who didn't seem to see her in a long-term girlfriend kind of way? Chin resting in her palm, she watched as Nash carefully wrapped a long noodle around his chopsticks. Maybe she could move things along a bit. See if he'd be her rebound guy. She'd keep him less lonely and he'd be her distraction as she mended her heart. When they were ready, they'd move on. No harm. No foul.

"You're so cute when you twirl your noodles."

He smiled and she realized she was close enough ... close enough to lean over and place her lips upon his. Seizing the moment she spun on her stool and gripped his face, placing her lips on his. She gave him a quick peck, leaning away so the kiss would remain light and airy--something that could easily be brushed off--when he gripped her shoulders, keeping her close. Knees touching, they stayed together, her light peck becoming a real kiss. It turned deeper, making her heart pick up its pace.

As he kissed her she pictured Oz kissing Mandy. Which was dumb. She hadn't even seen the kiss. But it had been public. Which said a million things. Such as the fact that maybe she needed a rebound man even more than she'd thought.

She kissed Nash hard, trying to keep her desperation at bay.

She should be happy. Happy that she was free to move on. Happy that Oz had made the final decision to cut the cord. She was free. No guilt.

But Mandy? Oz said he was never going back to Mandy. Why couldn't the girl just take up with Frankie Fall-Off-the-Water-Tower Smith who'd been chasing her for years and get out of her face?

Nash broke off the kiss and gave her a smile. "Wow. That was ... intense."

She sat back, feeling self-conscious. She'd totally lost track of the kiss. She'd probably freaked him out if her lips were anywhere near as furious as her thoughts had been.

Ducking her head she watched Nash out of the corner of her eye. His cheeks were slightly flushed, but he didn't seem anything beyond his normal cool, calm, and collected self. She let out a breath and took a swig of wine. It would be okay. She could do this. *They* could do this.

Nash resumed carefully twirling his long noodles, and desperate to keep the mood light, Beth hung a noodle from her lips, gnawing on the end before noisily slurping it into her mouth. Giggling, she slurped another while Nash frowned at her lack of manners. Everything about Nash and his condo was so neat and perfect, making it absolutely temptationalicious to act like an unmannered hick and make him cringe and roll his eyes. Laughing, she gave his arm a push and he grinned back, sliding his plate aside.

"Let's go for a walk you ill-mannered yahoo," he said, giving her curls another playful tug.

She slipped her hand into his offered one, a warmth spreading in her soul.

Happy that her out-of-control kiss hadn't freaked him out, she let him lead her onto the elm-lined street. She dropped his hand and linked her arm through his, leaning into his shoulder. It was refreshing to be able to spend time with him and not have the town anticipate marriage like they would if he were a local man. She inhaled the August air, permeated with a hint of the coming fall.

"I can smell autumn coming."

Nash inhaled deeply. "But it's still summer."

"It comes sooner in the mountains." She glanced at the trees. No signs yet, just the early warning scent of the upcoming change of seasons. "It's my favorite time of year. The earth is whispering to cozy up against someone warm." She tipped her head against Nash's shoulder, testing him. He placed a light kiss on top of her head.

Pass. This man was passing with flying colors. It almost made her want to drag him back to his condo and see what those smiling lips could do to the rest of her body.

"Speaking of the fall, I'm going to take ten days off in October and leave town for a bit."

Her steps faltered. The urge to follow him scared Beth. She didn't want to be in Blueberry Springs if he wasn't. At the moment, ten days without Nash felt as though it would be an eternity. She depended on him to smooth her brow when her shit-on-a-stick life got too covered in poop sprinkles. She forced her voice to be light. "Where to Dr. Leham?"

"I was thinking Europe. Maybe Paris."

"Holy crap. Are you serious?" He had to be kidding. She stopped and stared at him. Nobody from Blueberry Springs went to France-- Mexico, *maybe*--but France didn't happen even for high school trips or honeymoons.

"Paris is lovely in the fall. Nice and cool, not many tourists. It's perfect."

Beth blinked and studied him. "Wait. How do you know Paris is nice in the fall?"

"I've been there in October."

"You've been there in October? And you're going back?"

He shifted uncomfortably. "I try to go every couple of years."

"What!" She stared at him. He couldn't be serious. He took overseas trips--*expensive* overseas trips--repeatedly? To the same destination?

"What?" He took a step back, appearing almost offended.

"You're serious."

"Of course I am." He began walking again. She skipped to catch up. "If you don't believe me, come along and I'll show you around." Although he said it nonchalantly, she noticed he kept a studying eye on her.

"Serious?"

"Uh." Nash ran a hand through his hair, each strand falling perfectly into place. "Do you get any time off as a hospital minion?"

"Yes," Beth admitted slowly. "Probably." But could she swing that many days off in a row? And was he really, actually, honestly and truly asking her along on his vacation?

"Come with me."

Her knees weakened momentarily. What had she done to him in that kiss? *He* was inviting *her* to *Paris*? That didn't happen to women like Beth.

She sucked in a deep breath. Taking time off now would undoubtedly screw up her Christmas break, but it could be well worth it. Besides, it wasn't as if she needed more than a day or two to hang out with Gran and Cynthia while wishing her father was around.

She dared imagine Paris with Nash. An amazing, different life. Completely out of the norm from what she'd ever experienced or ever would, of that she was sure.

Glamorous. Exciting. New.

Only one problem.

"Um. Despite sharing rent with Katie for the last five months I'm pretty sure I don't have enough cash to fly off to Paris and stay there for ten days." She sighed as real life bitch-slapped her. Images of fancy dresses and laughter died away. It wasn't as if Paris would have been like that anyway. "Thanks just the same."

Nash scooped up her arm and tucked it under his so it was

pinned against his ribs. "Pick up your flight and I'll pay all expenses when we get there."

She paused for a second. "Serious?"

"Quit saying that, you know I am." He started down the street, pulling her along. "Think about it."

New beginning. Rebound of a lifetime.

Who was she kidding? She'd rob a bank to go along. Well, maybe not *rob a bank*, but she'd do whatever she had to in order to go as well as to find out what Nash was really like away from this place. She'd pick up a part-time job or beg and borrow from everyone she knew. She was going. She was going to eat one of those tiny packets of peanuts or pretzels or whatever they served on planes and see what people ate for breakfast on the other side of the world. It was time to live again.

"Let me in, Cynthia." Beth banged on Cynthia's apartment door. Her sister had to be home. She never missed the after-supper celebrity gossip show. Ever.

Beth's hands were shaking and her heart throbbed madly. She couldn't think. She had to move fast before her brain caught up.

Cynthia opened the door, a tube of lip gloss in hand. "For what do I owe the pleasure of your visit?"

"I need help. Is your computer on?" Beth slipped out of her sandals and headed down the hall to Cynthia's bedroom.

"No. Why? Are there naked pictures of you on the Internet? Because if there are, they can be tricky to get off unless you know what to do." She followed Beth, applying lip gloss as she went.

"No." She stopped to face her sister. "How do you know?"

She shrugged. "I watch a lot of TV."

"Right," Beth said without conviction. "Sorry for interrupting your show."

"Meh. It's about Tom Cruise. I can miss it." She pushed past Beth. "So? What do you need?"

"I need to book a flight."

"A flight?" Cynthia asked, perking up. "To where?"

"Paris."

"Can I come?"

"Oh God, Cynthia. I have a feeling I'm going to need help keeping my knickers on." Beth blushed, unsure whether taking a rebound romance as far as *knickers off* was something she was ready for.

"All right!" Cynthia high-fived her from the doorway of her cozy bedroom. She hit the power button on her computer and impatiently wiggled the mouse. "Who on earth would convince you to leave your little nest in Blueberry Springs? Surely not ...?"

Beth nodded and watched Cynthia for a reaction. Her sister's eyebrows shot up and back down again so quickly Beth almost missed it.

"And you think your knickers may come off, do you?" She gave Beth a coy grin and began clicking and typing away on her computer. "Very interesting."

"Well, no. Not really." Beth fidgeted with the cuffs of her light jacket. "According to the people of Blueberry Springs, they'll be off before I even reach the airport."

"Long before. You'll be eloping because you've already taken them off and City Boy needs to make an honest woman of his unborn offspring's mother."

Beth plunked herself on her sister's bed and flopped onto her back. "Ohmigod. Stop talking and book the flight." She dug Nash's folded note containing his flight info from her pocket. The neat, masculine scrawl almost made her head spin. She was going to Paris. With a *man*!

Cynthia took the note and, frowning, typed and clicked until she got to the site she needed.

Beth's mind raced. This was a blend of exciting and completely terrifying. She pulled one of Cynthia's pillows over her face.

Stop thinking, stop thinking, stop thinking.

"What if something crazy happens like Oz asking you back before ... October fifteenth?" Cynthia asked, reading the flight details.

"He won't," Beth said with a finality that surprised her. She tossed the pillow aside and glanced at her sister who had raised an eyebrow. "Look. You were right. It's time to move on. And Nash has offered me an opportunity to break away. I'm going to take it." Her sister didn't turn back to the computer. "If I go far, far away I'll get enough perspective that I'll know what to do about my life. What I want and need."

"Sticking with the British knickers slang, I'd say a jolly good rogering? 'Cause that's what's gonna happen."

"Cynthia!"

"Well, why else does a man invite a girl to Paris? Plus, you even said it yourself, knickers girl." Cynthia gave Beth's leg a shove. "Go have a Parisian fling and get being on the rebound out of your system. Your big sister is telling you to go live a little."

Paris. Alone. With Nash. Beth would never admit it, but over the past few days she'd had more than the odd fantasy about what that blue-eyed doctor might be capable of between the sheets, in her office, on the couch, in her car, and now on a plane. But it didn't mean she was going to make something like that happen. They were friends. Friends who were going on vacation together.

And maybe repeat a kiss or two. And engage in some fun rebound-type behaviors.

She snorted. Why was she even thinking about a fling? She wasn't the kind of girl who could pull off something like that without getting serious. And Nash was nothing but a charming distraction. A few kisses, etcetera. Nothing more. And if things *did* progress to serious for some reason, she still wouldn't be losing. Nash was a good man.

On the flipside, it wasn't as though she had to worry about Oz asking her back. He'd kissed Mandy--in public--for a reason.

End game.

Nash was waiting for her, hand extended. It was time to move on.

"Earth to Beth ..." Cynthia nudged Beth's leg.

She snapped back to the present. "A fling," she snorted, "yeah right. That would spell nothing but trouble."

"Dreamy look complete with blushing. You're sorely tempted aren't you? Although the peeved look? That was weird. Tell the guy it's an exit only."

"You're such a pervert." She stared at the watermarked ceiling and let her thoughts wash over her. "What if the life I want is a bit different than I've always envisioned? What if there is more to me than this small town? I mean, a man asking me to go to Paris with him? To travel? That's not who I thought I was." She propped herself up on an elbow. "But I like the idea so maybe I am? I mean, what if I'm that woman, but I was always too scared to find out? What if I like things like champagne and orange juice for breakfast and big diamond necklaces? I like cashmere."

"I think the point here is that everyone likes cashmere," Cynthia replied, her attention on the computer screen. "And nobody actually *likes* champagne. They just pretend to because it's glitzy."

Beth fell onto her back and fanned her face as heart palpitations set in. She didn't have a passport. She didn't even know if she had enough time to get one. Or how to book a plane ticket. Or if she got airsick. Or if she had a bag big enough for whatever she'd need to pack.

What was the weather like in Paris? What did they eat? French fries, French toast, and French bread? She couldn't even pronounce *merçi* correctly, how on earth was she going to deal with the language thing? She slapped her hands over her eyes and tried to calm her thoughts.

"It took a lot of convincing to even get you to apply for college in the city. And even then, you took Katie with you. I don't think you're truly a jet-setting gal in disguise."

"College was a good thing though," Beth reminded her.

"I know. It's just that this doesn't seem like your style." Her sister stopped uncertainly.

"To what? Be adventurous? To try something new? To see if I like wine--which I do. Cashmere--which I do. *Paris*?" Beth sat up, hands on her hips. She forced away the anger welling up inside her. "I can *do* this, Cynthia. I'm not going to be one of those old ladies wishing she'd gone and done something daring when she was young and free. That she had stepped outside of who she thought she was and what she thought she'd always wanted. I need to explore new dreams." Her back snapped straight as she realized what she said.

She sounded just like Oz.

What did that mean? That he was right all along?

No, it couldn't be. She still had her dream of having a family. She was simply testing her boundaries and living a little in the meantime.

Cynthia threw up her hands. "Whatever. I'm not arguing. It's just unlike you, that's all."

"Shove over." Beth squeezed next to her sister on the computer chair. "Let's book this stupid thing."

Step one, book a friggin' ticket out of here. Step two, figure out the details. Step three, panic later.

"I've got the airline and flight up already," Cynthia said. "Now what?"

"I was hoping you'd know."

"Well, let's just take it step-by-step. It can't be that hard." Cynthia started clicking little boxes and asking for information. "Confirm?" she asked finally, peeking at Beth.

Beth nodded.

"You can afford this, right?" Her sister squinted at the screen, her mouse's arrow hovering over the confirm-flight button.

Beth wet her lips and swallowed. "Barely."

Cynthia turned to face her full on. "Paris isn't cheap and the good doctor doesn't strike me as the slumming type. He's going to want to stay in fancy places." She tapped her fingers on her desk, thinking. "You're going to need more money."

"He's paying for everything but the flight."

Cynthia's fingers abruptly ceased tapping.

"I know," Beth said softly, ignoring her sister's probing gaze. She tried to ignore the heat spreading through her body, lighting her skin on fire. Nash wanted her. And she was going to put one foot in front of the other and see where it took her.

"Let me know how it goes becoming a member of the mile-high club when you *rendez vous avec le* doctor in the *avion*," Cynthia said dryly and clicked *confirm flight*.

She'd made it.

Paris was fantastic.

It was so fantastic she was never going home.

The croissants were crisp, fresh, and made with real butter. The champagne was lovely. Beth had fallen in love with the city and the romantic essence the very name evoked. And she hadn't even exited the plane. In fact, she wasn't even sure they were in France yet.

But she'd made it.

She reclined her seat and sighed happily. She'd made it to October. She'd made it to the passport office. She'd even made it to the plane despite having way too much luggage. Nash had laughed at her pile and she'd just had to shrug. What did she know about packing, foreign countries, and what she needed to bring?

Beth closed her eyes and relaxed. She hadn't chickened out and she'd found a replacement for work without a problem--despite Oz's cousin Justin, a man who was also her boss and in charge of her schedule, giving her a tough time. And while she didn't think anyone in Blueberry Springs bought her trip's cover story about the two of them backpacking through France--especially since it was pretty clear Nash wasn't the backpacking type and she had more luggage than even a Sherpa could comfortably carry--the misdirection made her feel better. The town could gossip about how neither of them were backpackers instead of what they might possibly be doing while overseas.

But heck. She didn't know a thing about France. Were the people of Paris called Parisians? Parisonians? Parasites? No, it couldn't be the last one. She laughed at herself and emptied her champagne flute, hoping to steady her nerves. It didn't matter if she didn't know anything about Paris. That's why she was going--to discover it. Plus, Nash would help her out. She hadn't been able to get French Euros from the Blueberry Springs bank--because nobody had ever needed any according to the teller and so they didn't have any on hand--and so Nash had loaned her some pocket money. That man would keep her from trembling and running back home early. He'd even gently guided her away from the little exchange booth with all its cool exchange rates displayed in red at the airport, whispering that he knew where she could get a better exchange rate.

Beth sucked in a deep breath and tried to quell her nervousness. It felt weird flying over the ocean to a foreign country. It should be someone like Katie who special-ordered French design and fashion magazines and had taught herself how to read basic designer-related French. But here she was. Off to France when she couldn't even order the food.

Nash groggily lifted his eye mask and squinted at her. "You should sleep. The time change is quite difficult."

"I'm too nervous and excited. I don't know what to expect. The airport wasn't the nightmare everyone said it would be even though I had to pay extra for my luggage being overweight." She lightly shook Nash's arm, prompting him to lift his mask again. "What do they say? The English say, 'bloody brilliant.' What do the French say when something is out-of-this-world fantastic?"

Nash looked at her for a long moment then murmured sleepily, "*C'est fantastique* or *c'est incroyable*. And you really should try to nap."

Beth relaxed into her seat and rolled her tongue over the exciting, foreign words. Nash groaned and slid the mask over his eyes while she willed the plane to go faster. The trip was going to be *incroyable*.

RIDING in the limousine to the hotel Beth felt as though she could be anyone in the City of Love.

She was free.

Nobody knew her. Nobody was going to judge her for vacationing with the handsome, single Nash. It was all perfectly cool in their glamorous, foreign eyes. And it *was* cool. Because she was single.

Deep breath.

"Single!" trilled an inner voice and pangs of excitement zinged inside her ribcage.

She could see anyone she wished. And she wished to see Nash.

All of him. Naked. No strings attached. Here. Now.

Her body sung with heat and she tried to quell the feelings of need mixed with her anticipation to see the city. He was just a friend, she reminded herself. A friend she'd kissed--twice. She was only excited about being here so she shouldn't go and jump on him, shove her tongue down his throat, and yank off all his clothes. That would just make the trip awkward. She had to play it cool.

Yeah, right. She was going to take matters into her own hands. That was, if she wanted anything to happen. She paused, thinking while she tried to focus on the sights whizzing by their limo's window. Everything was so overwhelming. Everything so different from Blueberry Springs.

"There is a lot of history," Nash was saying. "Did you see the damage on that building?"

"The big stone one?"

"Yes, it still has damage from World War II."

"Why don't they fix it?"

"Reminders, I suppose."

She nodded and continued to gawk out the window, pointing at every old building they passed, making Nash laugh and pull her hand down, gripping it in his.

"We'll have a view of the Eiffel Tower from our hotel. They built it for the World's Fair and had planned to take it down. We'll watch them light it up from a river tour at dusk tomorrow night. How's that sound?"

"Lovely."

Nash seemed so relaxed and at home. It felt as though the real man was being shown to her in a way none of their shared moments in Blueberry Springs had. It made her wonder if she seemed as at home in the limo.

She shook her head and smiled. "I still can't believe you hired a limousine."

"This is the proper way to be introduced to *mon Paris, chéri.*" He leaned closer, his breath warm on her cheek. He kissed the back of her hand, his eyes never leaving hers. Tingles rushed down her spine. French truly was the language of love. Romantic, frisky language. Hummuna.

She resisted the urge to push him onto his back and place her lips firmly on top of his. "A girl could get used to this treatment," she said, their lips almost touching.

"Please do." Nash brushed her cheek with a thumb as the car slowed. His attention flicked to the window and she reluctantly followed his gaze. Outside was an ornate, historic building spouting peaks, towers, and gargoyles. It appeared as though it should house a dozen princesses and have at least one fire-breathing dragon.

"This is it," he said.

Beth gasped at its beauty and held Nash's arm, allowing him lead her into the building while she gaped at the lobby's fresco ceiling. A uniformed porter followed them to the front desk, pulling their bags on a brass luggage cart. "Totally and utterly unreal." She had never-ever dreamed of stepping into a building this amazing, let alone stay in one. She wanted to plunk down in one of the cushy chairs with a bright, cold beer and soak it all in.

Nash pulled Beth aside and wrapped his arms around her. She slowly lowered her attention to Nash's clear, intense eyes. He placed his warm, minty mouth on hers, kissing her with an intensity and longing that made her insides jitter with anticipation of what might follow. She held him tight and inhaled his wonderfully clean scent, and kissed back, harder and deeper.

Finally, she forced herself to draw away, allowing herself a moment to refocus her eyes.

"Do you feel like ..." Nash blushed and hugged Beth's body tight against his, before lowering his voice to a whisper that tickled her ear. "A foreign affair?"

Oh. My. God.

Romantic. Spontaneous. Something that happened in books, but never, ever, to a woman such as herself.

She wanted it. She wanted it *bad*. A Parisian fling with a handsome, caring doctor--who wouldn't say yes to that? Plus, their kiss had her body throbbing and screaming, "Pick me! Pick me!"

But her mind, meanwhile, seemed to be sitting on the fence doing its nails. She didn't want to lose their friendship as it had become too important to her.

She closed her eyes, emotion and need racing through her. They would be hot together.

Beth reminded herself that half the purpose of this trip was to prove to herself that she could be someone different. Spontaneous. New.

She could do it. She could turn a friend who wanted a no-strings-attached fling with her--a girl on the rebound--into a passionate lover.

Every cell in her body was reaching out to Nash, pulling him in. Needing him. Wanting him.

And soon, taking him.

She opened her eyes and smiled. Damn the torpedoes, the hunk of male waiting for an answer could be hers for one week only. It was time to seize the day.

THEIR WEEK in Paris had been even better than she'd imagined. It had been a blur of wonderfully ancient, historic sites, sculptures, paintings, fountains, postcard-like settings, decadent food, and a most wonderful break from reality.

It had been a taste of what life could be like with a man who had a passion for seeing and enjoying the world as well as a little money.

"I never want to go home." Beth sighed and laid her head on Nash's bare chest. Last night they'd shared a loaf of fresh bread and a bottle of wine along the Seine, watching the twinkling lights turn on up and down the Eiffel Tower as the sun set. It was amazing. Romantic. Way beyond ordinary. And she liked it. She liked it a lot. Evenings like that could make a girl greedy for more.

Nash smiled, his eyes crinkling. He gently stroked her back with his fingertips and they snuggled quietly, listening to a cello playing what Nash had identified as Bach on the street below.

"Speaking of home," Nash said, breaking their silence, "did you return your sister's call?"

Beth's little bubbles of happiness began to dissolve, and determined not to lose them, she dismissed his reminder. "She was just checking in."

"You can use my calling card if you want."

She mumbled something noncommittal. The last thing she wanted to do was think about home. She'd be back to reality soon enough and this week had shown her how much of the world she had been missing by staying in Blueberry Springs waiting for Oz. She loved the freedom and spontaneity of traveling. She'd even enjoyed taking a lover, despite how it signaled a definite finality to her and Oz. She didn't miss home or anyone there and she vowed not to waste her last day thinking about it.

Nash teased an erogenous zone at the back of her neck, sending wake-up tremors of excitement coursing through her nervous system. She closed her eyes and savored the sensation. Tomorrow this would end. If she had the choice, she'd live like this for the rest of her life.

"I must say," she murmured, "med school was well-worth the tens of thousands of dollars. Was there a whole class on erogenous zones?"

"Nerve Endings 101. Any others in need of attention?" Beth laughed and offered an ear. He bit it lightly and whispered, "What do you want to do today?"

She ran a hand down the front of his boxers. "Something stimulating."

"An art gallery?"

"I do enjoy a good nude." She gave him a deep kiss, stroking him. "You've been *such* an attentive guide. I think you deserve a very *large* gratuity."

He sucked in a shaky breath as her strokes became firmer. "Gratuities accepted." He rolled on top of her and kissed her neck, his erection rubbing against her inner thigh's sweet spot. "How about I rent a car and we go see a vineyard?"

"Ooo ... yes, please."

An hour later, her cheeks still flushed, Beth leaned back in the cherry red convertible's leather seat and let her head loll to the side so she could watch Nash maneuver the car through the tight streets.

If only every day was like this. Or even every weekend seeing as Nash was a self-confessed workaholic. But being together back home wasn't part of the agreement. This was a fling and nothing more. When their feet hit the tarmac it was over. Back to being friends. Their time together would be tucked away as though it had never happened.

But she still had one day to be sexy and free and she was going to draw it out as much as she could. She slid her sunglasses over her eyes and raised her hands to let the wind whip around her arms. France was heavenly. Nobody was planning her life. Nobody was gossiping about the way she had to stop and kiss Nash every five minutes. Chocolates magically appeared on her pillow as if by fairies. Everything from food to fresh laundry was delivered to her room and beautiful sights were waiting every time she looked away from Nash. She was free. Happy.

She should have been born rich, nestled deep in Nash's arms.

She swiveled in her seat. "Ooo! Look at that!" She pointed at a meticulous vineyard with rows of vines marching over the rolling hills. Each row was as perfect as the next. Someone must have been very good with a measuring tape.

Beth laughed as they sped by the vineyard's driveway. "That wasn't it?"

"We're going a bit further. Wait and see." Nash geared down for a sharp turn. "You'll love it."

"I'll love anything you show me, Nash. Anything." Beth lifted her arms in the air and laughed as the air forced her arms back down.

EVERYTHING ABOUT VINEYARDS made Beth want to pack up and move to one. The bitter taste of grapes straight off the vine, rich soil running through her fingers, the subtle variety in the different wines, and most of all, the way Nash let his fingertips rest lightly on her lower back as they'd roamed the vineyard. It didn't help that he had pulled her from the tour group to press her up against a hidden trellis and make hasty, scorching love to her.

She'd never think of vineyards in the same way.

However, in an hour, their plane would land, crashing and breaking her fairytale world and romance, dissipating into the crisp fall air. Reality was already seeping in around the edges, staining her mood. No more convertibles. No more delivered breakfast. No slow lovemaking to the sounds of Parisian traffic. No more gilded everything. No more fresh croissants with champagne and orange juice for breakfast.

And most of all, no more Nash. No more sharing her days, thoughts, worries, dreams, and life with him.

No more. No more. No more.

Beth screwed her eyes shut, determined to cement every detail from their trip into her memory. Every day had felt fresh and full of potential.

She'd been alive. Truly alive. In Paris she had felt strong and confident. Adventurous.

Flying home, she knew the Beth she'd been in Paris would fade and her old life would slowly take over again.

She gave herself a shake. What was she thinking? This was her life. She could live it however she wanted. Hadn't she just proved that? She'd flown to France with a man. She'd taken a lover. Had a week-long affair. She was desirable. Independent. She had made her life happen by having the confidence and desire to do so. She'd find a great place to live. Her outreach would bloom. She wouldn't look back. And she most certainly wouldn't think about Oz.

Beth pulled the airline magazine from the seat pocket and flipped through it, pausing on a page of the Eiffel Tower lit up at night. She sighed. Paris. Beautiful, expensive Paris.

She tapped the magazine thoughtfully and glancing around the plane's cabin her eyes landed on a young family. She watched as the mother leaned over and wiped her daughter's face before handing her a coloring book and crayons.

Their trailer. There was enough equity in the home she'd shared with Oz that she could set up somewhere new. Live a new life. But only if she had her half.

She ordered a beer from a passing flight attendant and scratched all thoughts of home from her mind. She still had two more hours of fantasyland. Sipping her beer she turned to the same article Nash was reading: Romantic Getaways Around the World. She smiled at the idea that he might be thinking of another trip. She gave his hand a squeeze as her heart swelled. She already missed him and what they'd shared in Paris.

"We'll always have Paris," she whispered.

He squeezed back. "Yes, we'll always have Paris."

1 2

----

eth held the heavy present in her arms and yawned. Jet lag was a real hag with one heck of a backswing. Cynthia opened the door to Dan's parents' place and pulled Beth inside with a massive grin. "Is that for us? Engagement parties are the best!" She squealed and grabbed the package from Beth and gave it an experimental heft. "Oh my god, it's heavy. It's that Mix Master!"

"Shut up," Beth grumbled. Her sister always guessed her gifts within seconds. Even the year she'd added rocks to the gift box to try and throw her sister off, she'd piped up with, "It's that bracelet I wanted and a few rocks to throw me off." The girl was lucky Beth even bothered to wrap her gifts anymore.

Her sister tore off down the hall calling, "Dan! Beth got us the Mix Master!"

"Whoopee," came his reply. "Another thing I will never, ever use."

Beth entered the kitchen where a few gifts were already stacked on the kitchen island.

"Oh, be happy for me, honey." Cynthia wrapped her arms around Dan's neck, giving him a big smooch.

"For our wedding," Dan said, breaking free, "get us something we could both use, okay?"

"Like what?"

Dan shrugged. He grabbed a strawberry off a platter and dipped it in chocolate fondue. "One of these? They're wicked-awesome."

Dan's mother, Wini, entered the room and laughed. "That *would* be a lovely gift. And if you don't get one tonight--"

"Dibs!" Beth called.

Wini smiled and continued, "Beth will buy you one as a wedding gift."

Beth giggled at her sister's unimpressed expression.

Dan pointed his strawberry at Beth. "And lots of chocolate. The proper fondue stuff that you can't get in town. And it has to be a chocolate fondue fountain, not one of those silly pot things."

Cynthia rolled her eyes.

"Deal," Beth said and shook his hand.

Dan wrapped an arm around her shoulder. "You're going to be the best sister-in-law ever. Too bad you don't come with an equally awesome brother-in-law."

"Not yet anyway," she replied.

The air in the room shifted and Beth turned to see Oz standing in the doorway. "Hey," he said, addressing everyone. He glanced at Beth and said stiffly, "Have a nice trip?" He placed his lopsidedly wrapped gift with the others.

"I did, thanks." She bit her lip from sharing how wonderful it had been. She'd only been back two days and was still bursting with the thrill of having been away.

Dan handed Oz a bottle of beer and he chugged half of it back while everyone stood uncomfortably. Yeah, they were once engaged and now they were broken up. Elephant in the room. She got it. But it didn't mean everyone couldn't act like normal human beings.

"Neither of you brought dates?" asked Wini, rearranging the food platters to create room for paper napkins.

Oz and Beth shook their heads, giving each other side glances.

Wini raised an eyebrow but said nothing as she snagged her purse off the counter. "I'm off to play bridge with the girls, you kids have fun."

"Thanks, Wini," Cynthia said, following her future mother-in-law to the front door, Dan in tow.

"Where's Mandy?" Beth asked Oz. He shrugged in reply. "You didn't ask her to come?"

"Where's the doctor?" Oz stared straight ahead while taking a swallow of beer.

Two could play this game. Only she wasn't dating Nash or kissing him in public. At least not on this continent. "Dunno."

Oz gave her a side glance, shoulders tense. "Why do you think I'd bring Mandy?"

"Why do you think I'd bring Nash?"

He turned to face her, arms crossed, incredulously look on his face. "France! Rumor is--"

"And since when did you start subscribing to the rumor channel, Oz? And what does it matter to you what I do or don't do?" The front door opened and closed, Cynthia hollering her hellos as more guests arrived.

"Guys, time to play games!" Cynthia called from the other room.

Beth and Oz stared at each other, chests heaving. Oz wasn't a mortal enemy. He was still a reasonably nice guy, despite being an ex who'd broken her heart. She sighed and held out her hand. "Truce?"

Oz stuffed his hands in his armpits and rocked back on his heels. "You're different, you know that?"

"So are you."

He shook his head. "I only wish."

Beth gave him a puzzled look and he drove a hand through his hair and slowly kicked the air like he was punting an invisible football. He leaned against the island and blew out an enormous breath. "This whole finding oneself is unbelievably difficult."

"Tell me about it."

Oz let out a snort. "You already know yourself. At least a lot more than I realized."

"Hardly."

She looked away. She didn't want to explain that being around Nash had shown her there were things about herself she hadn't known and wouldn't have discovered. The biggest example being France and the outreach.

Oz was right. She was different.

And he wasn't. But there was still something about him that drew her in. It was beyond his strong shoulders, hard quads, kindness, and their shared history. It was the fact that it was still incredibly difficult--even seven months later--to imagine a future without him. He was more than a habit. He was her heart's pacemaker.

Oz pulled a hand down his face. "This is the hardest thing I've ever done." He glanced at her, his eyes soft and warm. "Second hardest."

Despite the warning bells ringing in her mind, she asked, "What was the first?"

"Guys!" commanded Cynthia. "Chop! Chop!" She swung into the kitchen. "Everyone's in the living room. Come *on*."

Beth stared at Oz, trying to read his mind. Was he hinting that breaking up with her was the hardest thing he'd ever done and that he regretted it and wanted her back?

She gave herself a little shake. Hello. Earth to brain. It was over. They were both moving on.

Following Cynthia, they entered the adjoining living room, their steps in sync. They awkwardly sat on the last seat available. The love seat.

Seriously? In a room full of couples. She felt a setup coming on. Oz gave her a helpless shrug and she let out a huff of laughter.

"Okay, it's like the newlywed game. Okay, it *is* the newlywed game!" Cynthia giggled and bounced on the couch next to Dan, acting like a giddy teenager that had sipped more than her fair share of Baby Duck and had just spun the bottle, landing on the boy she'd been chasing for months. Beth gave Oz a cross-eyed look and he chuckled as he leaned back in the love seat, draping an arm over the back. Great. Now she couldn't lean back without cozying up to him due to the way his weight would slip her up against his side. As tempting as that was.

Cynthia passed them a pad of paper and marker. "First question--
"

"Wait. How do we play? And am I on his team?"

"Hey!" Oz protested.

"Yeah," Cynthia said, not missing a beat.

Beth narrowed her eyes. Lovely. Total set-up. She sucked in a long breath, vowing not to spoil her sister's party. She was a big girl, she could handle this. She and Oz knew each other like nobody else in the room and would kick some serious butt. Her sister would wish she'd never dreamt up the game.

"What do we win?" she asked.

"Gloating rights," Dan said. The group of twelve groaned. "Okay, what?" he asked.

"Title of some sort," quipped Oz. "Like The Greatest Couple in Blueberry Springs."

Beth shot him a look. Why would he want to share a title like that with her? He ought to know she was not going to take this game lying down. Nu-uh. They were going to cream these pansies if it was the last thing she did.

"Deal!" yelled Dan, half-standing. "And you are so going down Mr. Best Man."

"Relax." Cynthia laughed, pulling him back onto the couch.

Beth narrowed her eyes and cracked her knuckles.

"Okay, here's how it goes," her sister announced. "I ask a question. If it is for the women, they write down *their* answer, secretly, and the guys write down what they think their women answered. If the answers match up you get a point."

"Wait, you wrote the questions?" Katie asked from her spot on a dining room chair.

Seriously? She chose a hard chair over the love seat?

"Foul play!" called her boyfriend, Will.

"Agreed!" said Beth.

Cynthia shuffled her notecards and looked put out.

"No way," protested Katie. "We ask questions of our own choosing."

The group agreed and Cynthia threw up her hands. "Fine. Each team asks a question for the group and the couple with the most points wins." She cleared her throat and chose a card. "First question."

"No way," said Katie. "All new questions."

"Seriously? For the title of The Greatest Couple in Blueberry Springs?" asked Dan. "You think we'd cheat?"

"You're going down whether you stack the deck or not," Beth said.

"That's my girl," said Oz, giving her shoulder a quick rub.

Cynthia rolled her eyes. "Okay, Fine. First question. Women answer. Where was your first official date?"

There were murmurings of, "That's easy," as the gals smugly wrote down their answers while the men's confidence flagged. Beth folded her sheet in half and decided she hated this game. Yeah, she and Oz could rock it, but it meant a lot of cruising down memory lane on a bicycle made for two.

"Women, show your answers!" Cynthia announced. "Annnnd men!"

Beth glanced at Oz's answer. "Benny's Big Burger." They nodded and slapped a high-five.

"How do you not remember where our first date was?" Katie complained to Will.

"This is where you first held my hand," he replied. "That was at least a full week before your so-called first date."

"Semantics. They'll get you every time," said Dan as he chalked up everyone's score. "Men, think like your woman!"

The next couple conferred on their question and asked, "What the men love most about their women."

Beth gently cleared her throat. This game was seriously not for the broken up. She tapped her pencil against her blank page. She hadn't a clue what Oz loved most--assuming there was still something. She wrote down *smile*. He used to say it brightened his day.

Oz wrote down *independence*.

"What? My independence? Since when?"

"You have all this secret independence hiding in there. You know. Like you're strong and don't even realize it."

Beth frowned. He was throwing the game. If he actually thought that, he would have trusted her to help him find his real life and wouldn't have broken up with her. He would have risked telling everything. She cracked her knuckles, determined to get the next one right.

The next couple of questions were gimme questions. Favorite colors, hated foods, favorite vacation, etcetera. They were one point behind Cynthia and Dan with two more questions to go.

Oz whispered in her ear. "Do you think we should give it to them seeing as it's their party?"

"Don't you dare!" Cynthia pointed at Oz. "I heard that. I want to win the title fair and square."

The next question was a double-header. What the man's dream job was as well as the woman's. Beth wrote down that she was doing hers and that Oz didn't know.

He wrote down the same.

"Woo!" Beth jumped up and gave Oz a double high-five up high and down low. If he'd been standing she would have given him a chest bump as well. She turned to her sister who had received half points, allowing Beth and Oz to catch up. "In your face!"

"This last question will break the tie between sisters and declare a winner. Drumroll please! What was your worst fight about?"

Beth closed her eyes and drew in a slow breath. Son. Of. A. Bitch. Why was she playing? She hated this game. She contemplated making a joke of it and writing down *Oz leaving the toilet seat up* or even storming out of the room. Instead she slowly wrote *Life*.

Barely breathing, she waited for the reveal. Tons of fights were displayed around the room and Beth shut her eyes. Fights about jealousy, misunderstandings, all fights they'd had since the break but had never known before then. Dan and Cynthia had both written down the same thing. The wedding. She glanced at Oz's card knowing no matter whether they won or not that she'd see one of their ugly, heartbreaking fights they'd had over the past few months. Seeing his tight scrawl she did a double take.

Love.

What? He thought their biggest fight was about love? He gently turned her held out paper to see her answer. They held each other's gaze for a moment.

This was starting to feel a lot like group therapy.

"Congratulations, Cynthia," Beth said as she stood up. "If you'll excuse me, I'll be back in a moment."

"Loser!" sang Cynthia, doing a victory dance.

Beth hurried to the bathroom, leaning over the sink to ease her riled up stomach. They'd been great together--she and Oz--but when the chips were down, had they ever actually been on the same page?

She smoothed her curls and dried her hands before returning to the living room. Her sister had moved on to opening gifts. She stood at the edge of the room, not wanting to be close to Oz as confusion and a million thoughts swirled through her. She hadn't thought of Nash and their Parisian affair all night. She'd been certain he was the right choice--the right path into her future. But now she wasn't sure. Oz was still such a part of her life and her history. When it came right down to it, weren't their final answers the same? Weren't love and life inexplicably tied together? Wasn't that exactly what all their fights had been about over the past seven months? She wanted to walk across the room and give him a big hug and suggest they drop the past and carry on from today forward like everything was brand new. No assumptions. No history. Just the two of them and their future together.

Beth watched Oz from the edge of the room. As Cynthia continued opening gifts his face took on a guarded, nervous expression. Cynthia unwrapped Oz's gift and turned a small, rough wood box over in her hands, giving Oz a puzzled look. "Thanks, Oz."

"It's whittled," he replied.

"Whittled?" Cynthia struggling to act pleased. Beth would have laughed at the scene if it weren't for the look on Oz's face. He'd never been worried about gifts before. Why now? What was going on?

Cynthia set it aside. "It's lovely, thanks."

Dan picked it up. "This would be great for cigars."

"You are *not* smoking cigars!"

"Still, it would be good. Thanks, Oz."

When all the gifts were opened, Beth yawned, begging off due to jet lag, saying her goodbyes.

Oz met up with her in the entry. He gave her an awkward fist bump. "We rocked that--even though we didn't win. Team Wilkineiter still has it."

She nodded uncertainly. She focused on tugging on one of her knee-height boots she'd bought in Paris, and not on the expression she knew she'd face when she asked him for what she needed. "I was wondering ..."

His cell rang and he ignored it.

"Aren't you going to get that?" she asked as it continued to ring.

He balanced her as she zipped up her last boot. He shrugged and glanced at the screen. His expression changed and he turned away muttering, "Sorry, I think I need to get this."

Beth zipped up her jacket, listening to Oz's end of the conversation. "When? Now? Are you okay?" Pause. "I'll be right over. No, it's okay. Everyone's leaving anyway." Oz hung up his phone and apologized.

She studied his expression and it hit her. Mandy. "What's wrong?"

"Nothing."

"No, what's wrong with Mandy?"

"She needs help." Oz tapped her arm. "I promised I wouldn't tell anyone."

She almost reminded him that it was her that he was talking to before she remembered exactly who she was to him, an ex. She didn't get to bear his secrets any longer. She was no longer his accomplice in life. She was nobody.

Lowering her head, she fiddled with her zipper. "I, um. It's time for me to move out of Katie's." She looked down at her feet encased in gorgeous leather. "And I, um, was wondering if maybe there was a way to get some of the equity out of the trailer?" Her voice rose and cracked.

"When?"

"I kind of don't have money."

"You did last month." He zipped his jacket with a sharp tug that just about broke the zipper and stepped into the crisp October night, his shoulders rigid.

She called after him, "What? I lose everything?" She stood on the front step and he turned, his eyes flecked with amber.

"Is this what you want?" he asked, his voice quiet.

"I can't stay with Katie forever."

"Fine, I'll put our place up for sale." He turned on his heel and strode off, his hands buried deep in his pockets, shoulders hunched like he was pushing against a snow storm rather than the odd falling leaf.

Beth swallowed hard, struggling to find her voice. To shout out not to sell the place. To ask if they could try again. Instead she watched as the darkness slowly closed around his form.

"So, tell me, what were the men in Paris like?" Mary Alice asked Beth, her eyes glittering with excitement.

"Mary Alice, you're married. Not to mention, have kids my age." Beth placed breath mints and a carton of milk by the register.

"So what?" She waved a hand and gave an impish grin. "I've heard about the Italian men and even met a few here and there, but the French? No such luck. Are they smooth and stuck up? Are they good lovers? I've heard they're short." She raised her brows. "In more ways than one."

"Mary Alice!" Beth scolded with an embarrassed laugh.

Mary Alice guffawed and leaned against the counter, arms crossed. She pressed her body forward, pushing her breasts upward and creating a deep gulch that hid great treasures of Kleenex, cash, cigarettes, and anything else Mary Alice wanted close at hand. "You can't convince me you didn't see the undercarriage of a man while in France."

"Mary Alice!"

"Look at you glow. You may as well take out a flashing billboard saying you got some in France." Mary Alice raised her eyebrows. "So? What *are* the French men like?" She paused, her eyes boring into Beth. "Or was it a more *local* man?"

Beth let out a snort and tried to look unimpressed. There was no way she was revealing to anyone in town what had happened between her and Nash. It was their little secret, not fodder for the town's gossip fest. In fact, to help curb any suggestion of them being more than friends they'd avoided each other for the past week and a half. At first, with the excitement of everyone asking about the trip she hadn't really missed him, but now his absence was starting to nag at her. In France, and even before, she had gotten used to leaning over to whisper her thoughts in his ear or to point out something unusual. Now, she had to sneak off to text him. And it wasn't the same. Going back to friends sucked. She missed Nash like an amputee missed their lost limb. It probably didn't help how her feelings about Oz had been stirred up at Cynthia's party last week.

"Well?" Mary Alice asked. "The French men ...?"

"It's hard to tell with the language barrier and all," Beth admitted truthfully. "Although, they do seem better dressed than the ones around here."

"Honey," Mary Alice wheezed with her smoker's voice, "that don't take much."

"The sights were amazing. We went to the Louvre, which is massive. I got lost trying to find the ladies room. There was more than one."

"You already told me about the stuffy art. I wanna know if you and that Nash fellow finally fit it together."

Beth gasped and took a step back. "Mary Alice! *Really.*" Beth gave her head an indignant shake. "I honestly can't believe you would ask such a thing!"

"Ha! And peanut butter is pink. You know the whole town is speculating and I'm the only one with the courage to ask."

"The word you're looking for isn't courage, Mary Alice."

Mary Alice laughed. "Look at you with your spunk. Something happened to you, girl. Something good." She gave another laugh and reached over the counter to give Beth's cheek a light pat, enveloping her in a familiar and strangely comforting waft of stale cigarette smoke. "You are so cute when you act all confident and are mooning about."

Beth slapped the latest edition of *In Style* on the counter. She gave Mary Alice a firm don't-mess-with-me look. "Ring me up."

"That all?" Mary Alice looked at the pile, then up at Beth. "I don't want you getting all the way home and finding you need yet more milk. Whacha makin' that you need milk every night after the grocery store closes, anyway? You didn't get yourself a French baby did you?" Mary Alice raised an eyebrow and eyed Beth's midriff.

"Very funny. You missed your calling as a stand-up comedian."

Mary Alice smirked and mentally calculated Beth's small pile of purchases before ringing them up. "You know, it's good to see the life back in you."

"Sorry?"

"That Nash fellow. I had my doubts about him, being all slick and citified, but he's brought you right back alive again."

"Oh," Beth managed to muster before scooping up her items. "Um, we're not together." She retreated to the safety of the street before Mary Alice could pull any meaningful information out of her.

Mary Alice called after her, "I hear you're moving out of Katie's; if you need a place our guest room is still available!"

Not on your big, fat life.

Beth let out a deep breath. Mooning about? And her and Nash? Could everyone really tell or was Mary Alice just fishing?

"Beth, wait up," Katie called as she scurried down the street in a woolly, fashionable hat. Since being away, the air had lost the heady scent of decomposing leaves and the first light snowfall had occurred making her disappointed she'd missed it. Thin patches of snow hung on the odd clumps of leaves still desperately clinging to the trees in the square across the street.

"Hey." She whacked Katie in the chest with *In Style*.

"Sweet! Thanks for the ones from France, too. *C'est incroyable!* The pictures are lovely, unfortunately the text is really hard to understand."

"I thought you knew French?"

"Yeah, but this season they're talking about things differently. I don't know. It's their frame of reference or something. I ended up ordering a French-English dictionary because Nash stopped translating for me. He *claims* it takes up too much patient time. Truthfully, I think his French isn't so hot." She rolled her eyes. "He doesn't even pronounce Christian Louboutin properly."

"His French is just fine, Katie."

"Ooh. Look at you sticking up for Doctor Boy." Katie nudged her with an elbow and a grin.

Beth rolled her eyes and opened her car door, vowing to never, ever hint about her Parisian fling to Katie. The really, really good Parisian fling. The one she would repeat in an instant. The one that kept bursting into her thoughts and dreams and was likely to have her panting and calling out in the night. Hello, embarrassing! Especially with Katie just one room over. The very definition of *awkwarrrrd*.

"Fluffy's up the tree again," Katie said. "And Oz is a bit preoccupied."

"What's that supposed to mean?" Beth said tightly, imagining his arms wrapped around Mandy's naked frame. She slung her purchases onto her Volvo's passenger seat. She didn't need Oz and he didn't need her. She'd started to want him at Cynthia's party and then he'd raced off to save Mandy. That was a good reminder of where they stood.

Plus, she had moved on, right? Right.

Well, mostly. It still burned to think that he'd chosen Mandy again over her. His fiancée.

Katie looked up and down the street then leaned in and whispered, "He's drunk."

Beth checked her watch. It wasn't even suppertime. "Drunk?"

"He's been having some ... issues."

"Did he and Mandy break up?"

"He says they were never together."

"Yeah, right." You didn't start rumors in town by doing nothing. Well, usually.

Katie shrugged and fiddled with her ponytail. "I don't know. He and Mandy are telling two different stories. I think maybe he's having troubles with the rumors about you and Nash. He hasn't been the same since Cynthia's party."

Beth's breathing stilled and she willed her eyelids to not flutter closed in defeat. Of course it wasn't just Mary Alice and a few others thinking something was up. "What rumors?"

"You two are an item."

Beth laughed despite herself. How could she be so stupid as to think she'd get off scott free and without Oz having some sort of fit about it?

"Yeah, I know." Katie shot her a relieved look. "Nash? Like, come on."

Beth climbed into her car. "Oz seemed fine at Cynthia's party." Although the rumor she'd overheard at work this morning was that he'd been best friends with the bottle since then. Question was, who drove him to drink? Her or Mandy?

She stared out her windshield, blocking out Katie's ramblings about how impersonal Nash was at work and the new protocols he'd put in place to prevent nurses from eating at their stations and how Beth would never go for someone like that and how she was silly to have believed the rumors even for just a minute.

"What about Fluffy?" Katie asked as Beth started up her car.

"Call the goddamn fire department." Beth caught Katie's shocked expression. "What?"

"Mrs. Everett is going berserk."

Beth sighed and pushed herself out of the car. "Oh, fine. It's not like I haven't seen it done enough times."

They crossed the street and stopped under the large oak in town square. Sure enough, Fluffy was perched among the snowy branches, yowling her little lungs out.

And just below the tree was Oz's groupie, Mandy. She adjusted the neckline of her tight, woolly sweater, a bright scarf obscuring most of her cleavage. "Where's Oz?"

"Why should I know? You're the one sticking your tongue down his throat."

Mandy backed up a step and opened her mouth a few times before saying, "Hostile much?"

Beth snorted.

"Oh, Beth," breathed Mrs. Everett as her mittened hand clamped on Beth's arm. "Poor Fluffy. She's been up there for twenty minutes!"

"Don't worry. I'll get her down for you." Beth slipped from the woman's grasp and tossed her fitted corduroy coat to the ground. She shivered as she sized up the oak. Why on earth had she agreed to this? Tree climbing--both up and down--was supposed to come naturally to cats, and an activity Beth should have left firmly in childhood.

Beth hoisted herself into the tree's branches, sending bits of snow and the odd stubborn leaf onto Katie. She was halfway to Fluffy when a familiar voice yelled, "Hey, Beth!"

Instinctively, she looked down and just about fell out of the tree. Oz was gazing up through the branches, his brown eyes filled with concern.

Beth stepped further out and stretched to get a grip on the branch above her. She walked her feet up the trunk and, with a soft grunt, hooked a leg over the branch. Sucking in a deep breath, she concentrated on not falling. In a feat of gravity-defying stupidity, she got herself on top of the branch before realizing that what goes up must come down.

No wonder Fluffy always asked to get rescued. Climbing down was going to be a task and a half.

Lovely. As lovely as poo pudding.

She tried to coax the cat closer as she risked a glance at the people below. She swayed dangerously and cursed under her breath. The ground was a *long* way down. Falling would definitely make the paper. It would also make her a laughingstock, get her a new nickname, as well as hit the rumor mill's frontline. Again.

Fluffy danced daintily toward Beth, gliding her tail across Beth's face as she strutted away. Beth rubbed her nose and waited for the cat to make a second flaunty pass, before grabbing the squirming body and tucking it under her arm. Fluffy wiggled and twisted until she was clutching Beth's shoulder with every single one of her dagger-like front claws. Beth slowly scooted her way back toward the trunk, resisting the urge to pull Fluffy's nails out of her skin and leave the cat to her own devices. How had Oz always made this look so easy?

"Here," came a voice directly behind her ear, just about causing her to toss the cat out of the tree. "Everyone knows it's my job to rescue Fluffy." Oz wiggled his fingers at Beth. "Come on. I have to get back to helping Benny with his cabinets."

"Are you sure? Katie said ..." She scrutinized Oz. He seemed sober. Shaven. Handsome.

"Just give me the cat." He stretched for the feline, refusing to meet Beth's eye.

"Fine." Beth thrust the cat at him, trying not to appear anywhere near as thankful as she felt. "Your funeral."

Oz placed Fluffy on his shoulder and was rewarded by a loud purr. Stupid cat.

In several quick moves the man and cat were safely on the ground. He had to be sober to do that, didn't he? Or maybe it helped to be drunk--you didn't stop to think, you just moved.

Beth dangled both legs off the same side of her branch. She was still several feet from the branch below.

"This is so not good."

She flipped onto her stomach, her legs still a hopeless distance from the next branch. She shuffled closer to the thick trunk and carefully reached out to hug it. Slowly, she slipped off the branch and allowed herself to slide down, as if hugging a rough, oversized firemen's pole. The bark lifted her shirt, scraping her stomach and arms as she slid to what she hoped was safety.

Her eyes watered as the bark stung her skin. "Ow, ow, ow!"

She loosened her grip as the scraping continued and plunged out of control, her left foot making flimsy contact with a young branch. She scrambled like an uncoordinated squirrel, grabbing a handful of withered leaves.

An "ooooh!" came from the crowd below and Beth bit back a curse. If she hadn't been blessed with such a curvy figure, i.e. big boobs, she was certain she could have climbed down with grace.

"Are you coming, Beth?" Mandy called. "Ozzie is already down!" She caught the brightness of Mandy's scarf and she fumbled to get out of the tree fast enough to gauge what was truly going on between the two of them.

"Enjoying the view!" Beth chirped. Her arms were covered with long, red scratches, stung like nothing she'd ever experienced, and felt completely useless. When she finally hit the ground she was *not* going to look good. She climbed down a few more feet and ignored Oz's offer of help.

Peering through the branches she saw the glint of a can as it met Oz's lips. If she was around he had to drink, it was that simple, wasn't it? By the time her feet touched the ground, she was pissed off and damp under the arms. Fluffy and Mrs. Everett had wandered off, as had most of the crowd. Oz rocked back on his heels and smiled at Beth.

"Best entertainment in town."

"Bite me." She dusted herself off and grabbed her jacket, hoping nobody would notice the sweat on her brow. Some hurry he was in to get back to Benny. The liar. His pants had to be rather uncomfortable considering they must have be on fire.

"Aw, come on, Beth," Mandy cooed, hanging off Oz's arm. "Everyone knows Oz rescues Fluffy because he's the best climber in town."

Beth turned away, sickened by how at home Mandy appeared on Oz's arm. She spotted Nash crossing the street, striding toward the action with determined purpose. Beth moved to head him off. In her current mood, she might find herself making out with her former fling in the center of town just to spite everyone.

"Hang on there, Beth," Oz drawled. She stopped and turned, hand on her hip, jacket slung over her shoulder.

Oz, a casual jumble of limbs, the can of beer hanging from his hand as though it had always been a part of him, stepped forward, slipping Mandy off his arm like he had so many times in the past.

"What?" Beth asked sharply, her eyes catching the amber glint in Oz's dark eyes.

He touched Beth's shirt above her left breast. She reached out to slap Oz, but a fist flew past her, knocking Oz to the ground before she could make contact.

Beth stumbled forward, turning to see who had come up behind her. Nash gave a primal huff, his blue eyes flashing like frozen blades.

Oz slowly raised himself into a crouch, rubbing his jaw.

Nash pushed himself in front of Beth, fists tight under his chin. In a flash, Oz lashed out with his legs making Nash do an awkward dance in order to stay upright.

"Stop it!" Beth shrieked.

The men, brows lowered, repositioned for another blow. Katie pushed her way between them, Mandy on her heels.

"You planned this!" Beth pointed a finger at Katie who slapped it away.

"Did not!"

"You don't grab a woman's breast in public," Nash bit out.

Mandy stepped in. "He didn't, you liar!"

Katie moved to stay between the two men and said calmly to Beth, "Your shirt is ripped."

Beth looked down to see her bra's pink lace exposed through a large tear.

"I was being a *gentleman*," Oz growled, pushing his torso toward Nash. Katie placed a hand on his chest to keep him at bay. "Which is more than I can say for you." Oz gave Nash a look loaded with judgment. "You may have intentions for my girl but--"

"You call--" Nash squared his shoulders.

"*Your* girl?" Mandy cried.

"Where's your sense of honor?" Oz asked.

"I was protecting hers!" Nash quipped.

"Well, it's a little late for that."

Katie stayed between the men, her face lined with anger, a glare aimed at Nash. "What are you? A Neanderthal? I expected more out of a man like you. Fighting and acting like Beth's your piece of meat."

The doctor's fists fell, the fight gone.

"Nash, let's go." Beth pushed at his tight shoulder and didn't dare look back. "This isn't worth our time."

13

Beth placed her silent phone on Katie's coffee table. She'd sent her résumé and application in to a nanny hiring service in Dakota an hour ago and called to make sure they'd received it. The director reviewed her application over the phone and was frank. No second language skills. No formal child development training. No experience as a nanny. She would be at the bottom of the pile. If she was lucky she might get a call for an interview in six months to a year, but due to the number of highly qualified nannies available and a slowdown in the local economy, the director didn't see someone like Beth getting a placement other than as a relief worker for three to six hours a week. Beth couldn't live off of that.

Meaning Plan Nanny swirled away like water down a gopher hole. She was truly stuck in Blueberry Springs with a pissed off best friend, an ex-fiancé, and an ex-lover. She was going to have to stick it out.

And after taking sides in the park yesterday things were going to be even tougher between her and Katie--assuming her friend ever came home again. The fact that she had stayed over at Will's place--something she so very rarely did--demonstrated how much Beth needed a massive gesture of forgiveness combined with a fortuitous alignment of planets and stars.

She unzipped her ratty suitcase. The airline had finally found her biggest bag and delivered it to her an hour ago. She dug under some laundry and pulled out a plastic bag with the Eiffel Tower on it. Perfect.

Footfalls echoed on the back steps and the door opened. A cool, crisp breeze roared in, winter having blasted in overnight reminding her how a mountainous November might as well be a December. Beth shivered and waited for Katie to enter the room.

"Hey." She watched Katie. Shoulders were stiff, mouth set at a firm line. Not good. Beth picked up the gift bag. "The airline found my luggage. This is for you."

Katie slowly pulled the snow globe out of the bag, her expression softening. "Wow."

"Do you like it?" She knew she'd just added the nicest snow globe to her friend's eclectic collection.

"This is very nice. Thanks." Katie shook the heavy globe and Beth stood beside her, admiring the fine sparkles as they floated down over the pewter scene of Paris, the Eiffel Tower sitting in a place of honor at the center.

Beth pointed to a spot near the tower. "We had a picnic right there." A contented feeling enveloped her thinking about that evening. It was an experience she'd never forget. The way she'd felt with Nash that evening. The way they'd laughed and carried on ... it was well worth all the BS piling up around her.

Katie's eyes narrowed and Beth realized she'd done exactly the wrong thing. Mentioned Nash. She backed up a step and tried to think of a way to show Katie that they could still be friends even though Beth hadn't chosen Oz's side.

Katie banged the globe down on the shelf with the others. "I only suggested Nash as a way to divert your attention and help motivate Oz, not destroy him."

"I--"

"Haven't you noticed what your trip has done to him?"

"What do you mean?"

"The drinking. Mandy ... I can't believe he *kissed* Mandy."

"That was before I booked the trip. And why do you think I left? I had to preserve a piece of myself."

"Is that what *he* told you?" Katie's eyes flicked to the snow globe, her head tilted to the side. She had a hard look that told Beth she'd never understand her side because in order to do so she'd have to abandon her brother, her own blood. And blood was always thicker than water. "Can't you see that it's you?" Katie asked. "You're the one pushing him to all this stupid-assed, self-destructive, humiliating behavior--"

"Am not!" Beth promptly clamped her mouth shut, knowing if she opened it again she'd lose her friend.

"You are *destroying* him." Katie prodded Beth's shoulder with a finger. "You need to stop seeing Nash and show Oz you still love him."

"I'm *not* seeing Nash," Beth said hotly. "And even if I was it wouldn't be anyone else's business because Oz *broke up* with me!" Beth tried to calm the shakes that had taken over her body. Her words came out fast and blurred. "Don't you get it, Katie? He broke up with me. He told me to move on so he could go kiss Mandy. He doesn't want me. He wants *her*."

"Nobody wants Mandy and certainly not Oz. And yesterday, why do you think he--"

"She was draped all over him."

"He shook her off like he always does. He still loves you. And he doesn't love her."

"Well, he has a really screwed up way of showing it. A real man would marry the woman he loves. He wouldn't tell her they were over so he could get back together with his ex."

The tenants upstairs banged on the floor for them to keep it down. The women faced off, puffing as their chests heaved, daring each other to be the first to take up the fight again, to prove the other one wrong and force them to admit defeat.

Beth picked up her suitcase. "I think I'd better find a new place to live."

NASH NUZZLED Beth's bare shoulder. "Why don't you move in with me?" he asked.

Forty-five minutes ago Beth had appeared at Nash's door, suitcase in hand. He'd let her in, no questions asked. He'd filled her with ice cream and listened without interrupting as she'd spilled the story of her fight with Katie.

As agreed, their Parisian fling had ended on the tarmac. But sitting on Nash's couch, his hand still slightly swollen from punching Oz, Beth found she hadn't been able to--or even wanted to--keep her hands off of him. She'd set her empty bowl aside and pounced. He'd greeted her renewed affections with the same desperate vigor and passion. The problem was, somewhere along the line her feelings had edged toward serious and she assumed Nash's hadn't.

"You have a guest bed?" she asked, gauging his reaction.

His eyes squinted for a split second and his body tensed. "Right. Of course. There's a Murphy bed in my office. You're welcome to take it over."

Was that disappointment in his eyes? Beth sat up and studied him, trying to see all of him without an enveloping cloud of hope. He was kind and supportive. Stable. Fun. A good lover. They'd been amazing in Paris. Add all that to the total package, along with the potential of him being ready to hand over his heart ...

But. But, but, but. Stop the bus. This had nothing to do with his heart. He said he wasn't looking for anything serious while in Blueberry Springs. He wasn't going to fall for a country bumpkin.

His offer was simply a lonely man seizing an opportunity. Nothing more. After all, living in a small town at their age, it was fashionable to be with someone. In the city it was fashionable to be single and independent. And they weren't in Dakota.

"You okay?" Nash asked, the air between them growing electric with tension.

"Say I accept your offer to stay here. Can we--would it be okay if I didn't tell people right away?"

Nash raised an eyebrow and crossed his arms.

"I mean," she said quickly. "I want to establish to everyone that we're friends, not lovers."

"Haven't we already done that?"

Beth paused. "Well ... yeah."

"Are you worried what others will think and say?"

She nodded. Of course she was. They could make their lives a living hell.

Nash gave her chin a light nudge with his swollen fist. "Since when did my Beth care about what others think?"

She gave a small smile, a warmth washing over her. More than anything she wanted to wrap herself in his arms and stay there. Instead she sat with her knees drawn up to her chest, thinking.

This was her life.

Was this her way to start over? A lifeline? A stepladder into the life she wanted?

She let out a hefty sigh. "I guess I just don't want Oz doing something self-destructive if suddenly it's like--*bam!*--here we are."

Nash ran a hand through his golden hair. "Oz. Right. I see."

"It's not that way," she said quickly, eager for him to believe he wasn't competing with her ex. "I just need to be sensitive to the fact that our actions might have a negative impact on his wellbeing. Every time I move forward I seem to set him back and it scares me how he's self-destructing." She watched Nash, hoping he'd understand that she still cared about Oz and what happened to him even if they weren't together.

Nash flipped the covers off his legs and stood. He pulled on satin boxers that urged her to forget talking and to pet its bulges. He paced the end of the bed, then eventually settled next to her.

"You know you deserve better than Oz and his issues."

"I just need to take things slowly."

"Take what slowly?" Hope lit up his eyes.

Beth pushed her chin deeper into her knees. Could she do this? Could she pursue something with Nash? Could she live up to this life? Could she fall in love again?

Had she already? Or were those feelings simply desperate need and lust?

Nash rested a hand gently over hers. "You can be free, Beth. You just have to decide to be. You don't have to run or hide. What this town thinks and believes doesn't define you. You are more than this town. You are adventure and independence."

Beth's eyes welled with tears. She loved how he always believed she was more than who she was, and maybe others did too. Oz thought she was independent. How did these two men see the woman she wanted to be but didn't feel like she truly was?

"I fell for that strong woman I saw in Paris," he said. "She's really something. Full of life, light, and hope. The future ... it's good." He tipped her chin to look her in the eye. "I know it's tough bringing that woman home to a town full of expectations and history, but you can do it, Beth. And I can help." He paused, still holding her gaze. "If you want me."

She gave him a crooked smile. "You fell for me?"

Nash smiled softly and pulled her against him. He gave the top of her head a kiss. "How could I not?"

"You realize I'm a country bumpkin, right?"

Nash roared with laughter. He wiped the tears from his eyes and held her face. "Even though you are a country bumpkin." He placed a kiss on her lips and wrapped her deep in his arms.

Her mind refused to process the conversation. It was as though it had become stuck in a groove and couldn't bump itself back out. She couldn't figure out if Nash meant move in together as casual lovers or as a couple in a serious, committed relationship. Had he fallen for her as in *love*? Real love?

He was supposed to be a light and easy rebound fling and nothing more. Something new. If she moved forward, it would strike a finality to any future with Oz. But the end had already been marked. And a new beginning was what she was seeking.

And it was right here just waiting for her to leap. To say yes to uncertainty and that feeling of it being not quite real. That was the exciting part--how this unexpected man had swept her off her feet. He assumed she was all these things she wanted to be. Plus, he was refreshingly confident that she would choose him--confident enough to put himself out there even when she was still hanging on to an ex.

He was good for her. He understood her.

Screw it all.

He was hers and she was his. Starting now.

She caressed the seriously high-thread-count sheet covering her. Life with Nash would be good. Different and good. Sometimes you were handed a second chance and all you had to do was close your eyes and step into it.

"So, do I have to stay on the Murphy bed?" she asked, peering up at him, head against his bare chest.

"You can sleep anywhere you like as long as I can be right there beside you."

1 4

The phone rang and Beth stretched across Nash's bed to reach it. His alarm clock said 11:37 p.m. meaning it had to be the hospital giving Nash yet another shift since he always said yes. It was starting to get boring hanging out in his empty condo all alone. It had taken her a whole two hours to get her life's possessions unpacked over a month ago and since then she had been dying of boredom whenever he went out. It was as fabulous as ever when he was home, but the man didn't return her texts when he was working. He used to, but now he said she was too distracting. She needed to convince him to get a game system or something. Anything. There was only so much hanging out alone before you started talking to the walls so your mind didn't turn to kibble.

She couldn't pester Cynthia because she was wrapped up in her wedding plans and didn't need help. And Katie was still in a snit. Well, she assumed so since neither of them had broken the weeks of silence. She was scared what Katie must be thinking about her moving in with Nash--even though she'd told everyone it was temporary. Although, holding Nash's hand last night while watching the carolers and fire performers downtown may have shown everyone it wasn't so temporary after all. That, or the kiss she'd given his chilled lips. And true, she didn't know one-hundred percent what

Nash was feeling seeing as she still hadn't shared the L word with him, but it felt real. It felt good.

She sighed and picked up the phone as Nash called from the bathroom, "Can you get that?" He ducked his head out of the en suite. "It's probably the hospital."

"Yeah, I know." Why was he always on the top of the list? She needed to teach him to live a little more. There was more to life than constant work with the odd big trip thrown in. Sometimes little weekend events like last night's Christmas festival could be just as memorable. Although obviously not as awesome as the pampering she had received in Paris. She lifted the receiver. "Hello, Nash's answering service. How can I help you this evening?"

She winked at Nash who'd stopped flossing his teeth to give her a stern look.

Silence.

"Hello?" she repeated.

"Beth?" The familiar voice made her hands curl into fists. She snuck a glance at Nash over her shoulder. "It's for me," she mouthed, and Nash closed the bathroom door, giving her privacy as he completed his fastidious oral hygiene regime.

"What do you want, Oz?" she asked in a low voice.

"I got in shome trouble," he slurred.

Beth took a quick intake of breath, her mind flitting from one horrible scenario to another. "What kind?"

"Can you bail me out?"

"Bail?" Her heart took up speed racing and she had to take long, drawn-out breaths to calm herself. "Where are you?" *Please tell me you didn't kill someone drinking and driving.*

"I didn't kill anyone," he said darkly.

"Sorry, I didn't mean to say that out loud."

Beth snuck a peek over her shoulder to check on Nash. Door still closed.

"What did you do?" She slid onto the floor, her back resting against the bed. Was she the only one he could call with his one call? And if so, how did *that* happen?

No, it couldn't be. He had his mom and dad, Katie and Will, Mandy, and a smattering of other relatives and friends. She was the one who had nobody other than Nash, Cynthia, and Gran.

"Why are you calling me?" She squeezed her eyes shut, reminding herself to push air in and out of her lungs. She opened her eyes and took in her now familiar surroundings. The cream colored walls, the original art, the bed that sent her off to sleep faster than if the sandman had personally bonked her over the head. And she had steady, reliable, loving Nash who didn't freak out at the idea of having kids. Who invited her in instead of shoving her out. She'd picked the right path. The right man. "Did you call your mom?" she asked.

"No."

"Well, since this is your first time I'm sure she'll come and get you. This *is* your first time?"

"Yes," he said immediately, although it sounded more like *yesh*. "Are you and Katie still fighting?"

"We aren't exactly talking."

Oz sighed. "She's stubborn."

"I'll send your mom in to get you, okay? I'm busy right now." She began to put the phone down.

"Don't." Something in his voice caused her to pause before hanging up.

She waited, listening to his breath come in puffs through the line. She wondered what he looked like. How his eyes seemed. Those windows into his soul--were they empty? Dark? Rimmed with red or wide open?

"You moved in with him."

Beth braced herself as Oz's hiccups were followed by strangled noises.

"That is what you wanted, wasn't it? For me to follow my dreams? To leave you alone? To move on?"

"Beth." His voice was anguished.

"What?" she begged. "What Oz? You don't want me in your life and have chosen Mandy again. What am I supposed to do? Wait for you to push me away one more time?" Desperation welled around her like floodwaters and she longed for him to snip the final thread between them and set her free. But he kept holding on. She wanted to buck against that thread and snap it.

She glanced at the closed bathroom door again. Why couldn't she simply hang up and move on?

"Mandy's just a friend. And I was making a point," he said.

"With who? Me?"

"A slick in leather pants was calling down small town girls. Calling you hicks," he slurred slowly. "I told him they were *babes* and that my ex-fiancée was small town and anything but hick." She heard him fumble the phone a few times as he relayed his story about how he felt the need to moon the man.

"Oz, tell me you didn't?" she groaned. To feel the need to defend her so-called honor at this stage was crazy.

"Right there in the bar!" he said with something that sounded like pride.

"Are they charging you with public indecency?"

"I don't know. I see a judge in the morning."

A chill raced through her.

"I don't get it. Are they letting you out?"

"I'm not done my story."

"Oh, God." She buried her face in her free hand. "It gets worse?"

"I kinda lost my balance and fell over and my pants came down. A lot."

"Oh, no." She could see it. How could he humiliate himself like that? "Tequila?"

"Shots."

"Oh, Oz. You know it makes you do stupid things."

"I might get charged with public indiscrepancy."

"Indecency." She sighed. Who was this man? "If you're seeing a judge in the morning I think you have to stay overnight." She rubbed her forehead, imagining him sleeping in a cell. She blinked away tears. "Just make sure you're honest with them, okay?"

"Yeah."

Silence.

Gripping the phone she asked. "Why did you call me?"

"I wanted to talk to someone who understands me."

"Oh, Oz," she said softly. "I wish I did."

BETH SNUGGLED next to Nash by the Christmas tree in Cynthia's apartment. Nash was flying out in the morning to spend Christmas with his parents. And even though he'd tried to convince her to come along she'd insisted she couldn't possibly crash his family gathering despite her longing to do so. And so tonight they were having a family Christmas at Cynthia's with Gran and Dan. Despite it only being the five of them it still felt like Christmas, only a little less bustling than Beth had always dreamed. She'd thought by this age the holidays would involve a house jam-packed with people and tons of excitement and bustle--kind of like last year at Oz's parents' place. Not this: five people and a tree crammed into her sister's miniscule apartment.

Cynthia handed Beth a tagless gift wrapped in newspaper, her expression blank.

"Is this is for me?" Beth asked, turning the small gift over in her hands. Her butt was getting numb, but there wasn't enough room to squeeze more furniture into the room.

Cynthia nodded.

"You run out of gift wrap?" she laughed.

"It's not from me, but I'm told you'll know once you open it." Cynthia trotted back to the love seat she was sharing with Dan, making the tree's tinsel flutter in her wake.

Beth frowned at the gift and glanced at Dan who shook his head. She peeked at Nash whose attention was absorbed by the radio gadget he'd given Beth. Even though they'd been living together for only a little over a month, she knew he'd never wrap a gift in newspaper unless he was trying to throw her off. And seeing as she'd already received her gift from him, this was a mystery gift. With a thrill racing through her, she ripped the paper off the small box and flipped it over, her heart's rhythm becoming unstable. The boxed set compilation of various musical genres was dog-eared, but otherwise fine. She pulled out the first CD and a small card fell into her lap.

"Who's it from?" asked Gran.

Beth hesitantly opened the card. Tight printing dented the tiny card and made her chest feel shaky. She closed her eyes as though concentrating to remember a flavor.

Oz.

She glanced at Cynthia who was intently focused on the blinking Christmas tree. Nash leaned against her shoulder to inspect the gift.

"Oh, CDs. We can get that stuff on your new satellite radio." He held up the gadget he'd been playing with. "We can set up song alerts."

"It's for my patients," she replied.

Oz wrote *love* on the card.

Did that mean love-love, or was it a leftover habit? Something slightly more fond than sincerely?

She turned the box over in her hands. Had he found this in his uncle's store and decided to send it along as a Christmas gift, nothing more? Just a little something to ensure they could still be friends and remain civilly in the same town? An apology for the drunken phone call? Or was it a hint? A keyhole for her to peek through?

She sighed. Why couldn't he just say what he meant and skip the little things that made no sense to her? And why was she trying to read intentions into his actions? The whole thing made her want to scream as well as flip him the bird.

Not like Nash. She smiled at her stable, reliable Nash. He didn't have weird stuff hiding under the surface that would mess up everything or cause her mass confusion.

Since the phone call, she'd stopped sheltering everyone from the fact that she was moving on with Nash. She no longer went out of her way to avoid ripples from her new life rocking Oz's boat. She no longer dropped Nash's hand in public, or refrained from kissing him in the grocery store. Protecting Oz had only landed him and his screwed up ass in jail anyway. She needed to live her life and be the Beth Nash had fallen for in Paris.

She set the CDs behind her. Out of sight. Out of mind.

Nash glanced at its dog-eared corners. "Second-hand," he scoffed, superiority lilting his voice. He leaned against her, digging in his pants pocket.

She shoved her curls from her face and stated, "It's a rare compilation. My first set was stolen from Oz's truck."

Nash turned slowly, color creeping deep into his cheeks. "Oz?"

"Yeah. It's from Oz." She met his eye, jutting her chin. As long as they stayed in Blueberry Springs, the man would always be in her life one way or another, just like they would be in Oz's.

With a smile Nash squeezed Beth's arm and boasted, "I can top that!"

"Ooooh, this should be good." Gran placed her hands in her lap, a snifter of sherry perched carefully on the arm of her easy chair. "He's a good gift giver," she said knowingly to Cynthia. She raised her eyebrows meaningfully at the bottle of sherry Nash had given her.

Nash stood and adjusted his navy cable-knit sweater. Clearing his throat, he addressed her family. "Thank you for sharing your Christmas festivities with me. I hope to share many more."

He gestured for Beth to stand and hesitantly she obliged. "What are you doing?" she whispered. Speeches were a bit formal for the Wilkinson clan. She blushed, shooting her sister an apologetic look, but Cynthia kept her gaze focused on Nash, her eyes burning through him as though they were secret-popping lasers.

Nash positioned an arm across Beth's shoulders. "As you all know, I love Beth very much."

Beth blushed. They'd only shared the L word a few weeks ago. She'd made them both wait, wanting to be sure it was an emotion she genuinely felt.

He lowered himself onto one knee.

Beth's pulse quickened like a panicked jackrabbit, and her eyes darted to the exit.

Gran squealed and clapped.

Her mind yelled *run!*

This couldn't be happening.

They hardly knew each other.

She still loved Oz.

No. No, she didn't. She couldn't love Oz any more. She loved Nash.

But Nash *had* to be joking. This was too soon.

She licked her lips and swallowed in an effort to moisten her dry throat. Her lungs became inflexible steel, refusing to draw air.

Oh, my God. She still loved Oz. Oh, my God. The room tilted dangerously to the right.

Nash was talking. Smiling. Looking up at her with such open trust and love.

Time. We need time.

Nash continued, smiling. In his sparkling eyes she saw calm, trust, stability, and love. Lots of love. And a chance. A chance to dodge everything from loneliness to heartbreak to infertility. With him she could be anyone. She could have her dream and the freedom and support to try new things.

Right now. There was no more waiting.

He gathered her sweaty hands in his own.

He was safe and he wouldn't hurt her. She focused on all she loved about him and that tiny, happy feeling deep inside her, beneath the worries.

"Bethany Anne Wilkinson, will you marry me?"

Her head started to bob.

She loved him.

Her voice wavering, she replied, "Yes," her head still bobbing.

Gran hooted and Dan gave a strange bird call in celebration. Nash slid a large ring onto Beth's trembling finger. The princess-cut diamond weighed heavy and swung upside down. Nash twisted the ring upright and it glinted in the room's light, the diamond perfectly proportioned and massive. She would never be able to slide her hand into her jeans pocket ever again.

The room tilted again. Beth swayed, unable to take her eyes off her finger.

This wasn't Paris. This was different.

She took a deep breath. Life was an adventure. She couldn't know what she liked and didn't like until she tried it. He was an amazing man and the potential was endless. And she loved him. This was just a ring.

"We'll get it sized," he said.

"Ha! Ha!" Gran shouted. "Guess what her new name will be?"

Beth closed her eyes and sucked in a sharp breath. Beth Leham. Bethlehem.

Tears stung her eyes as she folded herself into Nash's waiting arms, unsure whether to laugh or cry.

"So, what's the rush?" Cynthia asked quietly. "Are you pregnant, Beth?"

Beth let out a half-snort of laughter, unburying her face from Nash's sweater. "No."

Her sister watched the two of them clinging to each other. Dan slipped an arm around Cynthia's shoulder and gave the newly engaged couple a cheeky grin. "Why wait, Cynthia? Life's too short to wait around if you know who you want."

Cynthia looked away and swallowed hard.

Nash's chest expanded as if he was about to speak. Beth held out a hand to stop him. "You worry that I am on the rebound? That this isn't what I want?"

Cynthia gave a half-nod. "Sorry, Nash."

"It's all right. I appreciate your honesty. And I know you are looking out for your sister's best interests."

"Nash and I have been together as more than friends since Paris."

"I knew it!" shouted Gran, slapping the arm of her chair. "Woo!" She grabbed her wobbling snifter. "Close one." She took a large swallow and waved at Beth and Nash. "And in case anyone actually cares, I approve." She shot Dan a look. "He came by to ask permission. That man knows some manners."

Beth turned to Nash in pleased surprise. "You did?"

He gave a self-conscious nod.

She gave him a hug. "You're awesome." There was something about Nash that always made her feel honored and cherished.

Cynthia spoke again. "You two have only been together for two months?"

"We've been friends for a long time though." She stared at her sister, daring her to say more. Dan's eyes rolled back slightly, like he was counting months in his head.

"I know," Beth said impatiently. "I get it. This seems rushed, but it feels right to me. Okay?" Tears pricked at the back of her eyes.

Nash spoke up. "Beth is an incredible woman. I will do good by her. We get along well and there is no reason to wait. It would be wonderful to be married before I finish my contract here in Blueberry Springs." He took her hand and smiled. "I've made up my mind and it sounds like she has, too. I'd like to make an honest woman of her." He gave her a wink and a kiss and turned to her family. "Can I have your support?"

"Got mine already," said Gran, knocking back another snifter of sherry. "Damn fine stuff, my future grandson-in-law. As long as you keep me in this stuff you can have both the girls for all I care."

"Gran!" protested Cynthia and Beth together, but only Beth laughed.

"Oh, don't go getting your panties in a knot. You know what I mean. Life's too bloody short. You both know that. If you've found yourself some love, eat it up."

Nash piped up, "Exactly!"

"There's always divorce if you mistake lust for love."

15

---

*B*eth sat in the bedroom, twirling her engagement ring around and around her finger. Unspoken words circled her mind like a mantra: Live life. Have kids. Be happy.

Was life truly that simple once again? It was mind-blowing how, in less than a year, she was back to where she had started, only with a different fiancé. Somehow, she'd gotten lucky and had fallen in love twice.

Last week, sitting under the tree with all the gifts opened, something unexpected had struck Beth. The need to stay in Blueberry Springs. Not just until Nash's temporary contract finished, but forever. The town, crazy and buttinsky, was home. Always had been, always would be. The people knew her. Sure, they couldn't always see past her as more than who she'd been during her teens years, or see her as the adventurous woman Nash did, but they knew her history and the things she'd fought against. No explanations were necessary. And therefore, she knew in her heart that this was the town where she needed to raise a family. Blueberry Springs would take care of them. These were her people. As strange as it felt to admit it to herself, Blueberry Springs was *family*. Her family.

She flipped open a thank you card she'd received last week from a former patient's grown-up son. The card had brought home exactly why she was still a recreational therapist and hadn't run off during her more desperate moments. It was proof that what she did every day made a difference in the lives of others. During a tough time she could provide hope, meaning, and improve a person's quality of life just by being herself and doing her job. This was who she was. She was community. She was family.

Becoming an anonymous person where people didn't know each other when walking down the street was not what she wanted. That was not home. She wanted to fill Blueberry Springs with *her* people. She wanted to be known. Connected. Loved.

The only thing she needed to do was convince Nash that Blueberry Springs was the place. *Their* place. And that it would be good for them both. The first step in achieving that would be to convince him to have the wedding here. The second step would be to patch things up with Katie so the girl could put her style sense to work and help Beth show Nash that Blueberry Springs could be chic. Yesterday she'd sent her friend a wine basket, barely refraining from adding a little white flag. Now all she had to do was wait.

Nash entered the room with a cup of hot chocolate. He carefully handed it to her and cozied up beside her, flipping open a Moleskin notebook. "I called a friend in Dakota to see if we could get the stone cathedral on the corner of twenty-third. Dates for the spring and summer are gone, but there is a cancellation in April and one in late August. Unless we want mid-week or an early morning wedding?" He glanced up from his notes.

Beth took a sip of her hot chocolate and shook her head. A morning wedding wasn't the kind of affair she was looking for. That was for city people who were in a hurry. A wedding was an event.

"What we need to do," he continued, "is decide on a date. People are asking and it's been well over a week since our engagement." Nash straightened his faded med school T-shirt and paused to consult his list. He got up to flick off the overhead lights, leaving the bedside lamp to light up the room. Beth continued sipping her hot chocolate while he paced the room, pausing to tap his notebook thoughtfully.

Beth absentmindedly fidgeted with her ring. A spring wedding would be lovely, but felt a bit quick. She didn't want to seem desperate, but like Nash often said, there were no guarantees, and if you wanted something and could have it, why wait?

"Once we set a possible date we'll go to Dakota and look at available venues."

Beth rolled off her socks, tossing them in the growing heap of discarded clothes near the laundry basket. "I thought we were getting married here."

"In town?" Nash's brow furrowed, and his lips turned down. He dropped her crumpled clothes in the laundry basket and Beth laughed at his fastidiousness. She snagged him for a quick kiss.

"This is where most of our guests live and it's where we live." Seeing how he didn't look convinced, she continued, "It doesn't feel right to trek to the city for the wedding." She scrunched her nose at the idea of having to figure out the best cakes, facilities, flowers, and everything else in the city. That would turn her into a bridezilla for sure. She knew how to plan a wedding here. Not there. "We'd have to pay city people for flowers and cake. There are people here in Blueberry Springs who could use the business." If she was going to start a life here, a wedding would say loud and clear that this was the place she planned to make her home. "It will be a lot cheaper here, too."

"This isn't about money, Beth. It's about presentation."

Beth laughed. "You sound like Katie."

"Did she reply to your gift?" Beth shook her head and Nash continued his argument, "Is it fair to have my guests driving all the way out to the middle of nowhere?" He scoffed. "Are there even hotels here?"

"Of course there's a hotel. There are rooms above the bar."

Nash snorted. "That might not be what my friends are used to."

"Oh, tell them to live a little. They might find it quaint. Like the B&B outside town."

"That was last decorated in the '90s."

"It's cute!"

Nash raised an eyebrow and quirked his lips.

"Well, we think it's cute," she said with a giggle. "Are all your friends from the city?"

"Yes. Most of them. Some are overseas."

Beth slipped her arms around Nash's neck. "It would mean a lot to me to have it here. And it would also be so much easier to plan. Everything we need is here and you wouldn't have to miss as many shifts."

"Well …" Nash looked at his list of dates with reluctance. "I'll think about it. It would have to be a very different sort of wedding than I've been envisioning."

"Have you been reading my wedding magazines?" she asked playfully.

He turned away, slipping out of her grasp to straighten a picture. "We should pick a date."

"You have!" Beth clapped her hands together. "You are so great!" She skipped over and gave him a huge kiss. Planning their wedding together would be awesome. His attention to details would make this absolutely incredible.

"We need a date."

"Does that mean we can have it here?" Beth stepped back, hands clasped. She batted her eyelashes.

"I didn't say that."

"Oh. Okay." Beth turned back the covers and worked at keeping her mouth shut. This was an important battle. More important than cake, flowers, invitations, or even the band. She closed her eyes and envisioned them getting married in town, surrounded by familiarity and friends. Sort of similar to what she'd started to plan with Oz, only with a different groom. And maybe a little more extravagant thanks to Nash's input.

"You know I love you," he said, setting his watch on his bedside table. "I promised to take care of you. If it's important to you, it's important to me."

She met his clear blue eyes, trembles of excitement weaving through her.

He shook his head slowly in disbelief. "Let's do it. Let's have a Blueberry Springs wedding." He laughed and threw his hands in the air.

"I love you!" Beth bounded over the bed and leapt onto Nash. She wound her arms tightly around his neck and her legs around his waist.

Nash's legs gave out, and they crumpled to the floor in a heap. Beth giggled and peppered his face with kisses. "Oops. Sorry!"

"Warn me next time. You're heavier than you look."

Beth climbed off him, her cheeks burning. He could knock Oz down with one punch--a man who was able to catch her every time--but he couldn't catch her without collapsing?

Stop it! She had to stop comparing the two. She was engaged to Nash. They were two completely different men.

Nash picked himself off the floor, rubbing his elbow before testing its movement. "Should we pick a date and see if, what--the community center--is free?"

"Yes. The hall is great for the reception."

"Isn't there a golf club or something?"

"Out here?" Beth shook her head. "Nope. Not close by, anyway. Let's pick a date. We can have the service in the center, too." Or not, judging by the look on Nash's face. "Either way, picking our date shouldn't be a problem in terms of availability for venues." She knew full well that for Nash it was a church service, or pretty much nothing. But she may as well let him feel as though he was winning something substantial, too.

"Let's see what's available for April."

"That soon?" She tried not to look surprised or smile too big.

"Why wait?"

Beth looked into Nash's crystalline eyes and nodded. "Okay."

He'd soon see how easy and fast it would be to plan a wedding here. People would be efficient, helpful, and simply awesome. Just the way he liked. Within weeks he'd be talking about raising their kids here.

All she had to do was let Blueberry Springs win him over.

BETH EASED Oz's truck into a snowy parking spot outside Will's place, hoping Gran had her information right. She also hoped to have the truck back to Oz before word spread back to Nash that she was asking favors of her ex. True, she'd only had to send Oz a quick text when nobody else's truck had been available. He'd left it unlocked and warming up in the driveway so all she had to do was jump in and go. But, for some reason, it still felt as though she'd stepped across an invisible line. It didn't help that the truck's interior emitted a familiar, dusty man scent that felt like home. She only hoped that Nash would understand that borrowing Oz's truck was a last ditch attempt to get Katie back as a friend and had nothing to do with her ex.

Beth stomped the snow off her boots while heading into the entry of Will's apartment building. Having no security doors, she brushed by the new houseplants randomly dotting the entryway and let herself down the hall to the main floor suite and knocked.

Katie opened the door, her usual smooth ponytail looking as if someone had placed her head in a box of monkeys and given the thing a shake. "What?"

"I have a truck."

"Congratulations." Katie started to close the door.

"It's for you."

The door stopped moving. "What?" Katie narrowed her eyes, taking a second look at Beth who was wearing her old winter jacket and Levi's with the knee ripped out of them.

"I'm here to help."

"Oz is supposed to be bringing his truck."

No wonder it had been so easy borrowing the large vehicle, Beth had just freed him up to spend an evening at home, arms around Mandy, drinking beer.

She glanced at her left ring finger.

Not her problem.

Right.

Carry on.

Beth pushed on the door, trying to gently barge in before Katie turned her away and she ended up looking like a fool. A fool without a best friend. "It's Oz's truck. Now, do you need help or what?"

Katie stepped aside, her face a myriad of emotions. And all of them containing an undercurrent of snoopy, curiosity-driven intrigue that made Beth want to talk full stream so Katie wouldn't get a chance to open her yap.

"So?" Beth asked, quickly. "What needs to be moved? Gran said the couch?" She kicked off her boots and wandered into the living room. "What are you up to?"

"The big blabber mouth," Katie muttered. "It'll be a miracle if news of this makeover hasn't found its way to Will already."

Beth halted and looked at what used to be Will's living room. "Uh? When does Will come home?" She checked her watch. It was already 5:45 p.m. If this was the last day of his conference he could be home at any moment and the place was a disaster.

"He said nine."

Beth relaxed and peeked inside an open box. Fabric. The next box had throw cushions. She lifted one and refrained from asking Katie what she was thinking giving a man throw cushions.

"What?" Katie asked, hands on hips. Beth shook her head and dropped the cushion back in the box. "I know what you're thinking. That throw cushions aren't Will. But at my place he always tucks one under his arm and two under his head when he sprawls on his side to watch a movie. He'll like them."

Beth stroked the cushion's fabric. Okay, maybe the girl did know what she was doing. And the fabric was kind of manly. You know, for something that wasn't leather or denim.

"So, what do you have left to do in order to transform this place?"

Katie ran a hand through her hair, messing up her ponytail even further. She pulled out the elastic and redid it, smoothing it out. "I have to put the new coffee table and bookshelf together. Grab the plants from the entry, hang the curtains and put up the rods, put down the new throw rug. Haul the old couch out to the dump and pick the new one up at the depot."

"When do they close?"

"Seven. Well, there's someone there until seven. They closed at four."

Beth pulled the coffee table out of its box and looked at the legs. Screw on kind. Nice. She began screwing them in, one by one, trying to ignore the fact that Katie was simply watching, not doing anything. Keeping her head down, she screwed in the last leg and set the table upright. She brushed the specks of packing debris off the surface and finally looked up.

"Why are you helping me?" Katie asked quietly, her eyes resting on Beth's ring.

"Because you are my best friend." Beth blinked rapidly, trying to diffuse the silly tears that had appeared.

"Okay," Katie said finally. She stood and brushed off her pants. "How about we take the couch out next? It'll give us some room. Plus, the dump closes soon."

They began moving furniture out of the way in order to move the couch toward the apartment door.

"So, um?" Beth waited for Katie to look up. "Will you be my maid of honor?"

Katie blinked about twenty times before closing her jaw and composing herself. "Right. Sorry. Congratulations." With forced moves she gave Beth a quick hug. "That's exciting, huh?"

"I could use some help planning the wedding."

Katie laughed so hard she had to wipe tears from her eyes.

"What?" Beth asked, feeling slighted.

"You know more about weddings than anyone I know. You've got a zillion bridal magazines and have already picked out invitations and a dress."

"That was for Oz."

Katie jerked like a dog reaching the end of its leash. She carefully smoothed her shirt and reached for her coat. "Right. Well, let's get this smelly old couch out of here."

Beth refused to follow Katie's lead.

"Are you coming?" Katie asked, leaning down to shove the couch.

"You don't approve, do you?" Beth asked in a low voice. She knew Katie was peeved and didn't see the potential in Nash or even how much she'd grown to care for him, but she hadn't even once believed it was this bad.

Katie straightened, her face flushed with emotion. "You know what I did on Christmas Day? Late in the afternoon?"

Beth slowly shook her head, unsure whether she wanted to hear what Katie was going to say.

"I was going to come over and offer you congratulations, but I ended up getting Oz from the drunk tank. Too much eggnog and rum. And you know why he did that, of course."

Beth sucked in a sharp breath. Every move she took destroyed Oz. She placed a hand on Katie's arm. "I'm sorry."

"No." Katie pulled her arm away. "You're not."

"Excuse me?"

"It's because of you."

"What is?"

"That incident. He heard you got engaged and went off and got plastered."

"It's hardly my fault that I can't live my life without him acting like a dork."

Katie raised her eyebrows, daring Beth to fight. Beth let out a long sigh and raised her hands in defeat. When Katie got like this there was no arguing with her and, if she did, she'd only end up pushing her friend further away.

Beth fell into a heap on the couch, a waft of its fishy smell wrapping around her, as she burst into tears. "I can't live like I have forever, Katie. If I want a family--and I do--I have to keep moving forward. Oz doesn't want me. I waited eight years for him and had him for two and a half. I can't wait another eight just to see if comes back to me. You and I want him to want me, but he broke up with me." Tears streaming down her face, she looked to Katie whose expression was grim.

After a few moments Katie sagged onto the couch and wrapped an arm around Beth. "Okay."

"Okay what?" Beth asked once she got control of her emotions.

"Okay, I'll be your bridesmaid or maid of honor, or whatever. But I really don't think I'm equipped to help with the wedding. Anyway, I hear Nash is doing a fine ol' bang-up job of it." She gave a quiet, half laugh.

"Richard says the hall is booked." Beth's tears refreshed themselves and tore down her cheeks.

"Then pick another date."

"We did." Beth swiped at tears with the sleeve of her coat. "Everything we've picked is booked." She turned to face her friend. "How can that be possible?"

"Hm. That *is* weird."

"I'm trying to convince Nash to stay here. That we could raise a family in Blueberry Springs and I was hoping the wedding would solidify what a great place it is, but everyone's being such a bunch of dicks. I don't get it. This is my home." Beth fought off a fresh wave of tears and stood up. She took a deep breath and readied herself to move the couch and forget everything.

"He wants to leave Blueberry Springs?" Katie said, her voice sounding odd.

"He's always been clear that he's only here to fulfill his contract and gain experience."

Katie frowned. "Where would you guys go?"

"Dakota, I guess."

"The city?"

Beth nodded.

"You hated the city."

"It's not that bad," Beth said quickly. "I loved Paris."

"You were on vacation."

"Cities have their perks when you're with someone who knows and loves them."

Katie stood up and studied Beth for a minute. "You really actually love him, don't you?"

Beth gave a sigh of disbelief and barely refrained from leaving the room. "I'm not so desperate for kids that I'll marry the first man to come along."

"Sorry. I just didn't expect it for some reason." Katie frowned. "You know what?"

"What?" Beth asked, not sure she wanted to know.

"I think ..." Katie spoke slowly and carefully, seating herself on the couch again. "I think it is pretty brave of you. No, not brave."

Beth sucked in a slow, quiet breath, making herself wait for Katie to finish before she went volcano on her ass.

"I think it is honorable. Or maybe self-sacrificing. Or, anyway, it's cool that you let Oz go." Katie struggled with her words. "I mean, this isn't coming out very well. But what I mean is that someone like Mandy would have trapped Oz and made him be the man she wanted. You didn't slip up with the birth control." Katie looked up at Beth, her eyes dark and thoughtful. "You listened to him and respected his wishes even though they went against yours." Katie studied her hands. "And I guess I still wish that you and Oz would get back together because you guys were so *good*. It was like nothing I'd ever seen. But things change, and of course you have to move on. It's the right thing to do." She let out a loud sigh of defeat and looked up at Beth. "I hope you know you'll always be my sister, in my heart, even if it isn't by marriage. You're family."

Beth whispered over the lump in her throat, "Thank you." She gave her friend a long, hard hug. This is what Blueberry Springs was about. Right here. Now if only she could get Nash to see it and want to be a part of it. She blinked back tears, feeling torn between the man she loved and the family she'd been a part of her whole life.

Katie pushed her away and pulled out her cell phone. She swiped at her damp eyes. "Now. About the hall. There is no way it's booked. I'm going to get you a wedding date come Hell or high water."

"THANK YOU, OZ," Beth said, cutting the truck's engine in the driveway. "We really appreciated it."

"Glad to be of service." He tipped an imaginary hat, his eyes clear and bright. "Have to help out my lovely ladies."

She slipped out of his truck, gently closing the door behind her. She ignored the fact that he'd included her as one of his ladies, and that since his name was still decaled on the driver's side door, right above the handle, that her name could very well still be on the passenger side. Through all their errands, she'd carefully avoided being on that side of the truck. There was no reason it should still be there. But why did she feel a dark trace of disappointment thinking about it having been peeled off?

"You two managed okay? You were gone a while." He stepped from side to side in the cold, the snow crunching under his size ten feet. Soft flakes drifted out of the low winter sky and landed in his hair.

"She bit off more than she could chew, but we got it done." She looked away, uncomfortable standing this close and without a distraction.

"Thanks for helping her out." Oz looked up, his eyes quiet. "I'm sorry about the fight."

Beth paused, uncertain which fight he was referring to. "It wasn't your fault."

"It was."

Beth handed Oz the truck keys, hoping he'd step back so she could edge around him and make her escape. Her evening was going well so far and she didn't want to blow it by staying around Oz for too long. Katie had already proved her worth as a maid of honor by wrangling the hall manager into booking the hall--little did he know he was so busted for lying--and she was floating on a heavenly cloud of goodwill, hope, and anticipation. This was the beginning of everything turning around with their wedding planning and Nash falling in love with Blueberry Springs for what it really was. Family.

Family that fought. Family that looked out for each other. Family that was well-meaning even when it interfered.

"Well, I need to get ..." She paused, unable to choke out the word *home*. She glanced up at the trailer cozied into the snowdrifts behind Oz. It was up for sale and there had been no interest. She went to brush past Oz.

He let her by, her jacket brushing his hoodie. "How's the Volvo running?"

"Fine."

"I see you've lost the plug off your block heater." He followed her to the car and crouched down in front of the bumper. He lifted the frayed end of the electrical cord. "You need to get that fixed. We're due for a cold snap."

Beth paused by the driver's side door. "I know." She hesitated, then came over to look at it. "I bought one of those replacement ends you always got, but I was afraid I'd electrocute myself or blow up my car if I got it wrong."

"I'll grab my screwdriver. Do you have it with you?"

Beth shook her head.

"That's okay. I'm sure I have an extra in the toolbox. You can't be driving around like that in the middle of winter. You'll get stranded somewhere."

Beth opened her mouth to protest.

"It'll only take me a minute." He backed toward the trailer. "Promise."

Beth nodded and sighed. Fine. He could fix her car. He'd done it a million times. Or at least as many times as she'd driven off with her car still plugged in. She'd asked Nash if he could figure out how to do it, but he'd backed away as soon as she mentioned electricity.

Oz leapt down the front steps, holding up a part. "Knew I had one!"

Beth tucked her hands inside her coat sleeves and tried not to move so the cold air couldn't creep in.

Oz set to work unscrewing the new plug so it opened in half. He took her car's exposed block heater wires and slipped them into place, clamping them down to keep them secure in the new plug.

"You make it look so easy," she said, trying not to let her teeth chatter. She tugged up the hood of her coat and warmth finally closed in.

Oz explained what he was doing and how to tell the wires apart. "Next time you can do it yourself."

"That's what I keep telling myself."

He chuckled. "Maybe you should start unplugging your car before you drive away?" He looked up at her, a twinkle in his eye. She smiled at the familiarity of the déjà vu moment. Watching him fixing her car. Always promising to do better next time. Him teasing her. Only this time he wouldn't ruffle her hair, sling an arm around her and lead her back to the house with a kiss so they could enjoy a cup of hot chocolate and talk about their day.

She let out a mournful sounding sigh and, embarrassed, cleared her throat and looked down the street instead of at her ex.

"There you go. Good as new." Oz gave the new plug an experimental tug to ensure it was on firmly. "Do you have your winter emergency kit?"

"In my trunk. Thanks." She shuffled in the area of packed down snow she'd created while watching him work. Now what? She didn't feel as though she could just bolt back to the condo, but she didn't have anything to say and she most certainly wasn't heading inside.

Oz pulled an envelope from his back pocket and passed it to her. She fingered the thin package, immediately wishing she'd given up sooner in her quest for a truck to help out Katie. "What's this?"

He stepped back and ran a hand through his hair, making it spike in the front, snow falling onto his shoulders, joining saw dust. Saw dust? Her mind flicked to a rumor she'd heard about him making a racket in the back shed fixing up loose chair legs for his mom. She sighed, hoping that helping out others wasn't interfering with finding himself.

"I got an offer on Dad's business. I took it even though Dad got most of it. That's your share of our mutual fund we were saving for our ... that we were saving. And the equity." He tipped his head toward their old place.

He looked bashful and ashamed, and she fought the urge to slide into his arms to make it better. To make it them against the world. Consciously, she stepped back. She'd cultivate something like that with Nash. They just needed a little time.

"I'm sorry I kept you in money problems for so long. But I suppose that won't be an issue once you marry--" He broke off and cleared his throat.

"Right," she whispered as she caught his eye. "You sold the business though? Really?"

"While I don't think Dad understands my decision, I'm free to start a new career now."

"That's, well, that's unexpected. It's good though. I'm happy for you."

She closed her eyes. He was moving on now that she was taken. Not while she had been waiting, but now. She struggled against the urge to wallow in a severe sense of loss.

"How's your job going? I've heard your outreach is doing really well. You already help so many people. It's great. What you're doing."

"Yeah. Thanks." She fingered the envelope and glanced at Oz. He was staring at her, hands in the pockets of his jeans. "What are you going to do?"

Wait. Oz was wearing jeans. Not sweats.

She took a closer peek, trying not to be obvious. They were his old 501s with the tiny hole near the knee from one of his Fluffy rescues. Not only that, they seemed to be buttoned all the way up. He hadn't been in jeans in forever. And, dear Lord, they still looked incredibly sexy hugging his thighs.

"Tonight?" he asked, stamping his feet.

"I'm sorry. You're cold. I should go." She turned her body toward her car, her eyes still on Oz's lower half.

"I'm fine," he said quickly.

Beth snapped her eyes from his jeans, collecting herself. "What are you doing with your money? Your life?"

What was she doing? She couldn't--*shouldn't* be looking him over like this. And what did she care what he did with his life? It was no longer any of her business.

"My life?" He scratched the back of his head and gazed toward the horizon. "I'm not sure, but I feel ready to make some changes. I have ideas. But I'm still deciding."

Of course. A lightheaded sensation swept through her as anger rode in on murky waves. What was it with him that made her keep thinking she was a part of his life and that he would tell her about his secrets, dreams, and plans? He would never let her in to see who the mysterious, secret Oz really was.

"Great." She reached to open her car door. She remembered the envelope in her hand and gave it a wave. "Oh, um? We should arrange to get my name off the mortgage then?"

Oz stumbled back like he'd been shoved. "Right." He was breathing hard, looking panicked.

"What?"

"Nothing." He focused on his feet, swallowing hard. "I'll get the papers." He met her eye. "Is this the end?"

Her lips trembled. She bit down on them and slid into her car. "The end was a long time ago, Oz."

*B*eth stood still as Wanda placed the last pin in her bridesmaid's dress. Wanda spun her around and said, "There, how does that feel?"

"Pretty good." Beth twisted back and forth to admire herself in the mirror. Not bad for a bridesmaid. There was a reason Wanda's Wedding Store, even though being half way to the middle of nowhere, drew people from hours away. "What do you think, Cynthia?"

Her sister, pale and nervous, inspected the newly pinned seams and hem. She fluffed out the lavender skirt and stepped back. "That's *much* better, Wanda." She fiddled with the straps on Beth's bra, tucking them under the dress as Beth smacked her hand away. "You're not wearing that bra, are you? It's awful."

"I'll grab more pins," Wanda said, giving Beth's chest a frown. "Don't move."

Beth checked her chest in the mirror, on the lookout for drooping, sagging, boob-escapism, and other bad breast behaviors. Seeing none, she rolled her eyes. "You guys are so fussy." She did a twirl in front of the mirror. "So? Are you getting excited?"

Cynthia sucked in a sudden breath, her face blanching even more.

"There is *so* much to do. I have three weeks and *so* many details that still need to be taken care of."

"Don't worry, it'll all work out."

Cynthia gave her a look. "Don't say anything you don't want me saying to you in a month or two. I've had since the summer to plan my wedding. You have a mere three months until yours."

Beth looked at their reflections in the fitting area's wall-length mirror. Cynthia, slimmer than usual, was fussing around in the store's robe, one of Wanda's girls adjusting a dart on her wedding gown while she waited. Katie, meanwhile, was sitting cross-legged against the back wall, flipping through a bridal magazine. She held up a page to show them. "One of you two seriously needs to get an ice sculpture."

Beth waved her over. "Bring it here. I can't move until Wanda returns with more pins." She glanced at the offered page. "I like the one with champagne in it."

Cynthia clucked her tongue. "You know how much that would cost? And your champagne would get all flat and watery as the sculpture melted. Think of the mess. Besides, nobody actually likes champagne."

Katie considered the picture again. "Okay, so that one's not so practical." She pointed to a sculpture of a bride and groom. "What about this one?"

Beth pulled out her phone and snapped a picture to send Nash.

"Did you really just do that?" Cynthia asked.

"Do what? Ask my fiancé his opinion? Yes, I did." Beth stood proudly. "He's an awesome planner."

"Taking over, is more like it," Katie whispered to Cynthia behind her hand. "Which explains the lack of panic. That man's a total detail freak. She's got it easy. Unlike you." She patted Cynthia's shoulder and gave her a kind smile. "If you need me to take care of anything, let me know, okay?"

Cynthia gave Katie a hug that bordered on clingy and desperate.

"Um. Me too, of course. Again," Beth added. God, if wedding planning was making her sister--who always had it together--come undone, what hope did she have in the end? She didn't even have a dress. And yes, Nash was taking care of many details, but there was still so much to do and they had way less time than Cynthia'd had.

Katie pried Cynthia off of her, and sent her to try the latest adjustments to her dress.

"So?" Katie asked Beth. "Do you have your gown yet?"

Beth shook her head as Wanda crouched in front of her, adding two more pins to her dress.

"Don't move," Wanda warned.

Katie's eyes widened. "Have you narrowed it down?"

Wanda unzipped the back of Beth's dress as Katie held up a robe for her to slip into. "Not yet."

"Ohmigod. Beth!" Katie squawked.

"What?"

"You're getting married in, like, April! What if you have to order something?"

Beth and Wanda exchanged a look.

"Well," Beth said slowly. She led her friend into the main room where Wanda had the wedding gowns.

As if drawn by a magnet, her eyes settled on the featured gown of the month, its layered tulle barely fenced in by the ample display case. Spotlights highlighted the bodice piping, flecks of mother of pearl, and every dream Beth had ever had of her wedding day.

"No," Katie said firmly. "You can't wear that."

"Why?" Guilt warmed Beth's face.

"That dress has always centered around Oz-filled fantasies. You need a dress to center around Nash."

Beth cast a glance around the shop.

"You need new energy. Everything must be as different as the groom."

Realization hit Beth like a sugar rush. Head spinning, she sunk into a nearby chair. She was going to relive the excitement of trying on wedding gowns in her all-time favorite store. Today. All day. With her sister and best friend. "No wonder people bother getting remarried. This is awesome."

Katie grabbed two dresses and pushed them into Beth's arms. "These two would be good for your build. Wanda, come help. This girl is a sinking ship and doesn't even know it." Her friend headed toward the racks of designer gowns. "Nash can afford designer, right? Actually, he'll probably insist. You should pick a classy dress us small town girls will drool over, but can't afford. Turn us green."

"I'm putting you in charge of narrowing down the bridesmaid dresses," Beth called as she headed toward the most elaborate gown in a hundred mile radius. She set Katie's picks aside as she stroked a beaded gown. They barely had a guest list yet. They had the hall booked and were working on a color scheme. They were going to have to move head-spinningly fast to make up for lost time.

She pushed the heavy gown aside and flipped through the rest of the rack, moving around gushing women. All she had to do was pick a gown. No need to panic. She was marrying Nash. A solid, wonderful man whom she loved. He had lists upon lists already on the go. She didn't need to worry. When she got back to the condo with her dress she would figure out how to become more involved so they could pick up the pace. They could do this without morphing into Cynthia. They were team Bethlehem.

Dear Lord. Was she going to do the modern thing and keep her maiden name?

"Beth," Katie called. "I have the bridesmaid gown, pending your approval."

Wanda held out Katie's choice.

"That," Beth said, walking over to touch the dress, "is gorgeous!" She glanced at the tag and felt her eyebrows land somewhere near her hairline. Was Katie assuming Nash would shell out for designer bridesmaid dresses?

Taking a deep breath, she forced a smile and snatched up the beaded wedding gown as well as Katie's picks, fleeing to the change room. It felt as though everything she should be in charge of was being outsourced, making the wedding feel less real and less like hers. What if she chose the wrong dress?

Cynthia, dressed in jeans and a sweater, slid into the dressing room with Beth. "What's wrong?"

"The wedding doesn't feel like mine anymore." She caught sight of her pale reflection and sucked in a deep breath and blurted, "And I can't *not* love Oz. Every time he does something stupid or pushes me away, I think, *Well, that's it. I'm over him now. I can't possibly love him anymore.*"

Beth slipped to the floor wondering where this was all coming from. Was it cold feet? Was this how Oz felt when she began planning their wedding? With her eyes covered, Beth continued in a soft and wobbly voice. "It's like when it rains and the water table rises and the basement floods. You sponge up every last bit of water and go upstairs, figuring you have it licked. Later you go back, and there it all is again. It's seeped back in." She let out a shuddery breath. "Every time I turn around, Oz has seeped back in."

"Well," Cynthia said with a gusty sigh. "That's kind of heavy."

Beth sniffed and wiped her eyes, looking to her sister for answers.

Cynthia wrapped an arm around her. "This might be one you have to solve on your own, kiddo. But whatever you do, you need to choose one over the other and get closure so you can move on."

"I'm supposed to be getting married. I can't love two men."

They both sat silently, listening to the swish of material in the adjoining rooms. One girl said firmly, "This is the one."

Beth sighed, resisting the urge to ask through the wall: *How do you know? How do you ever know?*

<hr>

BETH STOOD at the back of the church, shifting from foot to foot, waiting to walk down the aisle. Oz, in all his handsome glory, was in position at the front of the church. Tuxedo, haircut, and a close shave had transformed him back into the Oz that made her heart go pitty-pat. The Oz who was currently nudging her body into discarding the memo stating he was persona non grata.

She sucked in a nervous breath, her bridesmaid bouquet

trembling in her grip. She inhaled its soft scent and tried to relax.

Damn that nasty stomach bug that had taken down Nash. She couldn't believe there were some things that had to be ridden out, M.D. or not. It was Valentine's Day for crying out loud! He was supposed to be stuck to her. And he was supposed to be the buffer between her and her mixed-up feelings.

Hearing her cue, Beth hoisted her bouquet and began marching down the aisle.

She couldn't help but stare at Oz standing behind Dan with the other groomsmen.

Tall, handsome, and delicious.

And now she couldn't look away. She also couldn't breathe right. Squeezing her eyes shut, Beth shoved down the hurricane of anticipation that was storming her body. She was *not* walking toward Oz. She was *not* getting married today.

They had *not* chosen each other.

But what if they had? He was like he used to be. His hands strong and capable. Fixing her car problems and so much more. That sweet smile was back and so much more.

What was she thinking? She had Nash. Oz had rejected her. Why couldn't she get that through her head?

Using every ounce of determination she could wheedle and whine from her preoccupied mind, she pried her thoughts away from her ex.

He was waiting for her to finish walking down the aisle. Toward him.

She risked opening her eyes. They flew to Oz who smiled. It felt right, walking toward him. The flowers. Feeling beautiful. His smile, as though they were the only two in the church.

Stop it! Stop thinking!

And stop smiling, dammit.

All she had to do was walk. No thoughts. No emotions. Nothing. Just move her feet.

She marched up the steps to where Dan and his men were waiting. She placed herself in position, ignoring the familiar, shadowy form on the other side of the groom. She swore she could smell Oz. Musky. Manly. Familiar.

The music changed and Cynthia glided down the aisle on the arm of a grinning Gran. Beth fingered the wedding band tied in her bouquet. Her eyes drifted to Oz.

No.

This was about her sister. She had a job to do and that was all. Smile, hand over the ring, sign as a witness, march out. No looking at the men. Eyes on Cynthia.

Gran released Cynthia and the ceremony began.

What if she had to pose with Oz during the photos? What if he was wearing his heavenly cologne? Of course he was wearing his cologne. It was for special occasions. She gave herself a mental smack. She needed to get a grip. She was promised to Nash. She would never risk that. Ever. He was her choice. Her new love.

Her eyes drifted to Oz who was absorbing the vows. Beth's breathing went funny as she took in Oz's tender expression.

She closed her eyes, unwanted tears floating through her coated lashes. Tuning out everything, she worked on regaining control of her emotions. A rough nudge knocked her off balance. Eyes springing open, she stepped forward, practically flinging her bouquet at her sister. The audience giggled and with shaking fingers Beth snatched back her bouquet and freed the wedding band.

The couple tenderly exchanged rings as Oz dabbed at his eyes, unshed tears blurring Beth's.

Today was not going to be easy.

AFTER CALLING NASH, who was still too ill to get out of bed and come rescue her, Beth mentally prepared herself for the most Oz-interactive part of the wedding, the reception. The photos had been a non-event, but the reception ... Well, she was half excited as well as half terrified.

She entered the hall's lobby, praying Cynthia had sprung for some form of champagne fountain like Katie had suggested. She was going to have to stand next to her gorgeous, knee-weakening ex-fiancé in the receiving line, share a table with him, dance with him, and, for her sister's sake, act as though it didn't bother her one iota.

Beth hung her coat in one of the rooms off the lobby and carried her gift to the reception hall. She gently placed the wrapped chocolate fondue fountain Dan had wanted on the gift table and dropped a gift card for her sister in a card basket. Beside the table stood a large, well-crafted china cabinet sporting a massive red bow.

She walked around the cabinet, admiring it as she went. Why would someone bring such a large wedding gift here? Why wouldn't they simply deliver it to the bride and grooms' apartment? Obviously, the gift giver wanted to display their generosity, not practicality. Damn show-offs.

Unable to resist, she ran a hand over the glossy, dark, half counter that broke the upper glass cabinet from the closed-in cabinet below. It was cool and smooth. Experimentally, she opened one of the glass doors and was impressed by how perfectly it swung on its hinges. This piece had been handmade by a master. Cynthia always had all the luck.

She checked for a card. Maybe she could invite the gift giver to her own wedding.

Nothing. It figured.

She lightly ran her fingers over the counter, letting her thumb rub the bumpy edge where she discovered an engraving. *May the circle of your love be like a golden ring: as giving, precious, and unending.*

Beth sighed. She wanted one of these. Bad.

Cynthia swished past, glowing. Beth pointed to the cabinet. "Where did you register, girl? Did Dad send this?"

Laughing, her sister propped the doors open to the lobby. "No. I doubt he even got the invitation I sent to Botswana or wherever the hell he is. I ended up sending invites to three different addresses." She straightened her back and proudly took her spot in the soon-to-be receiving line. "Oz made it. Now, come on. People will be arriving soon."

Beth faced the cabinet again, confused. Oz didn't do carpentry. She didn't think he even owned a hacksaw.

"Yeah, right," Beth muttered and gave the cabinet a last look. "Bought it is more like it."

She turned to join the receiving line and just about bowled into Oz.

"Oh." Embarrassment flooded her nervous system with lava, and she took several steps back.

"Hi." Oz gave her a calm, studying look and tucked his hands in his pockets. His eyes weren't nearly as relaxed as his demeanor. She glanced over his shoulder for his date, she'd been expecting Mandy to appear all afternoon.

Beth gave a little laugh. "Where did you buy this? It must have cost you a fortune."

Oz shifted, turning a shoulder to Beth. "I made it."

She leveled him with a give-me-no-guff look and waited.

He gripped the top of the cabinet, rubbing the varnish with a thumb. He propped up a card on an upper shelf that said *Handcrafted by Oswald Reiter.* "I had to keep myself busy." He met her eye. "This is it, Beth."

She laughed, staring at the card in disbelief. "This is what?"

He pushed past her in a wake of familiar cologne.

Beth stared at the cabinet. Saw dust. Saw dust on his shoulders. The whittled cigar box he was so nervous about giving. Benny's cabinets. She turned, facing his back. "Oz. I'm sorry."

He paused, half turning to judge her genuineness. "This is my debut. Nobody knew until now. Well," he looked over her head at the cabinet and sucked on his lower lip for a second before admitting, "I told Dad. He laughed and said I should focus on a real career. There was no way I could pay the mortgage and support you and a family playing with wood."

Crap. She'd just laughed at his dream like his father had. No wonder he didn't tell her this stuff. He probably felt as though it was either his life or hers--not their lives melded together.

Oz gave her a familiar half-smile and Beth lowered her gaze to stare at something safe, settling on the small, round buttons of his tuxedo shirt.

Instead of getting closure and finding that perfect reason to finally let go, she was finding more mysteries to pique her interest. Was this what love did? It made you greedy to know more about a person? Did it make you hold on even tighter when you should be letting go? Or was this simply an urge to tame and understand the unknown?

More likely, it was quite simply, old-fashioned regret for losing what might have been.

Whatever it was, it stung that he'd been right about her laughing at his dream.

"Did it take long to build?" she asked.

He stepped back, exhaled loudly, and ran a hand through his hair. "About two hundred hours."

She felt faint. Two hundred hours of dedication and perseverance. For his dream. And he was able to do it because she was gone. "You always knew this was what you wanted to do, wasn't it?"

"I had an inkling."

She ignored the painful twist forming in her chest and promised herself she would do whatever she needed to do to set him free. Completely.

THE BRIDE and groom took to the dance floor, their wedding song's bass thrumming in Beth's chest. People gave her sympathetic pats, telling her she'd soon be married, too. But it wasn't that. It wasn't that at all. She needed some space so she could come to terms with how she'd held Oz back from trying something daring and new. Something he was obviously good at.

But if he'd seen so many things about her that she hadn't, why hadn't he seen that he was more important than her dream of a family? Family was all around her in Blueberry Springs. Looking out, interfering, taking her in. Family was so much more than blood and marriage. It was something she'd had all along.

The couple's wedding song silenced, and Beth tucked herself behind Benny's ample height and width. Surely her sister wouldn't mind if she didn't dance. Surely she wouldn't hold a grudge and spoil Beth's own wedding dance two months from now if she hid out instead of joining the smiling wedding party on the dance floor. She risked a quick glance around Benny's arm to see if Cynthia had noticed her absence and a hand clamped onto her arm.

"There you are!" Oz grinned and pulled her toward the band.

Damn.

"It's too bad Nash isn't feeling well tonight," Oz said kindly. "Send my regards."

Beth kept her fake smile plastered in place and stepped on Oz's left foot. "Sure thing."

Oz winced, giving her a surprised look. He moved them smoothly around the dance floor with his old, easy athletic grace. The warmth from his right hand crept through the material at Beth's waist, creating an inner ache. If he accidentally brushed against her one more time, she was going to scream. Either that or do something stupid. She was supposed to be working on closure and letting him go, not whatever this was.

"Where's Gran?" he asked.

Beth flicked a gaze at Oz and clenched her jaw. "She went home. Why, do you want to drop her on her hip again?"

Oz's face reddened. "I never meant to hurt her."

His mouth set in a grim line, he twirled her out, yanking her back in again so quickly she had to put a hand on his chest in order to not smack into him. His surprisingly firm chest. She glanced up, but his attention was elsewhere.

A few weeks ago, he'd been granted special permission to enter the hospital in order to apologize to Gran. But had he apologized to Beth? No, of course not. She'd been on his parents' side throughout the breakup. Together, they'd pushed Oz to continue with a business and career he didn't want. Wedged him forward into a life he wasn't ready for. Laughed at what he wanted. How could a man forgive a woman for that?

Oz abruptly dropped her into a spin before whirling her back into his arms. She caught her breath as she was thrust up against him again. He could act as though they were friends, but she was still pissed off with him as well as herself. And doubly so for the way her body melted when in proximity to his.

She didn't need Oz. He didn't need her. She had Nash. Wonderful, sweet, lovely, detailed-oriented, list-checking Nash. Looking up, she gazed directly into her ex's eyes, unable to stop herself from trying to sort him out. He'd found his dream over two hundred work hours ago. He had never asked her back. Was it because she was already with Nash by the time he was ready? Or was it because the only way he could move forward was without her?

Oz met her eyes, holding them for a second. They collided into the couple behind them and Oz stepped on Beth's right foot.

"Ow!" she squeaked.

"Sorry," he called over his shoulder as he danced them to safety. He pulled her through a tight spot, leading with one hand as she danced around his moving body, his tantalizing cologne wafting over her.

"My patients miss you, even though you're a danger on the dance floor. When did you start woodworking? Exactly?"

Oz shrugged. "A few months ago. It's a good distraction."

"From what?"

He tipped his head toward his sister who was joining the dance floor with Will. "Katie says to smile." He boosted his own smile, making him look goofy.

Beth rolled her eyes and smiled despite herself. This was the way it was with him, wasn't it? Mad and upset at herself one second, lusting after him another, then sprinkle in some curiosity followed by laughter.

"Much better," he said, pulling her close. He spun her through the outskirts of the growing crush of dancers. She was starting to feel dizzy. She wasn't sure if it was from the dancing or the champagne she'd been using to fortify herself--and she noted, people seemed to like champagne just fine despite Cynthia's thoughts on the matter.

Oz gripped her right hand, the warmth of his touch heating her straight to the core. She looked into his eyes and there was warmth there as well. Everything about him was so achingly familiar. Her resolve fatigued and she wrestled with the temptation to rest her forehead on his shoulder. They settled into a gentle, quiet rhythm, Oz resorting to spins only to direct them out of the odd jam.

Beth smiled as the song's last beats wound down. Finally. Oz led her into a complicated move, her feet automatically taking the right steps as he continued to gently guide and lead. As the song ended he pushed her out into a fast spin, then brought her in to dip her low, chest to chest, before pulling her up and into one last, slow, attention-gathering spin, her dress flowing out around her.

Dizzy and exhilarated, Beth beamed. Without thinking she said, "Now, *that* I have missed!"

Their grins faded as nearby couples applauded.

Beth smoothed out her dress and gave a prim curtsy before removing herself from Oz and the dance floor. No need for people to get the wrong idea.

Oz caught her elbow at the edge of the dance floor. He whispered in her ear, "Can I talk to you for a minute?"

Beth steeled herself before turning to face his clean-shaven cheeks, her heart had stupidly forgotten that this Oz, just because he looked and moved like the old one, was not a man who loved her back.

Not that she loved him. She couldn't. She loved Nash. She just had to let go of Oz once and for all and all those mixed up feelings would vanish like Easter eggs hidden at dog level.

"Could I lure you to a secluded corner?" Oz winked and tilted his head away from Mary Alice who was closing in.

Beth acted nonchalant despite the way her body was begging and pleading to be shoved up against his. "Fine."

He led her by the elbow into the lobby and off into a large, unused coatroom which had become a storage area. Closing the door, the room filled with the scent of Oz's special occasion cologne. Honestly, she should demand he return it to her. That and open the door. Being in a closed coatroom with her ex was *not* the kind of rumor she wanted getting back to Nash.

"How are you doing?" Oz asked, smoothing out his shirt with a flat hand--which she noted went straight down from chest to pants, no belly stopover. While she'd failed at Nash's Buff Ex Plan, Oz had obviously succeeded. The bastard. Didn't he know that was unfair?

She shivered. "I'm great. Really great." She needed to get out that door. The one he was standing in front of. Yes, they needed closure. Yes, there was lots to talk about such as the small fact that he still hadn't sent over the papers to free her from the trailer's mortgage, but she couldn't bear to have more mysteries surface. She couldn't bear to be locked in a closed room with him. Not today when everything about him was wonderfully comforting from the tenor of his voice to the small scar skirting his eyebrow from the time Mandy chased him into a metal slide.

"I wanted to apologize," Oz said, running a hand along the high coat rail, acting as if he hadn't said a thing.

She'd waited so long to hear those words, but now they felt as though they would only usher in damage. She bit her lower lip to keep it from trembling. She couldn't do this. Not now. Not on Valentine's Day. Not at her sister's wedding. Not when her fiancé was tucked away, helplessly ill.

As she went to move past Oz, he spoke, "My dad was right." He gave a sad half-smile and ran a hand through his hair, making a piece at the back stand up and wave.

She stopped beside him, their shoulders touching. She flicked her eyes up to read the emotion on his face. He looked strained. Her worries slowly softened. Sighing, she resigned herself to having another tough conversation. She closed her eyes and asked, "He was right about what?"

"That if I didn't smarten up and be responsible, I'd lose you. That you wouldn't like the real me and that you'd run."

Exasperated, Beth said, "Did you ever even let me see the real you? And I didn't run anywhere."

"I know. I know. I meant the 'smarten up' part." Oz put up his hands in surrender. "I was afraid."

She leaned against a small round table situated behind her. "Do you know who the real Oz is now?"

He tipped his head up so he could look at her with one eye. He sucked in a deep breath and paused as if making a decision. He plucked a dusty wineglass from a box and idly twisted it in his hands.

"I've always felt like my father was running my life. Always telling me how to make a play in football. He'd even override the coach. I didn't know who to listen to." He raised a shoulder helplessly. "I don't know if I even *liked* football. It was such a relief when I twisted my ankle in my final season." He paused before continuing. "And with the business there was never really a choice. I was in there after school all the time." Oz let out a disgruntled snort. "My dad didn't want me getting into trouble with Mandy. I think he wanted me to date someone who was less likely to speak their mind and call him on his bullshit. And so he made me work in his office."

Beth raised her eyebrows, but kept her mouth shut.

"Since I was okay at it, Dad kept training me. It seemed like a good option for a kid like me who would probably never go to college. Not like you."

She gave an absent smile. If only he knew why she went away to college.

"Mandy used to encourage me to step out of my father's shadow and open up my own business. I think that's a good part of why Dad didn't like her." Oz looked thoughtful for a moment. "In some ways, I think she knew what I needed even before I did."

"She tried to trap you," Beth reminded him, upset that Mandy might have been a better choice somehow.

"Could you blame her? We'd been together for almost eight years and she still didn't have a ring on her finger. She was scared and we were growing apart. In some ways, I was all she knew and I think she was afraid of being alone."

"Yeah, except Frankie Fall-Off-The-Tower Smith was right there ready to catch her. Among others." Beth reigned in her jealousy, reminding herself that she understood exactly why Mandy had acted the way she had in trying to hold on to Oz. And even though things had always been tense between her and her rival, it wasn't as though Mandy deserved to be disliked by Harvey.

Oz let out a chuckle as she heaved a resigned sigh and the air between them changed. Brought them closer. Beth tried to ignore the fact that the lips in front of her had last kissed the very ex they were discussing in somewhat positive terms. And that he'd chosen that ex over her again.

But if Mandy was so great for him … "Why didn't you change jobs when you guys broke up then?"

"I thought the work angst was due to the tension between Dad and Mandy. By the time I realized it was actually coming from me, it was easier to keep moving. And, I got used to making a decent wage. Anyway, no job is awesome one-hundred percent of the time, right?"

"I guess." Beth rubbed her ring finger and thought of how there had been a few times in the past month where she'd wanted to stay cozied up in bed instead of going in to work on the weekend. "But you said you had an inkling about woodworking?"

"I thought it was intriguing. I didn't consider it as an actual career until a year ago when I talked to my dad about it. I didn't even know if I *could* do it. And then a few months ago Mandy needed help in the place she's renting. She ruined some of the cabinets in a toaster fire and was afraid her landlord would make her replace all the cabinets in the kitchen. She didn't have renter's insurance. And then Benny needed some help with renovations. I really enjoyed it. I thought maybe I could do it for a living."

Beth shut her eyes. Mandy. Saving Oz's day again. How did that woman always come out smelling like roses?

"When you and I got together and we started talking kids, I had these thoughts. Like, what if this isn't the real me? What if I burn out? How can I raise kids and be a good dad if I don't know who I am? How can I be an honest, genuine father who lets my kids be themselves if I can't even do that for myself? That's when I started talking to Dad about moving down to part-time so I could explore my interests."

"And?"

He shrugged, smearing the fingerprints he'd left on the wineglass. "I wanted to take some classes or something. Figure out who I wanted to be."

"What did he say? Why didn't you tell me this?"

Oz met her eye. "He said I couldn't support us if I did that. And that he couldn't get someone who was qualified all the way out to Blueberry Springs to fill in for me part-time and he wasn't about to take up my slack. He told me it was all in or all out."

"When? Why didn't you tell him to take a hike? Why didn't you quit?"

"We'd been engaged for a month or two. And he was right. We couldn't afford it and I couldn't give up a good career to blindly jump into the unknown. That's when I started teaching those computer classes at night. Just to see." He gave a short bark of wry laughter. "You know why I tried computers?"

"Why?" she asked, fearing the answer.

"Because Dad thought I was good with technology. And you know why I quit teaching the classes?"

Beth shook her head. She'd always figured he'd run out of students.

"I sucked at it. I didn't even have enough interest to find the answers when my students asked me something I didn't know. I realized then that I had to take more time to figure out what my real interests were. But how could I do that? We were saving up for a place and you want ..." With his free hand he grabbed one of hers and gave it a squeeze. "You *need* family. I realized I was going to end up stuck or else doing to you exactly what I'd done to Mandy. I couldn't pull you along for years when I wasn't ready. It wasn't fair. You don't trap the ones you love."

"Oz, I wouldn't have been trapped. And Blueberry Springs is my family."

"I know that now. But I couldn't just not give you what you wanted. I saw where we were heading and it wouldn't have been good for either for us." He leaned close, his hand still wrapped around hers. "You don't do that to the woman you love."

Beth blinked back tears, taking her hand back. "Why didn't you say something?" Why didn't he try to change their future?

Oz grew quiet. Finally, in a low voice he said, "I was going to, but Dad and I had a fight. A really big one. I caused his heart attack." Oz's shoulders shook as though he was at the epicenter of two rifting plates. The stem broke off the wineglass and he stared at the pieces in his hands as if he couldn't quite comprehend how they'd come apart.

Beth reached for him, placing a hand on his arm. His shoulders drooped and his eyes grew wet. He shook his head, gently setting the broken glass on top of the box.

"I told him I wanted out of the business. That I hated it. That I hated *him*. That he was ruining my life. He started having chest pains and I kept on yelling at him thinking he was trying to shut me down like he had so many times before. I had so much to get off my chest-- I felt like he'd kept me from figuring out who I was. There was so much I needed him to hear." His voice broke and he continued on faster. "He told me I couldn't do it to you. I couldn't change my life. That you'd never forgive me. That you needed and deserved something more. I would be giving up the best thing in my life. I was a spoiled baby if I thought I could drop my responsibilities and obligations to others so I could go play with wood. He told me to man up."

Beth sucked in a breath, unable to let it out. Hurt sliced through her trembling body. She needed to cover her ears, close her eyes, hide under the table--anything to escape this awful revelation of how their relationship had been destroyed by someone who thought he was saving it.

"Him giving me the business? That was his last trap. If I wasn't going to man up, he would make me. He didn't think I'd walk away and lose it all."

"But you still had your share of the business?"

"Six point five percent in the end."

"But that would hardly amount to anything!" Beth panicked, thinking how he'd given her what must have amounted to at least a quarter of his equity and how, if he was lucky and frugal, enough to live on for a year. A year before he would be back looking for a job that would suck his soul. A year wasn't enough time to build a woodworking business. He'd be stuck again.

"It's okay. It's given me enough breathing room. I know what I want to do with my life now." He gripped her hands in his and looked her in the eye. "Thank you, Beth. I know I hurt you, but you saved me."

"I didn't save you," Beth scoffed bitterly. *And you broke my heart.*

"You did. And I know it's been hard, and I'm sorry. But it's true, I couldn't have done this without you." He thumbed the diamond on her left hand and slowly released her hands. He stepped away and raked his hands through his hair. "It wasn't as if I would've ever measured up for Dad anyway. But the guilt. To give him a heart attack. To take away his livelihood."

"It's not your fault. He could have gone back to work. A heart attack could've happened at any time. At least you were with him and got help."

Oz brushed off her words. "It doesn't make me feel any better. I told him I hated him. What if he'd died? What if I'd killed him? What if those had been the last words--" His voice caught and they remained silent for a moment, the sounds of the dance echoing like a muffled heartbeat through the walls.

"He had you cornered, Oz. Quitting was the only way to escape."

He turned away, forehead furrowed.

Beth ignored her lie. Both of them knew he could have told her how desperately he needed to change things. That if he'd trusted her, trusted *them*, that maybe they'd still be together.

"I sold his legacy."

Beth gave Oz a soft punch in the arm. "That's what kids are for. They're our legacy." She winked playfully.

Oz laughed. "You're always thinking about kids, aren't you?"

"Not always." She smiled, feeling a closeness and kinship she'd missed. Letting him go was going to be even harder than she'd imagined.

NASH EASED onto the couch beside her, his face as pale as his old cotton tee. "What's up?"

Beth bowed her head and unclipped her necklace. The conversation with Oz had worn her out. The whole wedding had. She'd been hoping Nash would be asleep when she got home so she could curl up in bed and forget the whole night.

It was embarrassing to think how she'd let herself get sucked into the dream of her and Oz reunited when all he'd wanted was her forgiveness and understanding. She wrapped her arms around herself and sighed. Stupid. That's what she was.

Nash placed a blanket over her shoulders. "Did you see Oz tonight?"

Beth nodded.

"Is that what's bothering you?"

"He asked for my forgiveness." She couldn't bear to look Nash in the eye. She felt as though enjoying her dance with Oz and entertaining the idea of them being together again she'd betrayed Nash. Even though she hadn't acted upon it. Good fiancées were not supposed to double book their heart.

Although, she supposed she'd gained what she was seeking tonight, closure so she could snip the final thread between them. But if she'd gained closure, why didn't it feel light and easy? Instead, it felt like a heartbreak hangover and as though the world would never be bright or cheery again.

If this was closure, why did it feel just like the years she'd spent yearning for Oz?

Nash gave her a poorly disguised look of exasperation. "Of course he asked for your forgiveness. You're both moving on. This town is so bloody small everyone has to stay on good terms or you end up pissing off the only parts guy." He gave a resigned sigh. "And then where will you be?"

Beth's body stilled. "The rumor about you and Frankie is true?" She'd avoided asking about the incident, hoping so much that it had been a simple misunderstanding that had been blown out of proportion by the rumor mongers.

Nash's face rouged with anger.

Beth sighed. When was he going to learn how to live in a small town? "I've already heard Frankie's side, Nash."

"He was trying to break into my car. He said he was putting a part on the seat for you, but it was this tiny little thing and you weren't even shopping with me. Like you'd need *that* carried out. I can't believe he thought he'd get away with stealing from me in broad daylight!" He punctuated his sentences with finger jabs to the air. "Right on Main Street. I could hear my alarm from the flower shop. What a bloody moron. Now, if I need a part ordered in what am I going to do? He's the only guy in town who can get the right reflectors for my car and Lauretta keeps cracking them whenever she takes Sal out in a wheelchair."

Really? Mr. Smarty Pants PhD hadn't figured out that the spot beside the wheelchair ramp was always vacant for a reason?

"Nash, I asked Frankie to put the part in your car."

Her fiancé shook his head furiously, causing his face to pale. "You were at home wrapping your sister's wedding gift."

"Yes, but I knew you were shopping across the street from the parts place. You weren't answering your cell so I called Frankie and asked him to put the fuse I needed on my account and to put it in your car. He does that kind of stuff all the time."

Nash leaned back against the cushions, looking spent. "He called me Nash-hole."

A laugh escaped before she could stop it. "Aw, Nash." She knew that one was going to stick in her head and attempt to pop out every time they had a fight.

She shook her head, torn. It was going to take a long time before Nash fit into a town like Blueberry Springs.

"Did he ask you back?"

Beth snapped her head up to meet his eyes. "No."

Nash smiled and nodded, looking immensely relieved. "He's a better man than I anticipated."

She flinched. "What's going on between you two?"

"What kind of man would interfere with his ex moving on to a good thing?"

"What, Nash?"

"I heard rumors. I'm glad they are unfounded."

"Rumors?" Beth's heart quickened.

"Everyone's saying you're missing out and that he's the old Oz again. But I knew you wouldn't be interested." He laid a hand on her knee and cocked a grin. "You and your future family deserve love and stability. And that is something I can provide, plus some. You don't have to wait for me to get my life together."

"There's no race or rush, Nash," she said tightly. "We need to have a strong relationship first." She flicked Nash's hand off her knee. "My ex is not competition."

"You need family. You've said so yourself."

"Kids can wait until we're ready. Blueberry Springs is family."

Nash raised an eyebrow as if to say *some family*. "The right thing for you to do is to walk away from him."

She stood, exasperated. "I already have! I'm here with you." She clenched her hands by her side. "Can't you see you're the one I've chosen? What more do you want from me?"

Nash blinked and ran a hand through his hair, every strand perfectly in place even though he'd spent most of the day with his head against a pillow. "I'm sorry, Beth. I don't know what came over me. I love you. Come here." He pulled her into his arms. "I will guard your heart and keep it safe."

She relaxed against him, holding him tight. This time, no matter what it took, she wouldn't let a good thing slip away.

17

---

*B*eth studied Nash, his head bent low to study the medical journal on the kitchen island. He was handsome, loyal, and strong. Smart and endearing. Her heart swelled with love and she ran a hand along the back of his shoulders, leaning over to plant a kiss on his smooth cheek.

February and March had been rough. It felt as though every time she turned around there was a wedding roadblock whether it was the availability of the minister, the caterer hurting her wrist, or even just getting the baker to settle on whether or not he could make the cake they had chosen. She breathed a sigh of relief thinking of all they had gone through to pull this grand wedding together in such a short amount of time. And now they were within a week of saying their vows.

She rubbed his shoulders and he leaned his head back, resting it against her chest. "Hey, I love you."

"You can say that again."

"I love you," he said, laughter lifting his voice.

"Wanna work on our vows?"

"Sure." He tucked a bookmark in the journal and flipped it closed. He twisted to face her. "I meant to tell you earlier, the florist said their supplier is experiencing a blush rose shortage due to weather somewhere or other." He ran a hand down his face and forced a smile. He looked drained. He'd seemed tense for the past few days and she wondered if the idea of getting remarried had been weighing on his mind. "She's planning to place yellow roses in the bouquets instead. I told her that was fine. However, I was wondering if we should make a few minor changes to our color scheme?"

"It'll be fine." Beth smiled and climbed onto Nash's lap. He wobbled on the backless stool and she gave him a deep kiss. "Thanks for all your help with the wedding. You've been amazing." Despite the minor issues, she was nowhere near a bridezilla and that was directly due to him.

"It's no problem," he said, surprised. "It's kind of fun. Natasha kept me out of the planning when we got married so it's been nice." He rubbed his nose against hers. "I like working with you."

She smiled and gave him a kiss. "You've seemed tense. Are you worried?"

"About Oz?"

She frowned and leaned away. "Why?"

"Uh." He cleared his throat, throwing her a sheepish look. He ran a hand through his hair as she slipped off his lap. "I've felt a bit threatened."

Beth blinked. "Threatened? Has he been *threatening* you?"

"I love you, and want to marry you. My heart is intrinsically tied to yours. I can't bear the idea of harm ever coming to you in any way."

Chills ran through Beth. "What happened, Nash?"

"Everywhere I go, I hear about Oz. Everyone has such high hopes for him. It's threatening."

Beth crossed her arms, relieved but aggravated. This again? Really?

"Everywhere I go in Blueberry Springs, I have to measure up to Oz. The Before Oz. The New Oz. The Oz who knows everyone, is friendly, helpful, and was utterly devoted to you. According to half the town, you two were the perfect couple whereas I can't even find the right arena to compete with the guy. I can't be Oz. I'm Nash." He thumped a fist on the island and let out a rough laugh.

Beth swallowed hard. "I'm marrying you, not Oz."

"I know, but this is about me. My *feelings*. People refuse to accept that I'm the new guy and that I have different things to offer. Like money, prestige, success, and security, which has always been valued in Dakota where I'm a catch. But out here ...." He shook his head and turned his hands over, staring at his smooth, empty palms. "Out here, I'm just an outsider. A man who can't fix a snowmobile and is oblivious to when you plant winter wheat. What the hell does winter have to do about the wheat? Its color? When you plant it? Harvest it? What? I have no clue. It's like half the time everyone is speaking a foreign language. And there are so many industries out here to know about. Mining, exploring and tourism, lumber, ranching, farming. You name it, you have it."

He let out a sigh and rubbed his face. "I'm an intruder. I haven't lived here forever. I don't know everyone and everything. I'm clueless about everything deemed important here. I'm the outsider who drives a car from Germany. I will *never* measure up to Oz. I will *never* fit in. And even though Blueberry Springs is important to you, I just can't do it. I can't find the door to get in." Nash's forehead furrowed and his hands clenched. "People think I'm cold."

Beth stared into her fiancé's flat eyes, stunned. She had assumed his strength made him immune to caring whether or not he fit in. She felt for him, but she also knew that in the city she'd be in the exact same position and that if he tried--really and honestly tried-- that the town would warm up to him and bring him into their fold.

"They don't think you're cold." Beth swallowed the partial lie and reached for his hand, searching for a way to explain that people liked and admired him despite his differences. "They don't understand you, is all. They find you closed compared to everyone else. It's not fair to judge you by the same standards because you don't have the lifetime of training for all the minute social nuances--that's assuming you'd want to be like all us country bumpkins." She made herself choke out a half-laugh.

"Is that what it is? I need training?"

"Hey." She waited for him to look at her. "People admire and respect you because you are a doctor and you treat me right. You do good work, Nash. Those are very important qualities around these parts. Those make you a *real* man whether you're knowledgable about winter wheat or not."

She clung to his hand, rocked that Blueberry Springs had him feeling so insecure. The worst part being that she didn't know what she could do about it--if anything.

BETH SLID a sheet of paper and a pen across the kitchen island toward Nash. "Cynthia said they wrote down everything they loved about each other and that became their vows. Shall we try?" She took a swallow of her rum and Coke and cracked her knuckles. Despite Nash's earlier revelation she still wanted to get their vows crossed off their list, even if she wasn't feeling quite as inspired as she was half an hour ago.

Nash winced. "Don't do that."

"Do what?"

"Crack your knuckles."

Beth bit down a grin and slowly cracked her thumb. Nash closed his eyes and drew in a long, controlled breath. She let out a delighted laugh. She was looking forward to many wonderful years of torturing this poor, unexpected soul.

He reached over and pinned down her hands. "Let's write."

They sat quietly for a moment, staring at blank pieces of paper. Nash flicked his pen back and forth between his fingers. "I'm not good at this writing stuff."

"Just jot down what you love about me."

Beth tucked her head down, prepared to let her love flow onto the page. After thinking for a minute, her pen began scratching over the paper. She loved the fact that Nash helped people through his work and how his eyes became a lighter color when he was happy. Before his little revelation, she had admired his confidence and how he always seemed so certain about everything. Her pen hovered over the page. Was it all simply an act? Was he really as lost inside as everyone else?

Who was this man she was marrying?

Slowly, she began writing again. The man got things done. His refreshing efficiency never ceased to appeal to her. There were no hours of consultation with the guys or a two-hour trip to the hardware store, or even months of procrastination before he changed a faucet. He made his decision and got it done. It was that simple. Even though he usually hired someone else to do it.

Beth stretched her arms over her head and flexed her fingers. She peeked at Nash's piece of paper. One sentence. He frowned at her and covered his page with an arm.

Beth reread her notes. She kept thinking of Oz. Many of the things she loved about Nash, she had also loved about Oz. Yet, how could it be? The two men were so different. She read her list, bothered that the majority of her vows could also work for marrying another man. She tapped her pen against the island and cleared her throat. "Ready?"

His eyebrows jumped up and pen stopped moving. "To share?"

"Yep." Originally she'd wanted her vows to be a surprise, but seeing how he seemed to be facing some kind of writer's block, she didn't want to go on and on about him if he was going to sum up his love in one sentence. "I'll go first." Her cheeks warmed as self-consciousness crept in. "The way you look unguarded when you sleep. The way your whiskers are a different color than your hair. The way you--"

"Wait. I look guarded?"

"What?"

"When I sleep. You said I look unguarded. Do I look guarded when I'm awake?"

"Um, no. It's just that you look innocent when you sleep." She consulted her list again. "The way you--"

"Innocent? What do I look like when I'm awake?" She glanced at Nash in irritation.

"No, really," he insisted.

"Incorrigible." She flicked a hand at his list. "Did you want to go first?"

Nash furrowed his brow and cleared his throat. He ran a hand through his neat hair and began. "You're clean and don't have messy pets or friends. You're nice to people. You respect my space, and you have smooth skin."

Nash folded his paper, looking pleased with himself.

Oh.

He loved her because she was clean, nice, left him alone, and presented well.

That was not what she had in mind. At all.

BETH GROANED and handed Katie a cup of coffee. She sat in the chair across from her friend and banged her filing cabinet shut. "Keep on not believing in marriage, Katie. Wedding planning and details are complete hell."

"I thought Nash was taking care of most of it? At least that's what you were complaining about last month--that there was nothing for you to do."

"He has. It's just ..." Beth buried her face in her hands and groaned again. "I need to find a way to magically make Nash's vows half decent."

Katie quirked her head. "What do you mean?"

"I mean, his vows suck and we have less than a week to try and find an appropriate one. We shouldn't have put it off for this long. I had no idea he wasn't poetic. I just assumed he'd write an awesome vow."

"But all you have to do is make up some flowery gook and everybody gushes."

"According to Nash, I'm clean."

Katie burst out laughing and Beth scowled at her. "Not funny."

"But how Nash is that? It's perfect." She clapped her hands in glee and Beth contemplated kicking her in the shins. Her office was small enough she could reach her without getting out of her chair. Katie's humor suddenly died and she jumped from her chair. "Hang on. I've got an idea. I'll be right back."

A few minutes later, Katie returned, triumphant and waving a worn piece of paper. Beth hoped it wasn't one of Will's super sappy love notes. She'd made the mistake of peeking at one lying around Katie's a few months ago. The love letter had been one-hundred percent, over-the-top, romantic goop that had made Beth feel like a voyeur who had scooped out the sugar bowl.

Katie folded down the top of the tattered note. "Inspiration. It was written for me, but maybe Nash could borrow an idea or two."

Beth scrunched her nose but Katie failed to notice. Her friend cleared her throat and stood by the closed door. "*She can make any moment feel intimate.*"

Beth knew Will was a sap, but seriously? And Katie carrying this thing around with her all the time? Just as bad.

"Yeah, maybe not that one," Katie said quickly. "It sounds too personal. You don't want everyone in attendance getting frisky with each other."

Beth snorted a laugh and indicated that she should keep reading.

"*She smells like rain.*" Katie paused to consider it. "That's pretty good, don't you think? He could borrow that one. It's creative and sweet. We could somehow make him think that it's his idea to say that about you."

There was something about that last line that seemed familiar--a faint call on the wind, fleeting and undefined.

"Oh, here's a good one." Katie looked up. "What?"

Beth deftly snatched the note. Her friend tried to retrieve it, but Beth was already reading it under her breath. She brushed Katie off with one hand, her mind furiously taking in the tight printing, the words, the meaning, the emotions.

She unfolded the top of the note and glared at Katie. "*Reasons I*

Love Beth? Really?" She read a few of the lines, loudly. *"She smells better than rain. Her skin glows when she is happy ... smile lights up my gray life ... kindness makes me want to be a better person. Her voice wavers when she is trying to hide her emotions. She has faith in everyone and is forgiving."* Beth's voice shook, but she continued on, her tone growing softer. She needed to keep reading. To make this real. To solidify her thoughts and feelings.

The note was like an oasis. An oasis she wasn't sure she was looking for, but couldn't help torturing herself with nevertheless. *"She is tender and softly independent and strong. I want to wrap my fingers in her delicate brown curls and snuggle up in her trusting, warm, brown eyes."*

Tears trickled down Beth's flushed cheeks. Katie tried again to take possession of the note. Beth stomped a foot and held the paper behind her back.

How was it that Oz wrote lovely, appropriate words and Nash couldn't rise to the occasion? And why did it matter to her so much?

"Damn that Oz!" Beth snapped. "Did he put you up to this?" Maybe there was more to the so-called threat of Oz than Nash had let on. Maybe he had been the one quietly sabotaging things in the background just like his mom had when she'd tried to move out of Katie's place. It didn't seem like something Oz would do, but then again neither had many of his actions over the past year.

Katie shook her head and lunged for the note. "No. I'm just an impulsive mental case, okay? Give it back and we'll pretend I never showed it to you. He'll *kill* me if he found out I have it. I shouldn't have taken it. I shouldn't have even read it."

Beth grabbed her purse and shoved her office chair out of the way. "Move!"

Katie leapt from her spot in front of the door and Beth blew past.

"Wait! Beth. It was me, it was me!"

Beth rounded a corner at the end of the hospital corridor and could hear Katie in her soft-soled shoes scurrying to catch up. She moved faster.

"Wait!"

Nurses turned in alarm as they blasted by the station. In the atrium, she slowed to a fast walk, fake smiling at patients and guests who were engrossed in the news before storming ahead, finally reaching the exit near her car.

"You can't tell him you read it," Katie said, reaching to grab Beth's arm.

She whirled, just about hitting her friend upside the head with her swinging purse. "He can't screw with my emotions, Katie. Not without consequences." She resumed her march, exiting through the large emergency doors and into the blaring spring sunshine.

"Wait! He wasn't involved. I swear," Katie called.

Beth gunned the Volvo's engine and tore out of the parking lot. Less than a week until her wedding and Oz dared pull this crap? He had to be off his rocker thinking he could get away with sabotaging her future happiness. He'd given her up and she was going to remind him of that small fact right now.

She skidded down her old street sending a cat that looked a lot like Fluffy scuttling out of the way. Beth slammed her car into park outside Oz's trailer, jolting her seatbelt into its locked position. She tried to exit the car, and nearly strangled herself when her seatbelt refused to release for her fumbling fingers.

"For heaven's sake!" She threw herself back in her seat and impatiently tried again. Finally, she stumbled toward the front steps, tripping over a cedar whirligig.

She was going to tell that delusional man a thing or two. There was no way she'd allow him to illuminate Nash's poetic shortcomings and come out unscathed. *He* was the one who messed up. He had his chance and he blew it. Big time.

She stomped up the steps, yanked on the protesting screen door, and thumped on the inner wood door with a heavy fist. She continued to bang until her fist stung and the door swung inward, just about depositing her against a shirtless Oz.

Beth gaped at Oz's midsection, specifically, the faint outline of a six pack. And she was not referring to beer. She was talking stomach muscles. Large lumps of firm stomach muscles. More than she'd imagined when he'd smoothed his hand over his midriff at her sister's wedding.

Unable to tear her eyes off his gut, other than to make a quick visual to ensure that it was indeed Oz, she continued to gape. Lines of muscle ran down either side of his stomach region, narrowing to form an unfinished arrow. A trail of dark hair marched south from his belly button, drawing her eye to the top of his faded 501s. She lost visual contact with the line, but knew exactly how and where it ended.

Self-preservation kicked in and she sucked in a breath, combatting the lightheadedness that had taken over. Clutching the doorframe, she tried to recall why she had come and why she thought she should be angry.

Oz broke the silence. "I've been working out."

She blinked hard, turning her head so she'd stop staring at his midriff. She cautiously allowed herself to check his face. His eyes were crisp and bright. He looked healthy. Hot. Just like at the wedding. Only ... better. Lots better.

Sadness gripped her core with its freezing hand. Inside she screamed, *It's not fair!* He wasn't allowed to look this good when he wasn't hers. And he most certainly was *not* supposed to know it was affecting her. Comforting anger returned and she whipped out the note and waved it in Oz's face. "What do you think you're trying to pull?" She leaned forward and in the process caught a whiff of his sweet, memory-laden cologne. She steeled herself so she wouldn't sway, her breathing jagged. Why was he wearing it? It was for special occasions. This was most definitely not a special occasion.

Oz rested a shoulder against the edge of the inner door. Beth's indignation flagged as Oz's brow scrunched in confusion, a lock of hair falling into his eyes.

She waved the note again and stepped forward, the screen door banging against her butt. Oz grabbed her waving hand and plucked the paper from her grasp. His expression slowly closed as he unfolded the sheet.

The world felt as though it was turning. Something had changed.

"How did you get this?" he asked, a hard edge to his voice.

"What are you trying to do to me, Oz?" She watched as he took her in, leaving her feeling small and strangely guilty. "You're intentionally trying to sabotage my relationship with Nash."

Oz's eyebrows rose. "Wait a second, I--"

"Don't play games with me." She jabbed a finger at his chest. "I am not dumb. You're making everything difficult on purpose. You're being the old Oz and it's not fair! It's wrong. It's *all* wrong." She faltered, unsure whether to run or keep yelling.

Oz's expression softened, and her anger took over. She stepped forward, forcing him to back up as she went in for another verbal blow.

"You set me up. Me, Oz! Me!" She swiped at sliding tears. She sliced her index finger through the air, first at Oz and then at herself. "You and me? We're done!"

"Wait." Oz took a step forward, closing the space between them. "I don't know how you got this from my wallet, but I didn't set you up. You know me better than that, Little B."

The nickname cut through her core and she stumbled. "What?" She glanced beyond the entry and into the living room. Like a tease, it had transformed itself back into its former warmth. The room was clean, the plants green and healthy, the picture frames propped up. Her favorite video game was paused on the TV. It was as though the past had never happened--except she was now standing on the outside like she was part of an alternate reality.

She closed her eyes against the stinging flood of loss. She felt like a kite fluttering without its string, drifting and spinning on a breeze, unsure where the wind would set her down and in what condition.

Had all of this been simply to get her out of his hair? No. She shook her head. It was something else. She leaned over and breathed deeply. *Her* Oz. Chin crinkling, she tried to keep her lips from trembling.

He crouched so they were face to face. "I'm sorry, I don't know who is doing this to you."

Beth closed her eyes. Neither man was perfect. It was as though she had been idolizing rock stars only to find they had drug addictions, cheated on their taxes as well as their wives, and synthesizers had been making their voices falsely perfect and deep. But they were close. So close. And Oz felt like the closest even though he was the furthest. How could that be? How could she still think he was the one?

He slowly refolded the note over its creases and ignored the phone which had begun to ring. "I wrote this years ago. After the first time we slept together." His face flushed and he slid the note into his back pocket. Still keeping his eyes cast down, he continued, "I still carry it." His brown eyes, flecked with amber, met hers and took her in. "It grounds me."

Beth resisted the potent urge to fold herself into Oz's arms. She stood on the step, emotions roaring through her like a late summer storm. "We're over, Oz Reiter. Remember that. *Over!*" She stumbled against the screen door, pushing her way out.

How could she still have feelings for Oz?

How could she betray Nash by loving him *and* loving Oz?

And why couldn't she shove Oz out of her heart the way she wanted to? Why wouldn't he leave?

Beth folded her hands around her head, letting tears drip onto her denimed thighs. She checked the clock to make sure Nash would still be at the hospital and called her sister on the bedside phone.

"Yo, what's up bride-to-be?"

Beth sniffed, wiped her cheeks with the back of her hand, and sighed.

"What's wrong?" Cynthia asked. "Is this about Nash's bachelor party in the city? He let the stripper give him a blow job, didn't he? A blow job is a blow job, Beth. No matter who performs it or under what circumstances. Don't let him convince you otherwise."

Panic seized her mind. "He got a blow job from a stripper?"

"Well, I don't know. Did he?" her sister asked in a curious voice.

"*What?* No. I mean, I don't--you just said he did!"

"No, I didn't. But it seemed a likely explanation for your apparent distress. So, what *has* he done?"

"I hate you."

Cynthia laughed. "You get so wound up about men."

Beth took a deep breath and tried to relax. "I still hate you."

"So? What did he do? The Greatest Couple in Blueberry Springs has a date tonight. Can you make it snappy, or should I reschedule our public appearance?"

"He hasn't done anything. Not really."

"Not really? Or not at all? There's a big difference, especially when we're talking about men and upcoming nuptials."

"Not really." Beth let out a defeated sigh. Why did she bother calling Cynthia? Her sister couldn't figure this out for her. It was her problem. Her consequences.

"Spill."

Beth let out a painful hiccup. "Nash thinks I'm clean!" Renewed hurt washed over her and she chucked one of the throw pillows across the room, knocking over the laundry hamper. "Those are his vows."

Cynthia snorted as if holding back laughter.

"He says I've got nice skin and that my friends and I are clean. And that I give him his own space."

"And let me guess, you said some really nice things? Romantic things?"

"Uh, huh."

"Well, Beth, I hate to break it to you, but he's a *guy*. That's why there's a dozen women locked up in a Hallmark factory writing sappy cards for useless, unromantic men. Guys don't think all lovey-dovey. It's not natural."

"For some of them, it is."

"For the ones limp in the wrist. Nash is an acquired taste, like champagne. Not everyone likes champagne, but it gives an elegant impression and gets the job done. Nash is ready to go, right out of the bottle. You don't have to wait for him to figure out who he is in order to see if he wants a life with you. Vows are hollow, meaningless, Hallmark nothings."

"You're wrong. Not all guys." Beth paused, doubting herself. "Katie showed me a note Oz wrote--"

"Oz is a lemon drop, Beth. Everyone loves a lemon drop, even when it's covered in lint. Aren't you getting tired of sucking the lint and getting cavities?"

"He wrote it after we'd been dating for two and a half months. It was beautiful. Poetic. Romantic. He *knew* me."

Silence.

"He carries it around with him and has since he wrote it."

"Why are you telling me this? Are you hoping I'll magically make Nash poetically gifted? Or is there something else?"

"I'm talking to you because you're my sister and I need help."

"Help how?"

"To share the indignity of it all." Beth flung another satin cushion across the room. "I mean, I'm marrying Nash, who can't write a vow to save his life, and here's Oz carrying around an old note that would make perfect vows."

"Really? Is that all?"

"That's all."

More silence.

Beth would *not* tell her sister the truth. Ever.

"Do you know what I think?" Cynthia waited a beat before continuing. "You're still in love with Oz. Which is understandable since, from what I've seen and heard, Oz is getting himself back together. Back to the good ol', just-like-always, easy-to-love Oz who you've drooled over for years. But the problem is that Oz doesn't seem to want you back, now does he? He gave you up."

Beth blinked back tears and tried to swallow.

"So, little sister, you need to ask yourself, do you love Nash more than Oz and your perfect, unrealistic dream that goes along with him? Because you can't marry Nash in good conscience if you're dreaming of Oz and all he used to be. That man is gone. You need closure with Oz, and quick. You need to prove to yourself that he isn't sitting there waiting for you to come back to him so you can move on."

"Do you think he is? Waiting?" Beth asked, her voice small.

"He isn't acting like it and you've both moved on. You need to get your head in the game and start drooling after what you have, not what you used to have."

Beth stared at the ceiling and blinked back tears.

"Did you hear me? Get closure."

"Okay."

Cynthia was quiet for a moment, then added gently, "Oz is different now and so are you. You've both been through a lot and pulled some punches. Nothing can be the same as it was. You can't have the past. Only the future, and the future is, of course, completely uncertain. Whatever you decide, I'll support you. This is your life."

Beth closed her stinging, sore eyes and let a slow breath out from between her lips, spraying teardrops. She was going to have to say goodbye to the man she loved. A man who was just as good today as he had been the first time she said yes.

But which man was that?

III

—

THE WEDDING DAY AND WHERE THINGS BEGIN TO UNRAVEL

(April)

1 8

*B*eth paced the small upstairs room in the church. She hadn't gone to Oz for closure. And she hadn't broken up with Nash.

Of course she hadn't. There was no reason to do either. She'd merely had cold feet because she didn't know Nash as well as she knew Oz. It was so obvious now. Anyway, she and Oz had their closure ages ago. She had just been miffed that Oz was still a great catch. But not the catch for her.

She and Nash were in love and she was ready to get married and live a new life.

Pasting on a smile, she took a deep breath. She kept smiling and breathing until the smile felt real. Excitement started to build inside her. She was going to get married. To Nash. Today.

This was the beginning of something new. Nash was feeling more in tune with Blueberry Springs, her outreach program was in full swing, and now she was getting married. It couldn't get much better than this.

She paced the room in her bare feet and checked the clock. Where was Katie with her special order shoes from the city? And where was Cynthia with her necklace? She checked the time again. Maybe she should get someone to run to the condo and grab the stand-in shoes with the same height heel she'd worn for her fittings. She picked up her cell phone, debating who to call. She already had her two best gals on the job.

The large wood door squeaked open and Mandy Mattson hesitantly stepped inside. She was decked out in designer jeans that hugged her tush and she had a familiar tote. "I hope I'm not too late. Katie called from the city and asked me to get your stand-in shoes but I had trouble getting into your place. Nobody has a spare key and you keep the place locked." She frowned and thrust the bag at Beth. "Here are your shoes. Congratulations."

"What's wrong with Katie? I can't get married without her!" Panic raced up her spine.

"She said she ran into a slight problem and you might have to go down the aisle without her. Is there anything else I can help with?"

Beth clutched the bag. "Why are you being so nice?" Beth whispered.

Mandy's expression lost its friendliness. "I'm actually a nice person, Beth."

"I know. I'm sorry," Beth said quickly. "I didn't mean it that way." She waved the bag. "I just didn't expect this." As much as she wanted to give Mandy the benefit of the doubt and even thank her for trying to break Oz away from his father years ago, she couldn't help but think that Mandy was getting what she wanted, a single Oz to pursue once again.

But maybe it was better this way. Everyone got someone they cared about.

She met Mandy's eye. "Thank you, Mandy. For everything."

"It's just a pair of shoes."

Katie burst in, looking harried and unsettled. She was still in her jeans and ratty old winter coat. "Sorry, I'm late. Thanks, Mandy. I have the real shoes." She waved a shoebox. "These bloody shoes cost me my car."

"What?" Beth took the box as Mandy slipped out the door. "We prepaid for them. Please tell me they didn't charge you again?"

"I'll explain later." Katie shook her head and glanced around the room. "Where's my dress? Will better have brought my dress or I swear I'll…"

Beth slipped into one of the beaded new shoes and pointed to the garment bag hanging by the door. Katie snatched it up and bolted from the room. Holy moly, these shoes were going to kill her. She winced and shoved her foot into the second shoe. Oh well, all she had to do was wear them for a couple of hours and then she could change into the stand-in shoes.

The door squeaked again and Cynthia entered, tugging at her pantyhose. She was wearing a short T-shirt over pantyhose and nothing else. "Who pissed in Katie's cornflakes?" Cynthia grumbled. She stuck out a hosed leg. "Does this color look okay?"

"Why aren't you in your dress?" She checked the clock. "I'm supposed to be going down the aisle in five minutes!" She turned to shove her sister out of the room. "And I need my necklace."

"Right!" Cynthia snapped to, returning an instant later with the necklace in hand and her dress over an arm. She dropped the dress on the couch and held out an opened necklace. "Come here." She clipped the necklace in place for Beth, her gentle perfume reassuring as she adjusted it. Beth breathed in and tried to relax. Was everyone this nervous before they got married?

She fiddled with her engagement ring. Nash wanted her and she wanted him. They were in love. People in love got married.

But she couldn't help believing real closure should feel more definitive. That she should feel a little more sure of herself. Or at least a little less curious about what Oz was up to today.

Her sister spun her around and held her in place. "There, now you have something borrowed."

"Well, I suppose I'm ready to get hitched!" Beth's voice cracked on *hitched*, and her sister's grasp tightened.

"You can still back out, if that's what you need to do. I'll support whichever choice you make."

"Nash *is* my choice." Beth stood tall. "He's right for me."

Her sister gazed at her for a long moment. "You didn't get closure, did you?"

Beth turned away. "Of course I did."

There was something in Oz's eyes the day she smacked him with his love note. Something she couldn't put her finger on and it was making it difficult to let go. She shook her head. She was standing in a wedding gown, about to marry a great man and all she could think about was her ex? She needed to get her head on straight.

She quietly drifted to the window seat, mindlessly admiring how Mother Nature had gifted her with a lovely layer of snow for her wedding day. The snow twinkled in the bright spring sunshine and she sat at the window, trying not to think.

"Life's too short, Beth," said Cynthia quietly.

Beth looked up, having forgotten her sister was still in the room. "I know."

She could feel Cynthia staring at her while she slipped into her bridesmaid dress.

"Do me up?" she asked, coming over. Beth quickly zipped the dress and turned back to the window.

Her confidence sagged. What was she doing? She was like a yo-yo.

Up.

Down.

Yes.

No.

I do.

I ...

She tried to suck in a deep breath. If she could breathe properly, everything would feel right.

Her sister slipped out to check on Katie, and when she returned Beth mindlessly chatted, waiting to head downstairs. With her sister beside her at the window, she caught a flash of black tuxedo below and loud voices filtered their way up to her perch. She stood, nose pressed to the window in an effort to see directly below. She gasped, and ignoring her sister, fled to the heavy door blocking her exit. She wrenched it open and took the stairs as fast as she could. She reached the front doors of the church in time to witness Nash throw a punch at Oz.

Oz ducked. The momentum of Nash's swinging arm twisted his body like a corkscrew and his shoes slipped on the ice. His body arched through the air, a look of surprise, his mouth curving into a perfect, comical O.

He landed, head first, his body crumpling in slow motion.

A scream shredded the silence.

*B*eth stood on the condo's threshold, hating everything within it. Everything she used to admire about the place angered her from the decorative chair that sat uselessly at the front door to the silly ornamental kitchen lights that shone on dust-catching sculptures. She'd like nothing more than to break everything in sight. Nash's perfect condo lacked the comforting, cozy, homey feeling she craved. She wanted her saggy old velvet couch under her, not cool, elegant leather.

She dropped the small bag of things her sister and Katie had brought to the hospital, along with her blood-stained wedding gown. She held the door for Nash, offering her arm as he swayed.

"You okay?" she asked tightly.

"Just a touch of lightheadedness." His complexion matched the bandage spun around his forehead. "Hey, look. Nobody did up our condo while we were away."

Bitter rage brewed and her vision flashed with wild colors as she fought for control. "That's because we didn't go on our honeymoon." She fought back tears. "We missed the flight while you were in the hospital. And it wouldn't have been a honeymoon anyway because we didn't get *married*. And nobody rearranges your furniture when you end up in the hospital for acting like an ass instead of getting married like a civilized man."

She kicked the mangled pile of wedding dress and tossed her jacket on the floor, heading to the kitchen in search of a beer. Seeing how she'd hardly slept in the past day and a half, maybe she should consider a coffee. Either that or go straight to bed. Angry.

Really freaking angry.

And if she went straight to bed, she wouldn't have to discuss anything lack-of-marriage related with Nash, the one topic they'd carefully skirted for the past thirty hours.

The anger surprised her. Everyone expected her to feel hurt or disappointed. But it was anger. One-hundred percent, barely-bridled anger, and it was oozing from her pores like lava from a volcano during eruption. Anger at Nash. Anger at Oz. Anger at herself.

Nash appeared in the kitchen doorway, as Beth stood, frozen with indecision, staring at the oak cabinet door which was really nothing more than a dressed-up fridge.

"What?" she snapped.

"Are you okay? You seem upset."

Beth inhaled through her nose and bit her tongue. Nothing she would say right now would be good for their relationship.

Nash moved closer. "It bothers me that our wedding got ruined. It bothers me a lot."

Beth popped a hand to her hip. It bothered *him*? What about her? She'd only been waiting all her freaking life and then he went and ruined it with his stupid inferiority complex.

"Maybe you should have thought about that *before* you swung at Oz and landed on your head. Hmmm? Ever thought of that?" She stepped up to Nash. "Ever think that maybe you don't have to act jealous, because, oh, I don't know--I'm wearing *your ring*?" She thrust her ringed finger in front of his face. "That I chose *you!*"

Nash frowned and squeezed his right hand, the hand that had connected with nothing but air in his jealous, male rage. The hand that had ruined everything by doing nothing. "Beth, I've seen the way you look at your ex." He tipped his head, watching her.

"But I chose you, Nash," she said, her voice wobbling horribly. "I chose *you*. But maybe I need someone who knows me." She sobbed as the burning realization of what they were saying sunk in.

BETH HID IN THE BATHROOM, submerged in a hot bubble bath. When the water chilled she got out, checking to see if Nash had fallen asleep. She found him on the couch, cramped in the short space, a thin line of drool stringing down onto the leather. She grabbed her purse and skimmed the note he'd left on the kitchen island suggesting they book a local getaway and elope during their week off. Leaving the note as she found it, she slipped out the door.

She wasn't ready to move on as if nothing had happened. They needed to figure out their feelings if they hoped to ever be truly good together. And since Nash's concussion there had been an uncertainty in his eyes that made the idea of elopement feel similar to a wrong turn down a one-way street. A one-way street where they were speeding headlong toward an approaching semi.

She shook off the feeling, certain she was looking for a way out of something that would be right for her in the end. She strode aimlessly through the fresh spring air, and spotting Katie's dented car outside Will's apartment, went inside. Anything to get away from her whirling thoughts.

Katie opened the door and did a double-take almost as if Beth wasn't welcome. Beth stepped back and started to apologize when her friend opened the door wider. She paused half a second, then stepped into the hall, closing the door behind her. Katie crossed her arms, her shoulders hunched like she was cold. "What's up?"

"I was just popping by to ask what happened to your car, but if it's not a good time I can come back later." She hadn't talked to Katie since her failed wedding night. Beth had expressed how angry she was with Oz for crashing and ruining her wedding, as well as had hinted at finding out why Oz had shown up in the first place. Katie had been unusually reserved and simply stated that it had been Nash who had ruined the wedding, not Oz.

Either way, her friend had planted doubt in Beth's mind about Oz's intentions, making it easy to blame Nash for hurting himself and ruining everything. Especially when Katie had suggested that maybe Oz had simply been helping Mandy bring the shoes to the church and that possibly Nash had overreacted to her ex's presence.

A torrent of body-shaking anger consumed Beth just thinking about how stupid the men had been. How stupid *she* had been. She could have prevented all of this by getting closure and making certain Oz knew to stay away.

Katie licked her lips and glanced over her shoulder, lowering her voice. "Oz is here. You're welcome to come in, but I thought I should mention it."

The apartment door swung open and before Beth had a chance to beat a retreat, Will reached out and swept her close with an arm. "Beth!"

"I was just--I don't want to--I should--" Beth stuttered, resisting Will who was tugging her into the apartment. There was no way she was going to hang out in the same room as Oz. Someone was going to get hurt and it sure as hell wasn't going to be her.

Oz popped off the couch and flushed with color, looking uncomfortable. One of Will's favorite video games was paused on his television, coffee cups littering the table. A handmade toy box sat in the middle of the space between her and the sitting area, filling the room with the scent of fresh pine.

Beth stared at Oz, feeling as though someone had poured a jug of ice water down her back. She turned in Will's grip. "I've got to go."

Will held onto her arm, a serious look in his eyes. "Please don't. Stay."

Oz struggled to get a grip on the large toy box. "No. I'll go. Beth probably wants to talk to Katie."

"You have every right to visit your sister and best friend," Beth said tightly. No way was he going to be the better person in this situation. She was leaving. Besides, what had she been thinking coming here? She couldn't vent to Katie--she'd take her brother's side just like she had so many times before.

Will's grip remained steady and Beth glared at him, mere feet from her escape.

"No." Oz ran a hand through his hair, his eyes still cast down. "I'll leave."

"Before you go," Will said, coming to check out the toy box, his hand still gripping Beth's arm, "tell us what's up. Why did you bring this by?"

Beth glanced down at the box, its lid bordered with carefully carved alphabet blocks. She had to admit, its cuteness certainly did nothing to help quell her inner desire to have kids. She took in Oz's appearance as he dropped lightly to his knees, pulling a plastic bag from his pocket. There was the habitual tuft of hair poking up at his crown from running his fingers through it. The same broadness of his shoulders. The deep warmth of his voice. How every word seemed carefully chosen when he was feeling shy. But today, what had once been so familiar, felt almost foreign.

It was surreal. It was as though their love had been a dream. So vivid and real, yet intangible. And to know she'd never be with him again.

Blinking, she looked away.

Oz unwrapped the clinking bundle of metal handles, lining them up on his palm. "Which one would be best?"

Katie poked at the variety, choosing an ornate one for further inspection.

"You don't need a handle," Beth said, drawing closer. She leaned over, admiring the craftsmanship in the carving despite herself. Not only was he building magnificent pieces, he was carving. The man had surprisingly artistic talent. Despite what it had cost her, she was glad he was honing his abilities and developing his talent.

Oz looked up at her--eye level and closer than they'd been since Cynthia's wedding. His warm eyes rested on hers, making it impossible to look away. She leaned back, horrified that she'd been surreptitiously sucking in deep breaths of his aftershave. She took several steps toward the door. "The lid overhangs. You don't need a handle." She tried to say something about Nash waiting for her at home and that she needed to go, but she couldn't bring herself to say the words.

Will caught up with her. "No."

Everyone looked at him in surprise.

"No," he repeated, he pulled Beth back into the room. "Katie and I are going for a walk." He released Beth and took Katie's hand in his. He pointed at Oz. "You need to talk to Beth." He turned to Beth. "And you need to listen." He waggled his finger between them. "You two, talk. *Really* talk. Say it all. This is your chance."

Neither Beth nor Oz moved. Sighing, Will dropped Katie's hand and steered Oz to the couch. Beth crossed her arms and swallowed hard, taking several small steps toward the door. Will pushed her over to Oz, seating her next to him.

"Now," he said, standing over them like a peeved parent, "I recommend you two start by talking about what happened at the wedding."

He and Katie closed the door firmly behind them.

Beth folded her hands in her lap and cast a quick glance at Oz. He was pale. The sound of his jiggling denim-clad legs filled the room, making the couch vibrate. Instinctively, she applied pressure to his moving leg. Oz spun to face her and for a moment she thought he was going to sweep her into his arms and kiss her.

"Beth." His voice was rough as if he hadn't used it in days. "I know I've apologized for our relationship and everything you've gone through." He gently took her hands into his large, warm ones. She pulled the insides of her cheeks between her teeth and ignored the tightening in her ribcage. *Don't cry.*

He laid her hands on his chest, pulling himself closer as she tried to lean away. His worn flannel shirt was soft and warm under her fingers. It was comforting, real, and achingly *him*. "I am so very sorry, Beth. Really and truly, sorry." His warm brown eyes flecked with gold met hers and she relaxed. She knew and trusted this man. Despite it all.

"If you could only feel my heart," he said. Which was odd, because she *could* feel it. It was beating a million miles an hour, just like her own. "You would know."

Oz hunched his shoulders and bowed his head, dropping her hands. She searched his body for a sign of what she was supposed to know.

"I am sorry for what happened last Saturday," he said, his head still lowered. "For the pain I caused you. It's unforgivable. I ..."

She bit her lip, fighting the need to run. She needed to let him say the words she needed to hear so they could both move on. So she could marry Nash in peace.

He swallowed hard and paused as though wrestling with himself. "I came by your wedding to wish you luck. And for closure. I convinced myself that you needed that, when I think it was me who did."

Beth closed her flooded eyes. She would be married right now if she had followed Cynthia's advice. Instead she'd chickened out and not made a decision. And by doing that she'd screwed up everything.

Oz continued, "I didn't want to believe you were in love with someone else. It's no surprise you got swept up so quickly and by a guy with ... well ..." He struggled for words--like it seemed everyone did when it came to complimenting Nash and not his work.

"Yeah, I know," she said uncomfortably. "He's actually a great guy."

Oz cleared his throat and brushed a tear from her cheek, holding her face in his hand. "I never believed we were done." He stared at her as though memorizing every feature and making her feel as he always did--as though she was seen. All of her. Flaws, fears, and everything good. "I thought I would get you back. That you would see everything I was doing and know it was for you. For us." He dropped his hand and drew in a slow breath.

Had he bumped his head falling off his rocker? He'd kissed Mandy. How was that for her?

"It wasn't until you got engaged and were planning your wedding that I realized you'd made your decision and what I was doing no longer mattered." His voice grew quiet. "I went through a bad patch."

He held up a hand to stop Beth from speaking. "I know I told you to take a hike. I remember that painfully well. It's no excuse, but I needed space and it was so hard to figure out what I should do. But still, later, a part of me hoped that if I got myself together and you were watching, that you would ..." He sighed heavily. "Oh, I don't know." He moved away from her. "I was dumb. I needed space to get my head on straight and deal with the guilt about my dad, but I never thought it would take me so long and that I'd lose you for good." He looked at her with soulful eyes. "What a moron, huh? How long can a guy expect a girl to wait?"

"Why did you kiss Mandy?"

He rubbed a hand over his face and leaned back. "You and Nash," he said quietly. "I wanted you to feel the pain I was feeling. I hoped that if I kissed Mandy you'd see that you still loved me and would wait."

Was he kidding? They had been playing the same stupid game against each other all this time. She felt dizzy as a storm of unwanted, confusing thoughts swirled through her. "You didn't want me. I dated Nash to make you feel ..."

It was too late, too late, too late.

"I realized Mandy had known what I needed all those years ago. For a stretch I thought maybe she was the right girl--with her knowing I needed to get out of accounting, and all. But she's not. We never had that same click you and I had. That *something*, you know?"

Pushing his hands up and down the thighs of his jeans, his voice lowered as if he was speaking to himself. "I don't deserve a second chance. It's not fair or right. I ruined your wedding to a decent man without problems."

Beth couldn't help but snort. If there was one thing she'd learned in this whole ordeal was that nobody was perfect and everyone had problems. She paused, took in Oz's hopeful, questioning expression. "Wait." Chest tight, she watched, unblinking, as Oz's face turned red. She whispered, barely daring to breathe. "Are you asking me something?"

"I caused you pain. The things I've done aren't easily forgivable."

Beth tried to keep herself together. All she wanted was closure. Not complications and heartache. She only had to make it through this and then she could leave and figure out all these awful thoughts spinning out of control within her.

"But at the same time, I still love you," he said quietly.

She couldn't believe he'd wanted her back all this time and *still* let her go off with someone else and let her believe he didn't want her. She stood, her body shaking.

"You're asking me to put Nash on hold. My fiancé--the man I live with--and try things out with you again? How is that supposed to work, Oz? Do you hear what you are asking from me?"

"Pretty ballsy, huh?" Oz tilted his head to look up at her, his brown eyes brimming with emotion. She turned her back and moved to stare out the window.

"Why now? When over the past year you've done nothing but push me away? How do I know you won't do it again? That this isn't just a reaction to me finally moving on? To me marrying someone else?"

Oz drew in a long breath, his leg resuming its jiggling. "I broke up with you because I thought could save you the pain of me being lost. You could have a life."

"You'd have to be really fucking serious," she said, her voice hoarse. She couldn't believe she was providing him with hope. It would be so hard for them to trust each other again.

He stood, his hands loose at his sides. "I've never wanted anything more."

If she met his eyes she would never stop considering his words and the branch he was extending.

But for once in her life, she couldn't.

She had to get away from everything and everyone. She needed space to think. To figure out what was the best for her.

"You'd have to still want kids. You'd have to want a family and not feel like it was too much." She looked over her shoulder and he gave a slight nod. "It would have to be a sure thing, Oz. No messing around.

No leaving me hanging. No shutting me out. You'd have to tell me *every*thing. Trust me."

He nodded again, swallowing hard.

"And I'd have to be crazy," she replied softly, looking into Oz's deep brown eyes, her head shaking. "Really, really crazy."

20

Beth haphazardly stuffed items into her bag, her mind on everything but what she was packing. Time away with Nash would be good. A distraction. A way to reconnect. She wouldn't think ahead. She'd just keep moving forward. One day at a time.

How could Oz ask her back? And how could she even consider it? Why did she ask clarifying questions? It should have been clear cut. Instead of doing what was right, she asked questions, gave him hope, and then fled. Bolted. Ran. Escaped.

How was she going to elope with Nash--because that's surely what was going to happen during their getaway--if she couldn't shrug off her ex?

"This trip is a good idea," Nash said. "I think you'll really enjoy this area. It's near a gated community I want to show you. It's close to the airport, the opera, and a few other great places I think would be great for raising kids." Nash carefully tucked his folded underwear into his suitcase. "Beth?"

"Yeah. Great." She grabbed a tube of toothpaste from the en suite and shoved it into her bag along with her nightie and e-reader.

"Here." Nash held out his hand. "You're going to get toothpaste everywhere. Let me." Nash came around the bed to root out her toothpaste. "And don't forget your toothbrush."

Beth zipped her bag with a sharp tug. "Ready?"

"I need another ten minutes. Don't forget your toothbrush."

She released her bag, letting it thud onto the floor.

"What's wrong?" He turned, hands on his hips. He was pale in his uncharacteristic sweats and T-shirt, the bandage still covering his stitches and the worst of his hot and heavy smooch with the concrete.

"Nothing." She flicked off the movie Nash had turned on. "Let's go."

"Beth. What?"

"Nothing!"

She was not going to discuss the scary, tempting second thoughts that battered her nor all the thoughts whizzing through her mind about how wrong everything felt. It didn't matter what she did, there was no clear path that seemed like it was the easy, obvious, one-hundred percent right way to go.

"If you're mad at me, be mad at me." Nash's eyes flashed. "It isn't fair to act like this. I made a mistake. I admitted it. I apologized. I'm not perfect. Nobody is."

She stared at him.

"Beth!" He slammed his open hand on the bed. "Engage, damn it!"

"I can't do this," she whispered, backing away.

He rubbed his forehead. "Go on a trip? Get real. Pick up your bag and let's go."

"No."

He sagged onto the bed. "Why not?"

She took in their shared bedroom. Nothing said *ours* about the room. A photo of her and her sister sat on her bedside table and a bra hung on the closet doorknob, but other than that, everything else was Nash's. The exquisite bedspread, the trendy art on the walls, the fluffy towels in the en suite. Everything. At first it had been reassuring and luxurious, but now it felt lonely and exclusionary.

It wasn't their condo. It wasn't her home. It was Nash's. And it would always be that way. She felt as though she was the movie he put in the fancy DVD player when he wanted entertainment. And while she loved being Paris Beth, it wasn't the real her. She cared too much about everything and everyone and wasn't that free-flying independent adventure gal Nash thought she was. She was Blueberry Springs Beth. The woman with the job that wouldn't go anywhere big, but satisfied her heart. She was the person who provided hope and joy at the end of good people's lives and now helped others in need of therapy. She loved the fact that she knew all the faces walking around town and that if she fell down they would pick her up again. This town and all its flaws and aggravations accepted her, warts and all. It was home.

They knew what she wanted even more than she dared admit to herself.

She studied Nash. Perfect, perfect Nash. She closed her eyes. She loved him, but this wasn't where she belonged. When she was with him she wasn't her true self. If she wanted more people around her Thanksgiving table all she had to do was open her door and holler.

"I can't do this anymore, Nash. The real me is the woman you want to change."

Her ears blocked the sound as he lectured his way around the room. Detached, she watched his actions, demanding and pushy. Nothing similar to what would comfort and convince her to change her mind.

"It's been fun," she said, static pulling at her mind, "but I can't be with you, Nash. Not forever. Being together doesn't make us better people."

She hefted her bag and walked to the door, leaving him standing in the bedroom, jaw hanging low.

"Oz?"

A groggy, yet hopeful voice on the other end of the line replied, "Beth, is that you?"

"I hope I didn't wake you." Beth checked the alarm clock resting next to the hotel room's bed. Its bright red numbers announced the wee hours of the night. "I woke you, didn't I?"

The grogginess fell from his voice. "Are you okay? Everyone's worried."

"Sorry. It is too late, isn't it? I'm sorry. I shouldn't have called." Shouldn't have run away from Blueberry Springs. But the need to think, to be alone had been too strong.

Beth was about to lower the phone to its cradle when Oz said, "I'm here any time, Beth."

She paused, telling herself she only wanted to hear his voice. That it would never work out between them. That her hope would crush her. But she also wanted to reassure herself that his offer was real, and for a moment, believe that things could somehow work out for the two of them if she just reached out and took his hand again.

"What's new with you?" she asked.

He paused as if caught off guard. "I started a dining room table." He sounded perkier. "I'm working on going through the process of making the legs on my own, but I don't have a machine. I want to make the whole thing, start to finish, with my own hands." His voice lowered. "It's good for the soul."

"Are you going to buy one of those things they had in the school shop?"

He chuckled. "I haven't dared price one out."

"You have money though, right? You haven't spent it all?" The idea of him being broke already bothered her.

"I still have a bit of savings from selling the business, but I need to be frugal so I don't end up having to take a job I hate." He paused. "Right now I'm driving the recycling truck two days a week. It's a bit of mindless income to help me out."

"Oz?"

"Yeah?"

"... nothing."

There was a pause.

"Where are you, Beth?"

"Away, thinking."

"I heard you broke up with Nash."

"I guess so."

"You're not sure?"

She stared at the ring on her finger. "I'm confused." She wanted this to be easy, but was afraid if she ran to him he'd only break her heart again.

Silence stretched down the line.

"Make sure you do what'll make you happy. If he ..." Oz's voice broke off.

Anger burned through her, lighting her mind on fire. Oz had asked her back, but was implying that she shouldn't be too hasty in dumping his rival?

"What will make you happy?" he asked.

"How the hell am I supposed to know?" she snapped. "Why didn't you tell me what was going on with you, Oz?" Her voice wobbled and she clung to the phone. "Why did you shut me out?"

"I was scared." He paused, his deep voice soft and strong. "It seemed easier and safer than trying to live a different life. I was afraid of losing you. And then everything started to feel as though it was too late. And no matter which way I turned I wouldn't be able to give you what you needed. I couldn't find a way to be true to your needs. If I quit the firm we'd be broke and if I stayed there I'd be broken." He sucked in a slow breath and she could picture him running a hand through his hair, messing it up. "Sometimes I think we'd still be together if I'd been man enough to stand up and say I needed to make some changes in my life. That we would have found a way for us both to get what we needed."

She almost replied that of course they would have. But in her heart she wondered if the old Beth would have understood. If she would have been as accommodating and flexible. She'd been so determined that kids were the only thing worthwhile on her horizon that she may not have been able to give him the space he needed to find himself while they were together. "I should have known you weren't happy."

"The past is the past. You need to do what will make you happy tomorrow."

"I don't even know what happy *is* anymore!"

She slammed the phone down and let her tears breach the brim. She flung a pillow across the room, sending the vertical blinds jangling. Picking up the receiver, she jammed her finger down on *redial*.

"You're never going to let me in, are you Oz?" she said as soon as he picked up.

"Beth," he said with a hint of exasperation. "You're already in. You have been for years."

"But I don't even know you. I don't know *any*body anymore. Even myself." Knowing who you wanted to father your children should pretty much be a gimme kind of answer at this stage of the game. And the way she was feeling, kids didn't even feel that important anymore. She knew what she wanted and that was the old Oz. But the old Oz was gone. She didn't know the new Oz. What if he pushed her away? What if they couldn't get past their history and habits? What if she went back to him and it was a mistake?

She sniffed and swiped at her eyes, her anger building. "I used to know exactly what I wanted until you messed up everything. I'm different now. I'm *different*, Oz. I'm a good, caring person who makes a difference in the lives of people who are nearing the end of their time. And it feels good to be that woman. To be strong and to be needed. I'm independent and make my own choices. And I don't need a man, Oz. I don't *need* you. I don't even need kids. I have family, Oz. I have Blueberry Springs. There are people looking out for me. They aren't prefect, but they are mine. The problem is you, Oz. I don't know you. I don't trust you. How can I when you kept yourself from me? You ask me back but I don't even know who is asking me. I know *nothing*."

"Come get to know the new me. I'm an open book. All you have to do is ask."

"Fine," she said sharply. "Do we have a chance together?"

"I'm not a fortune teller."

"Oh, so, no then? Nice." Her eyes stung. "That's all I wanted to know."

"Beth." The pitch of his voice edged higher. "That's not what I said." He sucked in an audible breath, and his pitch slid lower. "It's what we make of it. Everything in life is what we make of it."

"So, I've made my life a big mess, have I?" She was unable to stop herself from twisting his words. "I'm the only one to blame since I'm not happy?"

"Beth, there's hope. There is always hope." He paused before continuing gently, "Where are you? Let me help you."

"I don't *need* help. I need to be *alone*. I need to make this decision and it sucks." She dug her fingernails into her palm. "I'm still totally in love with you, and I don't even know who you are!" She flinched at her words, not wanting to love Oz. It was complicated and it hurt. She swiped at her runny nose with a tissue. If she had Oz, she might not have kids. By the time he was ready it might be too late for her. And while the idea pained her, she couldn't imagine her future without Oz being there at her side.

"Beth, I still love you, too. More than anything. And that's more than anyone else can offer. Come home. Let me love you again."

Tears streamed off her chin and she wished she could close her eyes, click her heels, and repeat over and over, *There's no place like home,* and wake up to find herself at home with Oz, everything as it was before Harvey's heart attack. But she couldn't because she wasn't Dorothy. She was the cowardly lion. Except she didn't even have Oz.

And like everything in life, it was hard to go back.

IV

WHERE IT ENDS ... OR DOES IT BEGIN?

(April ... Still)

Beth slipped past Oz and into the trailer's living room. "You should take down the for sale sign for a while. And maybe forget those mortgage papers for a bit, too." She frowned. She was getting way too ahead of herself. "Not like you've ever been in a hurry to get them to me."

He lifted his hands in surrender. "A last ditch hope against hopes."

Beth frowned, hands on hips when he failed to say more. "Are you going to tell me everything? Or are you going to keep secrets?"

"If I sold the place it was letting go of my hope for us. And I couldn't. I turned down five offers. And I never sorted out getting your name off the place because I couldn't bear the idea of it. Your name is still on the truck's door, too. Even though Mandy wanted to peel it off."

Beth plunked onto the couch, excitement and nerves battling against each other. She could do this. She could start over with the one thing she wanted. All he needed to do was accept her and her terms and they'd see where the future took them.

Pulling in a deep breath for courage she blurted, "Let's date."

Oz scratched his head, making his hair stand on end. She smiled. If things went according to plan she'd have the right to smooth that unruly head of hair under her fingertips once again. He raised his eyebrows hopefully, but she saw fear lingering there as well. Did she show it too?

He took a lemon drop out of the bowl on the coffee table and popped it in his mouth. "What are you saying, Beth?"

"As in ... date. See each other. Start over. You and me. You're different. I'm different."

"Okay. A fresh start." His shoulders slowly lost their stiffness.

She stood and walked toward him. "We can't assume we know *anything* about each other. We have to act like we've just met. We need to see if we're still good together."

"Are you still living with Nash?"

"I moved out. I'm on Cynthia and Dans' couch until Benny's apartment over the mechanic's comes free."

Oz nodded, his face a myriad of expressions. She waited, watching him. Somehow she'd imagined this going a little more ... glad-to-have-you-back-let-me-sweep-you-into-my-arms-I've-been-waiting-for-this-moment-since-the-second-I-let-you-go.

"We're both different, but we're both still attracted to each other." She stepped closer. "Right?"

He gave her a goofy grin. "It's 'cause I've been working out, isn't it? I saw you staring at my abs when you came to chew me out." He patted his flat midriff.

Beth rolled her eyes. Too much talking. Not enough kissing. What did a woman have to do to get him to say *yes*?

"Look, Oz." She stood at full height. "I can't be that seventy-five-year-old woman sitting in continuing care wondering about the one that got away, torturing herself with 'what ifs'." Her voice rose. "God dammit, Oz. I can't shut you out of my heart. I want you. Nobody else. I always have. More than anything else out there." She held his face in her hands and looked him straight in the eye. "More than kids."

His eyes filmed with unshed tears, the windows to his soul warm and open. Inviting. She lowered his head to hers and gently kissed his lips. He tasted like home.

"I've always loved you, Oz. I've never stopped--even when I tried my hardest."

He wrapped her tight in his arms. "Thank goodness you failed because I've never stopped loving you, either, Little B. Everything I've ever done has, in some way, been for you."

Beth laughed. "You know, despite what others may think, I'm pretty sure I can handle having my lemon drop every day." She reached down and plucked a lemon drop out of the bowl. She popped it in her mouth and gave Oz a long, sweet kiss. "You've always been my favorite and always will be."

Jean Oram is a *New York Times* and *USA Today* bestselling romance author who loves making opposites attract in tear-jerking, feel-good, sweet romances set in small towns. She grew up in a town of 100 (cats and dogs not included) and owns one pair of high heels which she has worn approximately three times in the past twenty years. Jean lives near a lake in Canada with her husband, two kids, cat, dog and those pesky deer who keep wandering into her yard to eat her rose bushes and apple trees.

Become an Official Fan: www.facebook.com/groups/jeanoramfans

Newsletter: www.jeanoram.com/signup

Twitter: www.twitter.com/jeanoram

Facebook: www.facebook.com/JeanOramAuthor

Instagram: www.instagram.com/Author_JeanOram

Website & blog: www.jeanoram.com

www.ingramcontent.com/pod-product-compliance
Lightning Source LLC
Chambersburg PA
CBHW050337190726

48284CB00007BB/2046